FROM THE
NANCY DREW FILES

*THE CASE: While folding flyers for a political candi-
date, Nancy runs across a million-dollar mystery.*

*CONTACT: Nancy agrees to help a man who's broken
the law—to trap a robber baron.*

*SUSPECTS: Michael Mulraney—the handsome builder
has a shady past and a dark future.*

*Franklin Turner—the young political aide is rich,
well connected, and very nasty.*

*Tim Terry—the candidate for city council has
plenty of charisma, but he needs financing.*

*COMPLICATIONS: A mysterious kingpin is trying to
gain control of millions in city funds—and he
doesn't care how he does it.*

Books in The Nancy Drew Files® Series

Available from ARCHWAY Paperbacks

THE NANCY DREW FILES™ CASE · 33

DANGER IN DISGUISE

Carolyn Keene

AN ARCHWAY PAPERBACK
Published by POCKET BOOKS
New York   London   Toronto   Sydney   Tokyo   Singapore

AN ARCHWAY PAPERBACK *Original*

An Archway Paperback published by
POCKET BOOKS, a division of Simon & Schuster Inc.
1230 Avenue of the Americas, New York, NY 10020

Copyright © 1989 by Simon & Schuster Inc.
Cover art copyright © 1989 Jim Mathewuse
Produced by Mega-Books of New York, Inc.

ISBN: 0-671-74654-5

First Archway Paperback printing March 1989

10 9 8 7 6 5 4 3

NANCY DREW, AN ARCHWAY PAPERBACK and colophon
are registered trademarks of Simon & Schuster Inc.

THE NANCY DREW FILES is a trademark
of Simon & Schuster Inc.

Printed in the U.S.A.

IL 7+

DANGER
IN DISGUISE

Chapter

One

I'LL BE FOLDING FLYERS in my dreams tonight," George Fayne said, running her fingers through her short dark curls. She stretched to ease the kinks brought on by bending over a desk.

"Just remember you got us into this," said Nancy Drew with a grin that made her blue eyes sparkle. "Being a public-spirited citizen can be hard work."

George grinned back. She'd been doing volunteer work on Councilman Tim Terry's reelection campaign for the last couple of months. Occasionally her friends helped her out. That night they were using the councilman's office to organize a voter-registration drive.

"Well, this is the last of these," Nancy said, relieved. She tossed back her shoulder-length red-blond hair and stuffed the last flyer into the last envelope.

"Bess was smart to opt for the store distribution detail. Folding and stuffing isn't very inspiring." George pulled a denim jacket on over her blue button-down shirt.

"I have a feeling she had her strategy planned from the start," Nancy replied. She remembered how her friend Bess Marvin had grabbed the first batch of flyers from the copy machine. She had said she'd take them around to the shops in the neighborhood—including the video arcade where Jeff Matthews, her latest crush, sometimes hung out. That was Bess's idea of public-spirited volunteer work.

"I have to lock up, then we'll go find her," said George.

Nancy picked up the Emerson College varsity jacket her boyfriend, Ned Nickerson, had given her. Although it was early September and the days were still warm, the nights could get cool.

George piled envelopes into a shopping bag for mailing. "This really is a good cause," she said, "especially if people register and then vote for Tim Terry."

"You're really in the councilman's corner, aren't you?"

"He's a great guy and a decent politician. I'm not the only one who thinks so. He has some very influential people supporting him. He's even got big guns like Bradford Williams looking at him."

"That is impressive, all right." Nancy had often heard her father, attorney Carson Drew, talk about Williams. The Chicago businessman had become quite powerful in the past few years.

"It's important too. It takes more than stuffing envelopes to run a political campaign. With the right financial backing Tim Terry can go straight to the top."

"Where exactly is that?" Nancy looked quizzically at her friend.

George pondered for a moment. "After this reelection, I'm not quite sure," she said, "but he's on his way."

"And we should be on our way too." Nancy slipped into the varsity jacket. "I'll go turn off the copy machine while you finish up here."

Nancy was surprised to hear voices as she walked down the dimly lit hallway. She'd thought she and George were the only ones in the office—the last of the staff had left an hour earlier.

The voices grew louder as Nancy got closer to the copy room. She made out two men talking. One spoke in an unusually deep bass, and he sounded very angry.

"How could you have done something so stupid?" he rumbled in the first words Nancy could hear clearly.

Nancy ducked out of the hallway into a shadowed recess, so that she was near the copy room door but not visible through it. She'd made the move almost without thinking—something told

3

her the two men inside might not appreciate any interruptions. She peeked around the edge of the niche at the frosted glass panel of the door, but all she could see were blurred shapes. Quickly a second voice piped up.

"You made me nervous. All those threats on the phone—I rushed in here and out again and didn't think to check the basket of the machine. I must have left one of the copies in it by mistake." The second voice sounded pinched and shaky.

"You weren't supposed to copy them in the first place. You were supposed to turn the originals over to me and disappear." Nancy heard scuffling and then a squeal. "You were trying to pull a fast one, weren't you?"

"Let go of me!" The voice was choked as well as sounding nervous now, as if someone had the man by the throat.

"Oh, I'm so sorry." The rumbling bass words dripped with sarcasm. "Did I mess up your fancy suit? I guess I was thinking about how you might have gotten away with it—if I hadn't searched your briefcase and found those extra copies."

"I—I thought I needed them for protection." Squeaky wasn't choking now. The other guy must have let him go.

"The kind of protection you need, buddy, is from yourself. First, you try to double-cross me. Then you lose track of one of your copies," said Deep Voice. "Then we come here, and the copy isn't where you said it would be. Check the count one more time to be sure."

Nancy heard papers being riffled.

"There're only five here. I made six copies. I'm positive about that, and this is the only place I could have left the other one."

Suddenly the smaller of the two blurred forms came into sharp focus as Deep Voice pressed Squeaky up against the door. Nancy could see black hair and a gray sports jacket, and as Squeaky tried to wriggle away from his captor, she caught a glimpse of his hawk-nosed profile.

"Are you sure there were only six? You'd better not lie to me," the bass voice threatened.

"I swear I'm not lying!"

Nancy heard a sharp intake of breath. She could almost see the speaker being strangled. She peered around her in the gloom, looking for something she could use as a weapon. Poor Squeaky might need rescuing, but she didn't dare barge in unarmed.

"Why should I believe you?" Deep Voice was saying. "You made those copies after I told you I wanted those papers so I could get rid of them."

"But I admitted I'd done it."

"Not until I slapped it out of you."

"And I don't want you to slap me around anymore. I'm telling you the truth. There were only six copies."

That response was close to sobbing. Nancy tensed for action. She couldn't let this go on.

"I believe you, buddy. You're too scared to lie." The bigger man gave a sneering chuckle. "So what happened to number six?"

"Somebody must have taken it out of the copier basket by mistake."

"Or on purpose. Maybe somebody else besides me found out you'd been poking your nose in where it didn't belong. Maybe somebody else got more curious than it's healthy to be."

"No, I'm sure that didn't happen," came the hasty reply. "Nobody but me would have understood the significance of that printout. There'd be no reason for anyone to take it on purpose."

"I'll have to check that out for myself. I don't like loose ends."

"What are you going to do?"

"Somebody who works here must have taken that last copy. So I'm going to search the offices to see if I can find it or figure out who was here last."

Nancy slipped out of the recess. If he searched the offices, he'd find George. Nancy couldn't let that happen.

She hurried down the hall and around the corner, moving quietly along the wall and keeping low. Every nerve was taut in dread of hearing that deep voice boom out after her.

Easing open the office door, Nancy slipped inside and crooked a finger at George. "Come with me," she whispered urgently. "Don't ask any questions. Just hurry!"

George didn't argue. She followed without a word as Nancy darted out of the office and through a fire door into the back stairwell.

Nancy motioned for George to get behind her, then flipped off the light switch and eased the door back open a crack.

They'd made it to their hiding place with only a moment to spare. Nancy heard footsteps enter the office she and George had just left. The fire door had squeaked on its hinges when they had opened it. If she opened it wide enough to see, the man with the deep voice might hear it. She had to content herself with listening at the crack.

She and George hadn't picked up anything but their purses or turned out the lights behind them. The men would probably conclude that whoever had been using that office was the last to leave the building and had done so in a hurry. Nancy had no doubt Deep Voice would find that suspicious. Still, he'd have no way of knowing it was George and Nancy, since they were volunteer workers, not regular staff.

"What's happening?" George murmured just audibly.

Nancy raised a forefinger to her lips and pressed her ear closer to the narrow opening. A long moment lapsed before she silently eased the door shut and slumped back against the wall.

"What's happening?" George whispered again, close to Nancy's ear.

7

"They were talking about someone named Kathy Novello. Who is she?"

"She's a secretary—that's her office we were working in. What did they say about her?"

Nancy straightened up and answered in a tone that she forced to remain calm.

"One of them ordered the other to get rid of her."

Chapter

Two

WHAT?" GEORGE GASPED.

"Can you find her phone number? We have to get in touch with her right away," Nancy said grimly.

George searched hastily through the file, looking for Kathy Novello's card. Nancy filled her in on what had happened in the copy room, finishing up as she punched the phone buttons for Kathy's number.

"I've got her answering machine," said Nancy after a short wait. "She's not at home. We have to go to her place."

"She may actually be there right now," said George. "She lets the machine take messages even when she's home."

"Hello, Kathy Novello, are you there?" Nancy

said to the recording. Then she covered the receiver to ask George, "Why would she do that?"

"She always screens her calls. You know, in case she doesn't want to talk."

"Kathy, if you're there, please pick up the phone. This is urgent!"

"She won't necessarily hear you either," said George. "She turns down the volume, too, so she may not even know there's a call coming in. She says she hears more than enough jangling phones here in the office."

Nancy flashed an exasperated look at George. "Kathy, this is a friend calling. You are in danger. Please listen—get out of your house immediately."

"You have to meet Kathy to understand," said George. "She really keeps to herself. Sometimes she just turns the phone off for privacy."

Nancy slammed the receiver down and headed for the door. "Well, this time it could turn out to be the biggest mistake she's ever made."

George snatched the file card with Kathy's address on it and hurried after Nancy. "I hope not," she said with a worried frown.

They were on the way out of the office complex when they saw Bess, her long blond hair swinging over her shoulders as she bobbed her head in animated conversation with a security guard.

"It's after hours, miss," he was saying as Nancy and George hurried up. "Nobody's supposed to be in there after six o'clock."

Bess pulled herself up to her full five-feet-four inches, plumping up the shoulder pads of her red jacket in an effort to look authoritative.

"Here are my friends. They'll tell you. We have permission to be here."

"There're more of you? What's going on here?" asked the guard, who was beginning to sound aggravated.

"We've been up in Councilman Terry's office working on the voter-registration drive," said George.

"We're on an urgent errand," Nancy explained. "It could be a matter of life and death."

"Tell me another one." The guard moved to block the glass doors that led to the elevator and the underground garage where Nancy had parked her car. "I'm supposed to be notified of any nonofficial people on the premises after hours. I'm going to have to call the councilman about this."

"Of course you are," Nancy said quickly, cutting off George's protest before she could utter it. "You have to do your duty. In fact," she said, thinking fast, "that's just what I want to talk to you about."

Bess had a sheaf of flyers in her arms. Nancy grabbed a handful.

11

"River Heights really needs the help of a man like you who knows what has to be done and does it."

The guard had his mouth open to respond but couldn't get a word in.

"I want you to take these." Nancy pressed the flyers into his hands. He tried to push them away, and a few fell to the floor. "Oh, don't let those get damaged—they are *crucial* to the future of our community."

Looking bewildered, the guard stooped to retrieve the flyers, and Nancy gestured for Bess and George to move around him to the glass doors. "Thank you, thank you. You don't realize what a service you're performing for the public," she said. "I've got to run—good night."

Waving a cheerful goodbye, Nancy left the guard with his mouth hanging open and hurried to catch up with Bess and George. Her heart was beating fast. "Keep moving," she said.

"What was that?" asked Bess. "Some kind of comedy routine?"

"Something like that," said Nancy.

"What's the joke?" Bess looked confused. "I want to be in on it too."

"Don't worry. You're in on it." George grabbed Bess with one hand and shoved her along with the other. "But if you don't run as fast as you can right now, we'll all get stuck here cooling our heels till that outfit you're wearing has gone out of style."

"What's happening?" Bess scurried along as George nudged her to move faster.

"Don't talk. Run," said Nancy.

They'd left the guard in a pool of paper but knew he wouldn't be far behind.

They reached the elevator, and Nancy jabbed at the Down button. She doubted they'd have time to wait for it to arrive though.

She could hardly believe it when she heard the *whoosh* of the elevator doors parting. All three girls stormed the elevator, nearly mowing down a woman with a maintenance cart who was trying to get out.

"Sorry, ma'am. We have to take you out of your way for a minute," said Nancy as the woman opened her mouth to complain.

She saw the security guard rushing toward them and jabbed the Door Close button. The brushed steel portals eased shut just in time to keep him on the other side while George assured the cleaning woman that this really was an emergency, and—no, she wasn't being taken hostage.

Moments later they were in Nancy's blue Mustang, racing toward Kathy Novello's. The evening traffic rush had subsided and they were making fairly good time.

As they drove, Bess was filled in on what Nancy had overheard. "Nancy!" Bess wailed. "You're the only person I know who could turn stuffing envelopes into trouble. Believe me, this is going to become another case."

"I hope you're wrong," Nancy replied grimly.

They pulled up in front of a grimy brick building and jumped out of the car.

Kathy's apartment building wasn't in the best part of town, and it didn't have an elevator. The yellowing card by her downstairs doorbell said she lived on the third floor. Nancy and George took the stairs two at a time while Bess brought up the rear, puffing with each exertion. As they reached the third-floor landing, they heard a distant clatter, as though someone was clanging garbage-can lids together outside.

"Oh, no," George gasped as she dashed to the door with Kathy's apartment number on it.

Nancy's heart sank—the door to Kathy Novello's apartment was slightly ajar. That looked like trouble. She doubted that a young woman living alone would leave her front door unlocked.

Nancy gingerly pushed the door farther open and called out, "Kathy, are you here?"

There was a single, drawn-out metallic clang in the distance but not a sound from inside the apartment.

"Maybe she went out," George suggested.

Nancy didn't answer. She pushed the door wide and looked around the living room. It wasn't fancy: the furniture was worn and faded, and the off-white walls looked as if they could use a fresh coat of paint.

The window on the opposite wall had been pushed all the way up. Nancy walked over to it and looked out, down through the metalwork of a fire escape.

The body of a woman was lying facedown on the pavement below. Nancy knew from the grotesque angle of the figure that the person was dead.

"Oh, no."

It was the second time George had made that exclamation in the past few minutes. She was leaning out the window beside Nancy, and the shocked expression on her face told Nancy her guess had been right.

It was the body of Kathy Novello.

Nancy and her friends had just started telling their story to Detective Hicks when the ambulance pulled up with its siren wailing and lights flashing.

Nancy told the detective about the conversation she'd overheard in the councilman's office, and he wrote it all down, but instead of leaping into action, he remained in Kathy's apartment and questioned George about Kathy. George told him that Kathy had been dissatisfied with her job and that she'd also just broken up with her boyfriend.

Detective Hicks snapped his notebook shut. "Well, ladies, I'd say we've got a tough case here," he said, wearily massaging the back of his neck. "It seems to me that three scenarios are equally possible."

"Excuse me," Nancy said, trying not to sound impatient. "What are the three possible scenarios?"

Hicks walked over to the window. "One, Ms. Novello was murdered. Two, it was an accidental death. She slipped and fell. Or, three, she killed herself. In light of what this young lady"—he gestured at George—"has been telling me, I'd say suicide is as good a possibility as either of the others."

Leaning out, he called down for an officer to come up from the alley. "I want to see if they found anything unusual down there."

"But—" Nancy began to say, when she heard a sound that brought her bolt upright in her seat. She hurried over to the window.

One of the policemen below had reached up and grabbed the extension ladder to the fire escape and pulled it down toward him. The corroded metal was clanking and squealing in response.

"That's what I heard!" she exclaimed. "When I was outside the door to this apartment, I heard metal clanking. It must have been the ladder."

"How long between then and when you got to the window?" asked Detective Hicks. He sounded skeptical, but at least she'd captured his attention.

"Not more than a minute," Nancy answered.

The detective pulled his pen out again. "But you didn't actually see anyone?"

"No, but there could have been time for whoever it was to get out of sight if what I heard was the ladder coming back up after someone had climbed down it."

"Did you hear footsteps running away?"

"No, I didn't hear anything like that." Nancy couldn't help but feel exasperated with this methodical man. While he asked all his questions, whoever had caused Kathy Novello to fall to her death was getting away. "What I *did* hear was metal—clanking metal."

"I'm not surprised that you did," said a voice from the window.

Nancy turned to see the police officer from the alley climbing into the room.

"I'll bet there was a lot of clatter when she hit those trash cans. They're scattered all over down there."

"I see," said Detective Hicks as he closed his notebook and put it away.

Nancy gritted her teeth. "Please listen to me. I know someone meant to hurt Kathy Novello. And now she's dead. There *has* to be a connection!"

Detective Hicks sighed. "I'm not saying you're wrong, Ms. Drew. But I have no evidence. I don't even know where to start looking for this murderer of yours! The department *will* look into it.

But it's going to take some time. Now if you'll excuse me, I've got some things to take care of. The sergeant here will take your phone numbers, in case we need to contact you again."

Nancy knew Hicks was doing his job. But she also knew that the longer the case waited, the colder the trail would get. She *couldn't* sit by and do nothing while a murderer got away!

Bess had been right, she realized. She had found trouble—and she was in the middle of another case.

A half hour later the girls were still sitting in Nancy's car in front of Kathy's apartment building. Nancy couldn't bring herself to drive away with the cause of Kathy Novello's death hanging unresolved. Yet, she didn't know what else to do.

"You have to agree with Hicks that a conversation you accidentally overheard really isn't solid evidence," said George.

"I know it isn't," Nancy conceded, more discouraged than ever. "If I could just establish that there was a specific motive for those men to want Kathy out of the way—"

"You'd have to know what was on the piece of paper they were after."

"Right. And— Wait a second! *We* were the last people to use the copier. It could have gotten mixed in with the flyers we were copying," said Nancy, suddenly feeling revived.

A lead at last! This could be the starting point.

"Did either of you see an odd piece of paper mixed in with the flyers?" she asked eagerly.

"It wasn't in the pile we used for stuffing envelopes. I'm almost positive of that," said George.

"If it was in the tray of the machine before we started making copies then it would have ended up on the bottom of the first batch we did. What happened to that batch?"

"I took it," Bess chimed in. "I just hope I didn't leave off the paper you want at one of those stores I visited. I think I just handed out the ones off the top of the pile, but—"

"No 'buts' about it," said Nancy triumphantly. She'd been rummaging among the flyers Bess had tossed on the back seat when they jumped into the car. "Bless your heart, Bess. You dealt those flyers straight off the top of the deck, and look what we have here."

Nancy brandished the single sheet of paper that didn't match the rest.

"The motive!" she said.

Chapter

Three

THIS HAS TO BE what those men were after," Nancy went on, her eyes sparkling.

George and Bess pressed over Nancy's shoulder to get a look at the piece of paper that seemed to have caused the death of Kathy Novello.

"What is it?" asked Bess.

"Looks like a copy of a computer printout page," said George.

"It has something to do with the Immigration and Naturalization Service," Nancy added, skimming the contents. "And it looks as if somebody had folded over the upper right-hand corner before copying it. It has something to do with a Michael Mulraney."

"I know that name," said George. "I filed some papers about him at the councilman's office."

"Immigration papers?" asked Nancy.

"No, nothing like that. These files had to do with municipal contracts. Mulraney owns a contracting business—he was bidding on a job for the city."

"What does Councilman Terry have to do with that?" asked Nancy.

"He heads up an oversight committee to make sure the city doesn't hire any crooked contractors. A lot of towns have gotten into serious scandals over kickbacks and faulty work. Some have even been cheated out of millions. Tim Terry is determined not to have anything like that happen here."

"You're really stuck on this guy, aren't you?" asked Bess from the back seat.

"I'm not in love with him, if that's what you mean—I just think he's a good guy. What's wrong with that?" George sounded a little defensive.

"What did the oversight committee find out about Mulraney?" Nancy asked quickly.

"I don't have any idea. I was just helping out with the filing. That kind of information is confidential."

"Yes, I suppose it would be." Nancy thought a moment longer. "Do you know how to get in touch with him?"

"Mulraney? He has an office on the outskirts of town, if I remember right. I'm sure he's listed in the phone book. What are you planning, Nancy?"

"I feel a sudden urge to interview a building contractor," said Nancy, turning the key in the ignition and listening as the Mustang rumbled to life. "Maybe that committee found out something that wasn't quite legitimate about the way Mr. Mulraney does business."

"But he got the job."

"What?" Nancy had been about to pull out but hesitated instead.

"The city accepted Mulraney's bid, and he was given the contract," said George. "Nothing very big, as I remember. Nothing that would be worth risking jail for. And what would it have to do with immigration anyway?"

"I don't know, but there has to be a connection somewhere. I'm going to find it."

With a single, deft turn of the wheel, Nancy pulled the Mustang away from the curb. "If either of you sees a pay phone, yell," she said over her shoulder.

"Aaaaagh!" Bess cried promptly.

Nancy smiled. Count on Bess to bring a little lightness to any situation. "Thanks."

Michael Mulraney's answering service said he was still on the job, though it was nearly eight o'clock.

When the girls arrived at the construction site, they found him in the middle of inspecting the day's work. He was of medium height and compactly built; casually dressed in jeans and a blue work shirt, he could easily have been mistaken for one of his workers. As he held a portable work lamp aloft, Nancy saw thick, dark hair and blue eyes lit by its glow. He welcomed them with a wide, friendly smile.

"What can I do for you ladies?" He gestured toward the two-story duplex under construction behind him. "If you're interested in renting one of these places once they're built, I can give you the name of the agent."

Nancy barely registered the words he'd spoken. She was too busy listening to his voice, which was unusually deep. Could it be the one she'd heard earlier in the copy room? Her heart beat a little faster.

"Are you doing this work for the city of River Heights?" she asked to give herself something to say while she chose her next move.

If this was the man from the copy room, she had good reason to believe his jovial greeting was just a front, and he should be handled carefully.

"No, it isn't. I don't start that job till next month. Did you read about it in the paper?"

"Actually, I work for Councilman Tim Terry. I heard about it there," George chimed in.

Watching him, Nancy came to a decision. Knowing as little as she did about this case, she couldn't very well bluff her way through. Not when she didn't even know what she was trying to find out. She'd have to try shock treatment.

"I have something here that might interest you," she said, pulling the printout copy from her shoulder bag and holding it out for Mulraney to see.

If her purpose had been to break through Michael Mulraney's façade, then she had succeeded. He'd lifted the work lamp over the paper to read. His eyes were cast in shadow, but she could sense his whole body tensing suddenly. Nancy could feel anger there.

He grabbed for the paper with his free hand. Nancy whisked it out of reach just in time.

"Is that why the corner of the original is missing?" she asked. "Because you snatched it away from somebody?"

He'd moved the lamp, and she could see his eyes now. "Will you give me that?" he asked, the low tones of his voice rumbling. He was on the brink of rage. "It's my property after all."

"I'm not sure about that. I think I'd better keep it," Nancy said.

Mulraney glared at her. He wouldn't dare try anything in public, would he? Nancy wondered. She was suddenly glad she had her two friends there to back her up.

"Get off this site then," he said abruptly, "and don't come back."

His voice was different! Trying to conceal her surprise, Nancy stuffed the document into her bag and motioned for George and Bess to follow as she turned to leave. She remained silent as they walked back to the car.

"That sure didn't accomplish much," Bess said as she opened the door and climbed into the back seat.

"I'll say it didn't," George agreed. "What do you think, Nan?"

Nancy's hand was suspended in midair, with the key halfway to the ignition. She was staring out the window. She was remembering the deep voice she'd heard in the copy room.

"Earth to Nancy Drew. I asked what you thought," George repeated much louder.

"What? Oh. I don't think it was a bust at all," said Nancy. She fitted the key into the ignition. "We learned one very important thing."

"What did we learn?" asked Bess and George in unison.

"Well, both Mulraney and the man in the copy room have deep voices. In fact, they sound very much alike."

"But what does that tell us?" asked George. "Are they the same person?"

"Wouldn't you say that Mr. Mulraney was angry and upset?" asked Nancy.

"He sure was," answered Bess. "I thought he was going to try to make you into the Statue of Liberty, except you'd be carrying the lamp in your forehead instead of your hand."

"Well, the man at the councilman's office was

also very angry and upset," Nancy went on. "But did you notice what happened to Mulraney's speech when he got angry and upset?"

"Yes, I did," George piped up. "He started talking with an Irish brogue."

"That's right," said Nancy, "but the man in the copy room didn't have even a trace of an accent."

"So it wasn't Michael Mulraney you overheard today," George concluded.

"I don't think so."

"I'm glad that's cleared up," said Bess. "I think he's kind of cute."

"Good old Bess," said Nancy, smiling at her friend.

"But why did he get so mad when you showed him that piece of paper?" asked George.

"That's the other important thing," said Nancy, looking over her shoulder as she backed through the opening in the steel mesh fence that surrounded the construction area. "The one we *didn't* find the answer to."

But, she added to herself, tomorrow I can really start getting some answers.

The next afternoon Nancy was back home, lounging in the corner of the comfortable old couch in the den. She'd put on a blue skirt with a floral print and a white knit pullover, so she'd look neat and respectable when she went to the immigration office.

She was contemplating what kind of story she could tell there to get them to show her the intact version of the Mulraney document, when the front doorbell rang.

Nancy answered it and found herself face-to-face with the last person she expected to see on her front porch—Michael Mulraney.

"Uh—hi. What a surprise," Nancy said lamely. What was he doing there?

She noted with relief that the lock on the screen door was hooked. Although if Michael Mulraney wanted to, he could probably rip the door right off its hinges.

"I've come to apologize." He didn't sound angry, but Nancy remembered how quickly his mood had changed the night before. "One of my men who was working late recognized you last night. He told me you were a detective—he says you help people when they're in trouble."

"I try," she said, still cautious.

"I need you to help me with this."

He was holding a piece of paper up to the screen. There was a single sentence typed in the exact center, but Nancy couldn't make out what it said.

It took only a second for her curiosity to get the better of her caution. Opening the door, she stepped forward to read:

"The real Michael Mulraney is still alive."

Chapter

Four

NANCY READ that surprising sentence through twice before looking up at Mulraney. His expression was very intense. She couldn't decide if that was good or bad.

"It's a complicated story," he said, "and I can't stay away from the job site for very long. My men think I've gone to lunch."

"At three in the afternoon?"

He shrugged. "Some of us work odd hours. That has something to do with my problem, actually. I can tell you about it out here on the porch if that's better for you."

His brogue had begun to set in. Whatever he had to say to her was obviously pretty important to him. Looking at him, Nancy saw nothing but distress on his face. Her instincts told her she had nothing to fear from Michael Mulraney.

"Let's talk inside," she said as she held open the screen door.

He followed her down the hall to the sunny, spacious kitchen. She offered him a seat and brought him a cola. He didn't relax much and sat on the edge of his chair.

Nancy and her guest weren't likely to be interrupted. Carson Drew was spending the week at a New York legal conference. And the Drews' housekeeper, Hannah Gruen, was out shopping for groceries, which usually took her hours.

"Would you like a sandwich or something?"

"Thanks, but no." He shook his head, then stared down at his callused, red hands.

"What does that note mean?" she asked, hoping to get him talking.

He looked up at her, and what she saw in his eyes touched her heart.

"It means that someone's found me out," he said in a lilting brogue. "Somebody knows I'm not really Michael Mulraney."

Nancy took the seat across the table from him. "Then who are you?"

He hesitated.

"You can trust me," she said softly.

"I have to trust someone, I guess." He pulled at the collar of his blue work shirt and sighed before going on.

"My real name is Kevin Dougherty, and I come from Belfast, Ireland. The part of Belfast they call the Bogside."

He said the name in a way that told Nancy he had no happy memories of the place.

"My family is still back there. Ever since I came to America three years ago, I've thought of nothing but getting them out and bringing them here, especially my brother. But he won't come without my mother and sisters. So I must make enough money to bring them all together."

He was staring at his hands again, his face clouded by troubles that were an ocean away.

"Why is it so important to you to bring your family here?" Nancy asked.

"Because the Bogside is no fit place to live," he said almost angrily. "The place is like a war zone. And there are no jobs, especially not for young men like my brother. I know what it's like to have no work to go to and nothing to do. It's easy to get in trouble when you have nothing to do."

"Is that what happened to you? Did you get into trouble back there?" That might explain why he'd changed his name.

"Not quite, but I came close. And my brother Jamie is closer even than I was. My mother writes me that he stays out half the night with a gang from the streets. I had friends that did the same thing, and they're in prison now."

His hands were clenched tight together, knuckles showing white through his deep tan. His eyes pleaded for her to understand.

"Don't you see? I had to do whatever was necessary to get them out of there."

"What exactly did you do?" Nancy asked carefully. Her heart went out to him. But she had to know more before making a final judgment.

"I pretended I was somebody else, somebody I thought was dead." He sighed again and sank back in his chair, as if he'd been deflated by the words.

"Tell me how you did that." Nancy encouraged him to continue.

He leaned forward once more. "I saved up for two years. The plane ticket from Dublin took most of that, but a friend of my mother's had come over to River Heights several years earlier, so I had a free place to stay. Then, my second day here I was offered a job as a carpenter, the work my father taught me before he died. I could hardly believe my good luck. Just the work I wanted to do, and so fast. But there was a problem."

Nancy had become wrapped up in his story. "What problem?" she asked.

"The foreman on the job said I had to have a social security number and a green card. All I had was a temporary visa. Then, my mother's friend came up with a solution."

"Who is this friend of your mother's?"

"Her name is Dee Shannon. She lives on the other side of town from here. Sometimes she rents out rooms—that's how she got the papers she gave me. They belonged to one of her roomers who had died." He deflated again. "At least, that's what she told me."

"And you used them to get a job under an assumed name?" Nancy asked. She could see how uncomfortable that question made him, but she had to know.

"Yes, I did," he said.

"Did you understand that it was illegal to pretend you were Michael Mulraney?"

He shuffled his feet under the table, looking miserable.

"I know it's hard for you to understand," he said. "I'd come here from a place where there was no chance for somebody like me. I truly believed that this job offer was a fluke, and if I passed it up there would never be another. So I became Michael Mulraney. Then, I worked day and night till I could get a small crew together and start taking jobs on my own. I just kept on working and saving and praying I wouldn't get caught."

Nancy nodded. "Have you saved enough to bring your family here?"

"Almost. This job for the city will give me the rest. Then they can come here and have a decent place to live and something to get started on. My father taught my brother carpentry too, so he can take over my business."

"And what about you?" Nancy asked.

"I'll turn myself in and take what's coming to me," Michael said with a heavy sigh.

"What do you think that will be?"

"They'll probably send me back to Ireland, but I won't mind if my family is taken care of." He tapped the note, which he'd tossed on the table next to the cola he hadn't touched. "Only now it looks like I'll be going back before they come here."

"So, you think this note is a threat of some kind?" Nancy said softly. She couldn't help feeling sorry about the fix he was in.

"I think whoever sent this is going to use what they know against me somehow," Michael answered. "I thought it must be you when I saw you with that immigration paper last night."

"But that paper doesn't say anything that could prove you're not Michael Mulraney," Nancy objected.

"The corner was folded over where the birth date should have been. The date was proof." Michael sighed once more. "The real Michael Mulraney is twenty-five years older than me. I think that the person who sent me this note has the original of that printout with the birth date still on it."

"What makes you so sure the note isn't just a friendly warning?"

"If they wanted to help me, wouldn't they tell me more than this?" He unfolded the paper to show her the one sentence again.

Kathy Novello's death made Nancy inclined to agree. Good Samaritans didn't push innocent secretaries out of windows. But did Michael Mulraney qualify as an innocent victim too? That wasn't clear.

"What is it you want me to do exactly?" Nancy asked, curious.

"Find out who sent this to me, and then we'll decide from there," he said quietly.

"I'll have to think about this," she said, looking away so she wouldn't see the hope fade from his eyes. "You broke the law, and I don't usually take on a case for anyone who's done that."

"I understand," he said, and she could tell he really did. That didn't make her decision any easier.

It was past suppertime when Nancy got to the pizza parlor. Bess was out, having finally maneuvered a date with Jeff Matthews, and it had taken Nancy an hour to track George down at the gym and wait for her to finish.

Under George's peaked hood, her dark curls were still damp from the shower as she sat in the booth across from Nancy and picked up a wedge of double-cheese with everything—except anchovies. She was wearing a gray, hooded sweatshirt jacket over a T-shirt and navy blue sweatpants.

Nancy shook her head in amazement. "You work out like crazy—then top it off with a million calories."

George's dark eyes twinkled. "I'm just making

sure I don't get carried away with this fitness stuff." She creased the wedge deftly down the middle so none of the ingredients would fall off, then wound a strand of mozzarella into the neat package. "Speaking of getting carried away, what's got you looking so serious?"

Nancy recapped her conversation with Mulraney. She had to talk to somebody, and she knew George could be trusted with his secret. She was well into her second slice by the time the story was finished.

"Let's think about what could happen," said George matter-of-factly. "If you don't take the case, he'll probably get caught and be sent back to Belfast. His brother will still be on the street, and the family will be back where they started."

"On the other hand," said Nancy as George twirled the pizza platter in search of the piece with the most goodies on it, "if I do take his case, Michael may be able to keep all of his hard work from going down the drain." She caught the edge of the platter in midtwirl. "And I'll have time to figure out what really happened to Kathy Novello."

Nancy bounced out of the booth, taking the platter with her.

"Where are you going with that?" cried George.

"I'm having it boxed to go. We've got something important to do."

Nancy tapped her keys on the counter while

35

the remains of their pie were wrapped up. "Thanks," she said briskly when it was done. "Let's go, George!"

Michael Mulraney was working late again. He saw the blue Mustang pull in and hurried over to greet Nancy and her friend.

"I didn't think you'd be coming to see me so soon," he said.

Nancy could tell he was very nervous. "I've made a decision," she said.

"I see." Mulraney shifted from one booted foot to the other. "Well?"

Nancy smiled warmly. "I'll take the case, but I need to get some more information from you. Do you have time to talk?"

Michael Mulraney looked relieved. "Sure," he said. "Just give me a minute to put the outside lights on."

Before Nancy could answer, he was off across the dirt yard.

She was getting out of the car when Michael suddenly went rigid beside the circuit breaker box. He began to twitch, first along his arms, then through his entire body.

Nancy gasped and ran toward him. "Come on!" she shouted over her shoulder at George. "He's being electrocuted!"

Chapter

Five

"DON'T TOUCH HIM, NAN! You'll get shocked too!" screamed George.

"I have to get him off that handle somehow!" Nancy tore away from her friend's grip on her arm and looked around her. There had to be something— "Wood!" she muttered, remembering that it was a nonconductor.

She pulled a two-by-four from a stack of lumber and thrust it at Michael, trying to pry him loose. He quivered some, but remained clamped fast to the circuit breaker.

"Harder!" cried George. "He's got a death grip on that switch."

She grabbed the board along with Nancy. They lunged forward together. The board struck Michael with a thud in the chest. *Whoosh!* The impact knocked the breath out of him.

At the same instant his hand popped off the charging handle. He slid to the ground, unconscious—but alive.

"Is he—is he all right?" asked George.

"Call an ambulance" was Nancy's only reply as she bent over Michael.

The lights had pulsed off and on while he held the shorting handle. Now they were out completely.

"What's going on?" called a workman who had come out of the building. Then he spotted Michael crumpled on the ground and Nancy hovering over him. "What happened to Mike?" the workman shouted in alarm.

"He got a heavy jolt from that circuit breaker. I'm trying to bring him around."

She slapped Michael's cheeks and called to him, but he didn't come to. Meanwhile, the workman was examining the circuit breaker box, being careful not to get too close. Nancy jumped up to peer over his shoulder.

"This thing is wired all wrong," the man said, sounding amazed. "There should be a negative and a positive here, but look"—he pointed—"there're two positives instead."

"What does that do?" Nancy asked. She bent down to listen to Michael's respiration. He was breathing steadily, but he still showed no sign of waking up.

"It means that, instead of alternating like it's supposed to, the current went around in a circle," the workman answered, making hand motions to demonstrate. "When Michael touched the handle he became part of that circle with the current going straight through him. It's a miracle he's still alive."

"Could those wires have been rigged wrong by accident?" Nancy asked.

"I don't see how. They were fine earlier."

"Then you think somebody must have switched the wires deliberately?"

"I don't think anything!" the man snapped, suddenly on the defensive. Then he hesitated. "Still, I don't see any other way it could have happened." He eyed her with suspicion. "Who are you, anyway?"

"I'm Nancy Drew. Who are you?"

"The name's Pete Donaldson. I'm Mike's foreman." He still sounded skeptical.

"Does Michael turn these outside lights on every night?" Nancy wanted to know.

"I guess he has done that, ever since the wiring was finished," said Pete.

"Is he usually alone on the job this late?"

"Usually, unless we have something big to finish. Sometimes I stay around, but most of the time he's alone," Pete answered.

Nancy nodded. Michael's routine would make him an easy target for a would-be enemy, she reflected. She knelt to check his pulse again. Rapid, but steady.

"Would you ever inspect this outside area, or

was Michael the only one who did that?" she asked, though she could already guess what the answer would be.

"He was the only one," said Pete. "Say, what's going on here?"

"I'm not sure what's going on," said Nancy. She debated what to tell him. Pete seemed to be exactly what he said, a guy who worked for Michael. Still, somebody with access to that box had rigged those wires, and Pete appeared to know how that would be done. She stood up.

"I suspect somebody's been trying to scare Michael," she went on, watching Pete carefully, "or maybe even kill him."

Pete stared.

"That's all I need," murmured an unsteady voice from the ground. Michael had regained consciousness.

He tried to sit up, but Nancy wouldn't let him.

A few minutes later the ambulance arrived and medics checked Michael over. They moved him to a cot in the construction trailer nearby. There'd been no serious damage done, except for the nasty bruises where Nancy and George had struck him with the board. The men tried to talk him into going to the hospital, but Michael wouldn't hear of it. Finally they left.

"All I need is a little rest," Michael said to Nancy. "And one *other* thing."

"What's that?" Nancy asked.

40

"To find out why someone would do something like this."

"We'll find out," replied Nancy seriously.

A broad grin lit up Michael's face, and he seemed to be a little less pale beneath his tan. He sat up painfully and grasped Nancy's hand. Then he looked dismayed and sank back down on the cot again.

"What's wrong?" she asked.

"I may have ruined our chance with the only lead we have," he said. "Yesterday, after I left your house, I was sure you were going to turn me down, so I thought I'd better check things out on my own.

"I went to see Dee Shannon, the woman who gave me Michael Mulraney's social security card. I'm afraid it didn't go very well."

George had been listening and looked suddenly worried.

"What do you mean?" Nancy asked Michael.

"My nerves were a bit on the ragged side. That's my only excuse for what happened," he said. "I lost my temper and started yelling at her for giving me the card in the first place." He hung his head. "Instead of getting information, I got kicked out and was told never to come back."

He looked so unhappy and ashamed of himself, and he'd been through so much in the past few days. Nancy couldn't bring herself to tell him that if he really had ruined their chances of

41

getting Dee Shannon to cooperate, then they could really be in trouble. Michael Mulraney's hot temper might very well have cooked his own goose!

Late the next morning Nancy visited Mrs. Shannon. Michael had said she was a real TV buff and that it wasn't a good idea to interrupt her during the afternoon soaps or evening prime time.

She lived in a white, wood-frame house. Green flower boxes brimming with orange and yellow marigolds lined the wide porch. Dee Shannon answered the door, but it took some fast talking from Nancy to keep her from closing it again the minute Michael's name was mentioned.

"Please, believe me," Nancy pleaded, "Michael is in very serious trouble. You know him—normally he would never have acted the way he did yesterday."

"And you're asking me to get myself in trouble along with him?" Dee Shannon's naturally high-colored cheeks were even redder from the agitation of the moment. "After all, I'm the one who gave him that card."

"Why don't you let me in for a few minutes? We'll talk about what we can do to keep everybody out of trouble."

Mrs. Shannon was short and wide. She filled the doorway so Nancy couldn't possibly get past.

Instead of stepping aside, Mrs. Shannon moved back several steps, letting Nancy into the entryway but no farther. She knew she had to calm the woman down or they'd never be able to talk sensibly about Michael's situation.

"Something smells good," said Nancy. "Were you cooking?"

"Yes, I was."

"Don't let me stop you then," said Nancy with a bright smile. "I'll come into the kitchen and we can talk there while you cook."

Mrs. Shannon looked Nancy up and down suspiciously one more time, then turned and walked down the hallway.

"I do my cooking early so I can watch the soap operas when they come on," said Mrs. Shannon as Nancy surveyed the array of steaming kettles on the kitchen stove.

Nancy remembered what Michael had said about Mrs. Shannon being a real TV lover. Maybe that could be a way of getting to her.

"I met Rick Arlen once," said Nancy. "You know, the guy from 'Danner's Dream.'"

"You did?"

Nancy could see Mrs. Shannon beginning to thaw, and it wasn't because of the steamy kitchen.

"I can hardly watch that show since they had him die. It's just not the same without him."

Nancy nodded before steering the conversation back in the direction she wanted it to go. "Michael wishes he hadn't lost his temper with you."

"He shouldn't have talked to me the way he did." Mrs. Shannon sounded as if she was getting angry again.

"Well, he wasn't thinking straight at the time," Nancy said apologetically. She told Mrs. Shannon about Michael's problems.

"I think he snapped under the pressure," she finished up. "After all, he could lose everything."

Mrs. Shannon stared at her for a moment. "Yes," she said finally in a much softer tone. "I see what you mean."

Nancy tried not to let her sigh of relief be audible.

"I can't really help you much though," said Mrs. Shannon. "That other Mulraney—the real one—kept to himself. He didn't even eat his meals here the way most of my roomers do. Tall, handsome fellow—but not very memorable, for all that. He never smiled. He made it very clear that he minded his business and wanted everybody else to do the same. Then, the next thing I heard, he was dead, killed in some kind of construction accident."

Construction! That was the present Michael Mulraney's business too. Was it just coincidence, or was there more of a connection than that? Nancy realized she'd have to find out more about the first Mulraney.

"Did he have any friends that you know of?" she asked Mrs. Shannon.

"If he did, he never brought them here. He was quiet and neat, and he paid his rent on time. That's all I can tell you about him."

Nancy couldn't hide her sigh this time. It looked as if she'd hit a dead end.

"Wait a minute. Now that I think about it," said Mrs. Shannon, wiping her hands on her apron, "there was one thing I heard."

"What was that?" Nancy asked eagerly.

"Supposedly he hung around a pool hall in the neighborhood sometimes. It's called the Side Pockets Club." She frowned. "I remember it seemed strange to me. He struck me as too much of a gentleman for that crowd."

"Thanks, Mrs. Shannon," said Nancy. "I'll check it out."

"Don't you be going there by yourself," said Mrs. Shannon. For the first time, Nancy heard a bit of a brogue in the woman's voice. "As I understand it, that's no place for a young lady."

"Oh, it can't be that bad," Nancy protested, but Mrs. Shannon shook her head vigorously.

Mrs. Shannon wouldn't let Nancy go back into the hallway until she promised not to go alone. Nancy hated to deceive the woman, but it wasn't a promise she could keep.

However, when she saw the pool hall, she wondered if she shouldn't have taken Dee Shannon's advice.

The sidewalk in front of the Side Pockets Club was littered with bottles and cans. The windows of the one-story building had been painted over in dark green with black lettering. Nancy couldn't tell anything about what or who was inside. She remembered Mrs. Shannon's warning. Still, it was a bright, sunny afternoon, and Nancy was anxious to get on with the investigation. She was following a trail that had been cold for a few years, and she had the feeling it could get colder by the minute. She opened the door and stepped inside. It could have been midnight instead of broad daylight. The long, narrow room was lit only by green-shaded light bulbs suspended from the ceiling over a dozen or so pool tables. By the time Nancy's eyes had grown accustomed to the gloom, she heard someone move in behind her.

The man blocking the door was tall and dark-haired and was staring straight at her. Nancy looked around and saw more guys gathering, forming a semicircle with her at the center. She could feel their silent challenge fill the dimly lit room.

This was a scene she'd have to play just right, or she could be in *big* trouble!

Chapter

Six

DOES ANYBODY HERE feel like shooting pool?" asked Nancy, trying to sound confident as she elbowed her way through the lineup of guys. She half wished she was back watching the soaps with Dee Shannon.

She could see that the swaggering character at the door had been thrown off guard by her question. He obviously didn't expect a "nice girl" like her to be a pool player. He watched as she made a ritual of selecting a cue from the brace on the wall. She took each one down and tested it for balance across her palm and for straightness by eyeing it along the shaft.

Nancy had learned to shoot pool in the billiard room of one of her father's lawyer friends several years earlier. She'd been at a very determined age and went back again and again until she got her technique down pat. She made a silent wish that all that practice would pay off now when she needed it most.

"First game is mine," said a stocky, tough-looking guy who had been leaning against a nearby table.

Nancy guessed from the way the others deferred to him that he was a leader here.

"What're we playing for?" he asked, looking her up and down.

"How about information?" Nancy answered.

"What kind of information?"

Nancy knew it was always safest to keep a half truth as close as possible to the whole truth.

"I'm trying to help out a guy I know," she said. Snickers rippled through the crowd, as if a girl like her was the last person a guy would turn to for help. She had to gain some respect and do it fast.

"My break?" she asked her opponent.

"Sure. Why not?" he said. "What's your name anyway? I don't like to shoot with anybody unless I know their name."

"Nancy Drew," she said, then wished herself luck and crouched down to line up her shot.

She stroked the cue complete with follow-through, just as her father's friend had taught her. There was a murmur of approval as several balls rumbled into the pockets, and she realized she'd been holding her breath since her shot. She let it out slowly so no one would notice.

"What should I call you?" she asked her opponent as she chalked her cue and forced herself to appear at ease. It wasn't easy, with a roomful of tough characters watching her.

"Ace."

She saw some knowing looks exchanged around the room and no snickers this time. She called her next shot and sank it.

"So tell us your story," said Ace.

"Like I told you before, I'm here to help a friend," she said, improvising a story rapidly. "In fact, he's from this neighborhood."

She walked slowly around the table, sizing up her next shot. Then she aimed and sank that one too. Still in her crouch, she peeked under her outstretched arm to check Ace's reaction. She had to be careful not to make him look foolish in front of his buddies, and being beaten by a girl could do just that. Yet she didn't want to cheat if she could help it.

"My friend is in pretty big trouble," she went on.

She tried to sound calm, but the situation was making her nervous. Her hand was shaking slightly as she took her shot. She missed, honestly.

"Let her take it over. She was shook up about her friend," said someone in the crowd.

"No thanks," Nancy answered quickly. "That's not my style."

There was another murmur of approval as she stepped back from the table. Ace looked a little guilty as he lined up his shot, but he took it anyway. To Nancy's great relief, the ball sped across the green felt and into the side pocket. Right then, she'd rather lean against the wall and watch Ace show off his moves.

"What is it you're trying to find out for this friend of yours?" he asked as he sauntered around the table, sizing up the position of the balls just as she had done.

"About the guy who's behind all his troubles," said Nancy.

"Don't you know any guys who could take care of this for you?"

"It isn't the kind of thing I can let other people know about, and he's counting on me."

"Since when does anybody count on a girl?" the character by the door piped up, and there were snickers again.

Nancy looked hard and straight into his sneering face, her stomach flip-flopping. She held her breath a minute before answering.

"Since I promised to help him," she said.

"All right," said Ace, clapping her shoulder as he sauntered past her toward the other end of the table. He turned to the guy by the door. "Now, let the lady tell her story, McCarthy," he said with a hint of a warning in his tone.

"How's *she* going to help someone?" McCarthy muttered. This time there were no answering snickers. He scowled and skulked back against the door.

"You got a name on this guy you're after?" asked Ace.

"Michael Mulraney."

Another murmur traveled around the room, and Ace straightened from his crouch to study her face for a moment before responding.

"I'm afraid you're a little late," he said. "Somebody beat you to the punch with that one. Old metal-mouth's dead and gone."

Metal-mouth, how odd, Nancy thought. She studied Ace. She'd swear he was telling the truth. As far as Ace knew, Mulraney was dead, just as Dee Shannon had said he was. Nancy didn't exactly know what she'd expected to find out, but she was disappointed.

"And you're lucky he *is* dead and gone," Ace added. "I don't care how tough you are, you wouldn't want to go up against Mulraney."

"Tell her what he did for a living," said McCarthy in his smart-aleck way from the sidelines.

"He was a professional." When Nancy showed no sign of comprehending, Ace went on. "He was a hitter."

"Yeah. He killed people for fun and profit," said McCarthy in a mocking tone. "From what I heard, he did it mostly for fun. Is that what he did to your boyfriend?"

"Not my boyfriend, my friend," she said as firmly as she could manage. Her mind was reeling. The further she delved into this case, the more dangerous it became. A hit man!

"Lay off, McCarthy," Ace warned.

Nancy could feel the tension between them.

"What happened to Mulraney?" she asked hastily to cool them down. The last thing she wanted was to end up in the middle of a brawl between these two.

"Word on the street was he did exactly what you claim he did to your friend. He let somebody down. Only this time he did it to the wrong dude, and that dude cashed in Mulraney's chips for him."

"Permanently," McCarthy added with a nasty smile.

"That's right," Ace confirmed. "There was a big construction project over on the west side at the time. Rumor was they dumped him into the foundation."

"How do you know that's true?" Nancy asked.

"Because nobody ever saw him again, and he left a lot of loose ends behind, the kind of stuff a guy would clear up if he had a chance to."

"What kind of loose ends?"

"Like people who owed him lots of money," McCarthy interrupted again. "And Mulraney always made a point of collecting his debts, one way or another."

"Did he have any friends?" Nancy asked Ace.

"Why do you want to know that?"

She heard the edge of suspicion in his voice. "I guess I want to hear the details to satisfy myself that he's really dead."

"You can take my word for it. He is. Mulraney was alive one night, hanging out on the street, acting like his usual miserable self. Next day he was history." Ace took the shot that clinched the game for him. "Besides, he was too mean to have friends."

Nancy looked crestfallen as the ball rolled into the trough. Since that was actually how she felt about what she'd learned so far, it wasn't too hard to pretend.

"Sorry," said Ace, sounding as if he really was.

"Good game," Nancy said.

She walked to the brace on the wall and hung up her cue, then extended her hand to Ace for a shake. He took it solemnly. "Any time," he said.

Nancy moved toward the door, but McCarthy stepped in front of her to block her way just as he had when she first came in.

"McCarthy, you called for winners, didn't you?" said Ace, chalking his cue and giving Nancy a conspiratorial grin. "That means you're up against me."

Nancy saw McCarthy's sneering façade slip a notch as mocking laughter rippled nearby. This was a weak moment for him, and she'd better take advantage of it. She walked around him to the door, paused a moment to salute Ace, then was outside the pool hall at last. She let out a long sigh of relief.

Walking to her car, Nancy thought about what she'd learned. It looked as if the original Michael Mulraney really was dead. Nobody'd seen a body, but that was probably how things were done in the circles he frequented.

She opened the door of her car and slipped gratefully inside. Her visit with Ace and company had left her more than a little tense. She switched on the ignition and pushed in the tape she had left in the deck. Maybe some music would help.

But instead of the song she'd expected, an all-too-familiar deep voice rumbled from the speakers. "You'd better watch your step, Nancy Drew!"

Nancy's hand dropped from the tape deck as she listened. It was the same menacing voice she'd heard that night from the copy room.

"You could get hurt—maybe you could even get *dead!*"

Chapter

Seven

NANCY DIDN'T LIKE being threatened. She frowned. So the man with the deep voice knew who she was, and he thought he could scare her off. Well, she wasn't backing out now!

With a screech of her tires, she pulled out into the traffic and drove to the Municipal Building.

At Councilman Terry's office, George was in a planning meeting, so Nancy sat down to wait for her in the reception area. The receptionist smiled at her. "Are you coming to our big fund-raiser tomorrow night?" she asked Nancy.

"I don't know—am I invited?" Nancy asked, surprised.

"Oh, of course," the receptionist assured her. "Didn't George tell you? All the staff members are encouraged to bring a few guests. You know, the more money we can raise for the councilman's campaign, the better."

"I can see the logic." Nancy laughed. "The more the merrier, right?"

"Mmm-hmm." The receptionist nodded. "All of Mr. Terry's biggest backers are going to be there. Even Bradford Williams—he's coming from Chicago for it. He's such a *wonderful* man!" She looked slightly starry-eyed. "Handsome, generous . . ." Her voice trailed off as a door opened.

"Nancy! What are you doing here?" George walked over to them, looking crisp and business-like in her tailored jacket and slacks.

"I came by to ask your advice," Nancy said, trying to signal with her eyes that she needed to talk to George alone.

George winked. "Just call me Miss Lonelyhearts," she joked. "Let's talk on the way out. I got finished early today."

Saying goodbye to the receptionist, who seemed disappointed to lose her audience, Nancy and George headed to the elevators while Nancy repeated the details of her eventful afternoon.

The elevator doors eased open, and a young man of medium height with slicked-back black hair stepped out, moving fast and not bothering to look where he was going. His briefcase grazed Nancy's leg as he pushed past, but he didn't stop.

He turned to give her an annoyed look as if

she'd run into him instead of the other way around. Then he hurried on his way, hawk nose in the air, walking faster than ever in the direction of the councilman's office.

"Who was that?" asked Nancy, staring after him. Something about him struck a chord in her memory. Maybe it was just his unpleasantness. She was beginning to think this must be her day for running into unpleasant characters.

"His name is Franklin Turner," said George, grimacing. "He's one of Councilman Terry's aides."

"I thought politicians were in the business of making friends. Terry won't win any popularity contest by having that guy on his staff."

"Turner is what you might call a political appointee," George explained as they got on the elevator. "His parents are old friends of the councilman's family. The way I heard it, they want Turner to get into politics and thought working here would be great training for him, especially since the councilman's next stop will probably be Washington."

"From what I saw, Turner needs all the training he can get!"

"You're right about that. If he had to depend on his personality to get ahead, he'd be in big trouble," said George as they got off the elevator. "But, if it's any consolation, he's even less enthusiastic about being here than we are to have him.

The job doesn't interest him much. It was completely his family's idea."

"Hmm." Nancy couldn't feel much sympathy for someone whose parents' money was greasing his way into public service.

"Punctuality isn't one of his strong points either," said George, checking her watch. "Three o'clock, and he's just getting to the office. He was probably out late last night. I hear he loves the Chicago club scene."

"Hmm," said Nancy once more. "Well, he sounds pretty awful. Let's not talk about him anymore. Is there a pay phone around here? We should call Bess and see if she wants to help out."

It was time to get down to some hard-nosed investigating of the Michael Mulraney case. They gave Bess a call, but she wasn't home, so Nancy and George were on their own.

There was just time for George to get to the newspaper office and check the articles morgue before it closed for the day. Maybe she could find something about the accident that killed the original Mulraney.

Meanwhile, Nancy went to the police station to see if she could find out what was going on with the investigation into Kathy Novello's death. Though she wasn't hopeful, there was always a chance that Detective Hicks had turned up something she could use.

"We did the standard follow-up, looked the

place over, talked to the neighbors," he said. "We didn't find a thing. We're still doing background checks on her, but so far we've come up blank everywhere."

Of course Nancy wasn't about to give up that easily.

"Was there anything unusual about any of the neighbors you questioned?" she asked.

"The guy downstairs seemed disappointed that he had been out at the time and missed the excitement."

"Would you mind giving me his name?"

Hicks squinted at her. "Unofficially, all right? Norman something." He shuffled through some papers in his Out basket. "Norman Fredericks, but I'm telling you he's no lead. He doesn't know anything. He wasn't even around when it happened."

"You're probably right," said Nancy.

But whatever Hicks might say, she intended to have a talk with Mr. Fredericks.

"I didn't find out a thing," said George when they met at the pizza parlor later. They couldn't find Bess—she was probably out with her new heartthrob again. "There's no record of Mulraney's death—or of his life either, for that matter."

"Interesting," murmured Nancy, half to herself.

"What's so interesting about it?" asked George as she contemplated her hero sandwich unenthusiastically. "Seems pretty much like running into a blank wall to me."

"First of all, this makes it look like the guys at the Side Pockets Club could be right about how Mulraney died, and Dee Shannon was probably lied to."

"How do you know that?" George delicately popped a shred of lettuce into her mouth.

"The fact that there's no record suggests to me that it could have been a contract killing after all, a professional hit with no loose ends and no trace left behind. If his death was a simple accident, as Mrs. Shannon said, it would have been reported in the paper." Nancy took a sip of her diet soda while she thought a moment. "Even so, she could be partly right. Both Mrs. Shannon and the Side Pockets guys said his death had something to do with a construction site."

George and Nancy looked at each other.

"And the *new* Michael Mulraney is in the construction business," said George slowly.

Nancy nodded unhappily. She knew George was thinking what she herself had tried to avoid thinking. She liked Michael Mulraney and wanted to believe he was just a hard-working guy struggling to help his family. She didn't want to believe that struggle had made him so desperate he might have killed for it. She picked up her shoulder bag and started fishing for the keys to her car.

"I think we'd better get on with this investigation," she said.

George looked down at her half-eaten hero. "Don't bother saying it. I know the routine." She sighed out loud. "I'll have this wrapped to go."

Norman Fredericks lived on the second floor, directly below Kathy Novello's apartment. He needed no softening up to talk.

"I keep a close watch on things around here. I guess you might say it's my main form of entertainment," he admitted.

Glancing around the barren apartment, Nancy could believe he needed to look elsewhere for his interests.

"Some people watch television," he said, "but I prefer real life. Then I can use my imagination to make up the bits that go between the little pieces I see." He was small and very thin with pale, wispy hair.

"What pieces did you see of Kathy Novello's life?" Nancy asked.

"Nothing much, really. She was very quiet. I had to do a lot of imagining where she was concerned, but I never thought up anything like what ended up happening to her."

Nancy could hear in his voice the disappointment Detective Hicks had mentioned. She was disappointed too. Norman would have made an excellent witness, but he said he hadn't witnessed anything.

"I did see something yesterday," he added. "I might call the police about it and I might not. They wouldn't even take the time to come inside and talk while they were here, and they wouldn't tell me a thing about what was going on. So why should I tell them what I saw?"

"If you'd like to, you could tell *us* what you saw," Nancy suggested, trying not to sound too eager. "We came in and talked."

"Yes, you did," he said, looking her over thoughtfully for a moment. "I suppose I could tell you.

"Well"—he leaned forward in his seat—"there was this young man in the hallway, and I'm almost certain I heard him upstairs trying the Novello girl's door, but the police had put on a special lock so he couldn't get in."

"Did you actually see him?" asked Nancy.

"Yes, I did," Fredericks answered, his tiny eyes glittering at the prospect of having an interested audience at last. "He was about medium height. And he had black hair. I only saw him from the back." He looked disappointed. "But from the way he stomped out he seemed pretty upset."

Nancy's heart sank. "I see," she said. Standing up, she held out her hand. "Thank you for your time, Mr. Fredericks. You've been a big help."

Later, as they were walking away from the

building, George said what they'd both been thinking.

"You know who that description sounds like, don't you?"

"Yes, unfortunately, I do."

"Michael Mulraney."

Nancy nodded agreement, though she wished she didn't have to.

"Maybe we should call him Kevin Dougherty," George remarked.

"Whatever we call him, we'd better do it while we're asking him some tough questions about where he was the night Kathy Novello died. And there's no time like the present for doing that."

Nancy hurried toward her car with George in her wake. She didn't bother calling Michael's answering service this time. She figured he'd be at the job site.

But when she pulled up to the curb, the steel link gates were closed and locked and a small crowd had gathered outside.

"What's going on?" George asked.

Nancy parked as fast as she could, half in and half out of the space, and both girls rushed to the gate. They could see that the outside lights were off around the building once again.

"There's been an accident in there," a woman carrying a grocery bag volunteered. "They say a big scaffolding collapsed and somebody got killed!"

Chapter

Eight

THE WAIL of an ambulance siren told Nancy this was no narrow escape like the incident with the circuit breaker. The gate swung open to let the ambulance pass. Nancy grabbed George's hand and they slipped inside.

They found Pete Donaldson, and Nancy repeated George's question. "Michael was up on the scaffolding correcting a mistake in some window trim when the support rope broke," the foreman explained. "He doesn't usually wear a safety belt. Thank heaven, he had one on tonight. That belt saved his life."

Nancy had kept her distance from the spot where the ambulance team was huddled around the dark-haired form on the ground. Now she pressed forward to make certain that Pete was right and Michael was safe.

"He was lucky in another way too," said Pete. "That block and tackle over there came down just inches from his head. If that had hit him he'd be dead now for sure."

While Michael was being lifted into the ambulance, Nancy went to take a closer look at that scaffolding cable. Unfortunately, there was no way of telling if it had been tampered with. If someone had cut this cable partway through, then they'd done so strand by strand to make it look like a fray.

"Excuse me," Nancy said to one of the paramedics. "Is he going to be all right?"

The paramedic looked at her. "Friend of yours?" she asked. "Sure, he'll be just fine. We'll take him in for observation, but I'll bet you he'll be on his feet again tomorrow. Don't worry." She gave Nancy and George a reassuring smile, then climbed into the back of the ambulance.

Nancy frowned. So far Michael had had two near misses. True, he'd survived both, but either could easily have been fatal. He couldn't possibly have arranged them, could he?

No, it seemed highly unlikely. And even if it was possible, Nancy couldn't believe it. Her instincts kept insisting that Michael was the victim, not the villain here.

So then who *was* the villain? Who had caused Kathy Novello's death—and who was trying to kill Michael now?

Just then something that had been nagging at

the edge of Nancy's consciousness leapt into focus. She grasped George's arm and pulled her friend around to face her.

"Remember the description Norman Fredericks gave of the man he saw at his apartment building?" she said urgently.

"Sure I do."

"Well, could it fit somebody else besides Michael? What about someone Kathy knew from the office?"

George paused a moment to think. Then her eyes widened. "She had a crush on Franklin Turner," she said, staring at Nancy. "And he fits that description too."

Nancy nodded. "I thought there was something familiar about him when I saw him this afternoon," she said. "I just figured out what it was. I saw the profile of the guy who was being threatened in the copy room. It looked a lot like Turner's."

"But he's such a—such a wimp!" George protested. "Could he kill someone?"

"I don't know," Nancy said grimly. "But I'm going to find out."

Nancy, Bess, and George spent the next morning at the hospital. Michael was being discharged, and Nancy had volunteered to drive him home.

"Do you really think this guy Franklin Turner could be involved in Kathy's death and what's happening to Michael too?" asked Bess as they waited.

"Why not? He had access to the copy machine. It could have been him I overheard that night threatening to take care of Kathy. And it was Michael's document he was after."

"But Turner's rich! Why would he need to blackmail someone like Michael?" George asked, looking doubtful.

"We don't know for sure that this *is* a case of blackmail," said Nancy. "We're not sure yet what's going on. There hasn't been any demand for money. In fact, whoever is doing these things to Michael seems to want him out of the way permanently, and that's no way to get somebody's money."

"That's true," said George with a grim smile. "But then, the question is, why would Franklin Turner want Michael Mulraney out of the way?"

"I don't have an answer to that yet." Nancy was well aware that her theory had gaping holes in it, and she was a long way from filling them.

"I'm not saying I don't think Turner could do such a thing. He strikes me as one of those rich kids who thinks he can get away with anything," George commented. "Still, he'd have to have a reason."

"I agree. I think it's time for a closer look at Franklin Turner. Will he be at that fund-raiser tonight?"

George shrugged. "I guess so."

"I think Councilman Terry just found another supporter," said Nancy with a smile.

"Hey! I want to go too," Bess chimed in. "Is it a formal?"

"If you're talking about a party, how about inviting me along?"

The girls looked up to see Michael Mulraney limping toward them, grinning rather crookedly. His right arm was in a soft sling, and he appeared to be listing in that direction.

"You don't exactly look like you're up to celebrating," said George skeptically.

"Could you deny a condemned man his final wish?"

There was that crooked grin again. Nancy tried to smile along with him but couldn't. The events of the past few days hadn't put her in the right frame of mind to appreciate that kind of humor.

They all dressed in their best for the Pinnacle Club. George had on a navy blue dress with a short white jacket that emphasized her slim figure.

Nancy's two-piece outfit was just the right color blue to set off the shine of her red-blond hair and put a blush in her cheeks.

"What a place!" Bess said as they entered the elegant foyer. She paused and stared at the gleaming chandeliers and marble columns. "I bet there'll be a lot of great-looking guys here too!"

"I thought you were only interested in Jeff Matthews," Nancy said, teasing her a bit.

Bess smoothed the skirt of her yellow silk dress. "Well, he's wonderful, of course," she replied. "But he's not the only guy in the world. Anyway, I can look, can't I?" she added with a mischievous grin.

George laughed. "Poor Bess. Being in love is almost as hard as being on a diet, huh?"

Nancy looked around curiously. She was only interested in one guy tonight, and Franklin Turner was hardly great looking. But she didn't care as much about looking at him as listening to him. She was certain she'd recognize his voice if it was the one she'd overheard in the copy room.

There was a sudden clatter behind her, and she turned to see a half-dozen nails bouncing across the parquet floor.

"Sorry," said Michael, retrieving the hardware and stuffing it into his suit pocket. "I stopped off at the site on my way here, and I guess I brought some of the job along with me."

They moved into the main gallery where the reception had already started.

"I hadn't expected anything quite this fancy for a local politician," Nancy remarked.

"I don't think he'll be local for long," said George. "I hear he's planning to run for Congress soon—maybe even the Senate."

"Does he have the kind of support it takes to do that?" Nancy asked.

"That's what he's after here tonight."

"These are mostly businesspeople, aren't they?" asked Nancy. She'd recognized several associates of her father's.

"That's right," said George and began pointing out the big names. "We're expecting some potential backers from as far away as Chicago."

"So I heard at the office yesterday."

"I wish businessmen were younger," lamented Bess, still scanning the crowd.

Nancy laughed. "It takes a few years to get this successful."

"There's one closer to our age, but he's not exactly my type."

Nancy looked across the room where Bess was pointing. It was Franklin Turner!

He wore a tuxedo, and he had a very sophisticated-looking young blond woman on his arm.

"There's Turner," said George, who'd made the same discovery.

"Who's that with him?" asked Nancy, adjusting the jacket of her blue outfit and wondering how she'd look in a sleek black number like the one Turner's date was wearing.

"One of his friends from Chicago, probably. He doesn't have much to do with anybody from River Heights. Not unless they're very important, that is," said George. "See those two men he's walking up to? They're big-time lawyers, Jethro Serkin and Maxwell Edwards. Turner's probably trying to convince them he's running the councilman's operation single-handedly."

Nancy had heard Carson Drew mention both of those names. She wished he were here, so he could refresh her memory.

"We got word today that Jethro Serkin wants to cosponsor the voter-registration drive," said George proudly.

"Congratulations," said Nancy. She was only half paying attention, because she'd been watching Franklin Turner.

Two other men had joined his circle, and Nancy was about to ask George who they were when Councilman Terry and his wife came up to introduce themselves to Nancy and Bess.

They had a good talk until the councilman stopped in midsentence as a distinguished-looking man entered the room. Terry excused himself without finishing whatever he'd been saying and hurried away with his wife in tow.

"Bradford Williams just came in," said George, nodding toward the new arrival. "He was one of the people we were hoping would come tonight." There was a flash of gold as Williams smiled down at Mrs. Terry.

"He's nice-looking," Bess commented through a mouthful of pâté. She'd sent Michael after a waiter with a tray. "How old is he?"

"Old enough," George answered dryly.

Meanwhile, on the other side of the room, the group Nancy was interested in had dissolved.

Maxwell Edwards was talking to someone she'd never seen before, and she couldn't find Franklin Turner.

"I'll see you later, guys. There's something I have to do," said Nancy, and she launched herself into the crowd.

She moved purposefully through the two rooms, looking for the distinctive silver-blond hair of Turner's companion. She'd be easier to pick out in a crowd than he was, but neither of them was anywhere. Nancy even checked the ladies' room. She should have guessed from what George had said about him that Turner might not stay too long at a party with what he would consider local yokels.

"There you are," said George, hurrying up to Nancy as she emerged from the ladies' room. "Gee, it's great to be friends with the daughter of the famous Carson Drew. I have a feeling that's why we got this." She held up an elaborately hand-lettered card of heavy, cream-colored vellum.

"What is it?" Nancy asked.

"An invitation to a private supper given by Terry and his wife for their special friends and associates. They're picking us up outside and we're being driven there in a limousine."

"All of us?" asked Bess, who had just walked up with Michael. "Right now?"

"That's what it says," George answered.

Nancy really wasn't in the mood for another party. Then a thought occurred to her.

"Will Franklin Turner be there?" she asked.

"I wouldn't be surprised."

That made up Nancy's mind and the mention of the limo had sold Bess on the idea. Michael agreed to tag along.

Bess was in seventh heaven as the long, sleek car eased away from the portico of the Pinnacle Club.

"I absolutely love limos," she exclaimed, as she explored the backseat cabinet. It was equipped with a television, CD player, and fully stocked bar.

Bess had served them each a soda with crushed ice in a crystal glass and was starting on the assortment of munchies when the car pulled over to the side of the road. The outside view was mostly obscured by the black glass and surrounding darkness, but Nancy could tell they'd left town and were on a country road.

The partition between the front and back seats was made of heavy, opaque Plexiglas. It was closed as it had been from the start. It occurred to Nancy that the Pinnacle Club doorman had helped them into the car, and they'd never actually seen their driver.

She had her hand on the intercom button when an all-too-familiar deep voice came through the speaker.

"End of the line" was all it said.

Nancy heard the front door on the driver's side open and slam shut. She pressed herself up against the window, but could make out only an indistinct form hurrying toward another car up ahead. The figure climbed in and drove away.

"What's going on?" asked George.

Nancy didn't answer. With rising dread she reached for the door handle and pulled it. The door didn't budge.

"Nancy, what's happening? Why are we stopped?" Bess asked, alarmed at the look on her friend's face.

Michael sniffed the air. "What's that smell?" he cried.

Nancy swallowed hard. "Guys, I think we're in trouble," she said. "That's the car's exhaust—and it's loaded with carbon monoxide!"

Chapter

Nine

EXHAUST FUMES WERE HISSING steadily into the car. Bess opened her mouth to scream, but the sound was choked off as she started to cough.

Nancy knew they had to remain calm and act fast. Carbon monoxide didn't take long to knock a person out.

"Give me your sling," she said to Michael.

He winced as he yanked off the piece of black cloth and handed it over. Nancy grabbed the seltzer spigot from the wet bar. Her eyes had begun to water. She had to concentrate just to see clearly.

"Let us out of here!" shouted Bess between choking sounds. She started pounding on the door.

"Don't panic!" said Nancy in a voice so stern

and loud it made Bess snap around to look at her. "And don't waste your energy beating on a locked door."

She barely got that out before her first fit of choking overtook her. Time was dwindling now. Once the coughing turned to spasms she'd have a hard time doing anything.

She saturated the sling with seltzer water and handed it to George. "Tear this into four pieces and give each of us one," Nancy instructed. "We'll put them over our faces and breathe through them."

"Let me," said Michael tensely.

"You can't tear cloth with one hand. Anyway, I need you for something else." It was getting harder for Nancy to speak now. "Do you have any tools with you?".

She remembered the nails falling from Michael's pockets in the foyer of the Pinnacle Club and prayed they weren't all he'd stashed away. Michael rummaged in his pockets and pulled out a four-inch level. The bead of yellow liquid at its center bounced crazily in Nancy's blearing vision as she shook her head vigorously.

"Something to get us through to the front."

She gestured at the partition between the seats. They had to get to the controls up there. The doors and windows were electrically controlled, and the controls had to be in the front.

Bess had taken off her shoes and was pounding on the back and side windows with them. It was a futile gesture, but Nancy didn't tell her that. She'd seen the tears streaming down her friend's face and knew they weren't just from irritated eyes. Bess was terrified.

George handed out the pieces of wet material. Nancy slapped hers over her nose and mouth and breathed in. The bubbles from the seltzer tickled her nose, but the mask did help her to breathe. And at this point, every little bit helped.

Meanwhile, Michael's foraging had produced a tape measure, a notebook and pencil, and more nails. Then from his inside jacket pocket he pulled a small screwdriver. Nancy gestured toward the mechanism that held the partition window in place, and Michael started prying at the clasp. When Bess heard Michael chiseling at the lock, she spun around.

"I'll help," she choked as she scrambled across the seat, clambering over George. Before Nancy could comprehend what was happening, Bess had grabbed the screwdriver handle along with Michael and gave it a furious jerk.

Extreme fear can make a person very strong all of a sudden. And that had happened to Bess. Fueled by terror, the force of her pull on the handle was too much for the screwdriver. The long blade snapped with a crack that made Nancy sick to her stomach.

Michael wrestled the handle away from Bess and went on jabbing at the lock with what was left, but Nancy could see it wouldn't do any good.

"Spray!" she choked at George, gesturing toward their nose cloths.

George spritzed them each with another dousing of seltzer. The dancing bubbles didn't feel like tingles this time. They burned like tiny, hot needles searing Nancy's nostrils.

Still, that wasn't what worried her most. She could feel herself getting woozy. She knew how dangerous it could be to slow down in a situation like this. Fast thinking was more crucial than ever.

A clever idea was desperately needed to save them from what was beginning to look more and more like their fate. But no idea came.

Nancy felt her muscles growing slack despite her efforts to keep them taut and action-ready. Bess was racked with choking spasms now. She sounded as if she was on the verge of strangling, and George and Michael would not be far behind.

Nancy had to think! Her powers of reasoning and deduction had been her mainstay in times of trouble for as long as she could remember. They were clearly failing her now as she felt herself fading from consciousness.

The gas had slowed the others down too. Bess

was back at the window, but the results were closer to tapping than pounding now.

Then, through the fog of Nancy's gas-clogged thinking, came the faint glimmer of an idea.

"Backs against the seat!" she rasped as she plopped back onto the cushioned leather that had seemed so luxurious such a short while ago.

The other three stared at her instead of moving. Their brains were obviously as sluggish as hers right then.

"Do this," she ordered in a hoarse voice. Her throat had begun to constrict, and she doubted she'd be able to say much more.

She pressed her back against the seat and forced her legs upward into a tuck against her chest, gesturing for the others to do the same. Michael was the first to respond, and George after him. They crawled to the seat as quickly as their slowed reactions would allow, one on each side of Nancy. George grabbed Bess's arm and pulled her down also.

Nancy made a slight kicking motion at the partition in front of them to show what they were supposed to do. They'd need to kick together, but she could no longer speak so there'd be no countdown. She raised her arm as a signal. Her hand seemed to float through the air.

The rest of them had pulled their knees up and apparently understood that they were supposed to kick the partition together. Even Bess was in position. Their heels glanced off the Plexiglas out of sync in a random pattern.

Nancy's heart fell. It was their last chance. She looked at each of them in turn and in that glance she willed herself to convey the words she could not say.

Once more, she urged them silently. This is the one that counts.

She clamped her knees to her chest, staring at the partition through her tears, looking directly at the spot where her feet would hit—concentrating all of herself on that spot as if it contained the entire universe.

From somewhere deep inside her, out of a corner of herself she'd hardly known existed until that moment, came a surge of determination like nothing she'd ever felt before. It rocketed through her with a power she wouldn't have thought herself capable of.

"Now!" she shouted.

At that very instant, four pairs of legs shot forward in a single, mighty movement—hitting the partition and punching it forward to burst from its frame on Michael's side. He was out of his seat and pushing himself through the opening before Nancy had recovered from the jolting impact of the kick.

She could hear him fumbling with buttons in the front seat. With her last ounce of strength she reached over and grasped the door handle and pushed it down. It hardly budged at first, only clicked against the secure lock like the sound of doom.

Then the handle moved a few inches farther, and the door swung open with Nancy falling after it, tumbling into the cool night air—choking, sobbing, gulping her way back toward life.

Chapter

Ten

THEY ALL LAY on the ground near the limo and choked and gasped till they could breathe normally again.

Bess sat up and brushed weakly at an enormous grass stain on her dress. It had been made when Michael had dragged her away from the car. "My dress is ruined," she said with a shaky laugh.

They all could have made the same complaint. Evening outfits weren't made for scrambling around in life-or-death situations or kicking out partitions or sprawling on damp grass. Michael's white shirtfront wasn't gleaming any longer. In fact, it didn't even look white. Nancy's blue skirt had ripped when she had made that last desperate kick, and her stockings were a mass of runs.

"We're alive," croaked George. "That's what matters."

"They didn't mean us to be," said Michael. He'd been over at the limo, checking it out under the hood. "That car has been rigged with a switch on the dash to direct the exhaust back inside. They could have killed all of you just to get to me." He was holding on to his injured arm. He'd probably hurt it more pulling Bess from the car.

"I don't think they're only after you," said Nancy.

She told him about Kathy Novello's death. Michael's eyes widened as she retraced the scene in the copy room.

"So," Nancy concluded, "Kathy may have been killed because they thought she knew about you. But I'm not really sure how it all ties together."

"I swear I've never been anywhere near Kathy Novello's apartment building," Michael Mulraney said. "I didn't even know her."

"I believe you," said Nancy.

"Is all of this over that note I got about the real Mulraney?"

"Maybe somebody doesn't want us to dredge up the fact that he was probably murdered," George suggested.

"Could be," said Nancy.

"Franklin Turner couldn't have done all this," said George, gesturing toward the limo.

"If he did, he wasn't alone," said Nancy. "There was that other guy. The one with the deep voice."

"How would somebody like Turner be connected to the kind of people that probably killed Mulraney?" asked George, sounding confused.

"Only one person has the answer to that," said Nancy, standing up and brushing herself off. "I think I'll pay Turner a visit, but I don't think I'll be talking to him," said Nancy.

"But I thought you said you were going to visit him," Bess objected.

"I am." Nancy replied. "But, actually, I'm hoping he won't be home."

"Well, we're coming with you," Bess said. "It sounds too dangerous—" She stopped, overtaken by a fit of coughing.

"Bess, you're the greatest," Nancy said with an affectionate grin. "But you're obviously in no shape to do anything more right now. I'm sending you home to bed.

"You, too, Michael," she added, raising her hand to silence his protests. "You shouldn't have come out tonight in the first place. I want you to rest and recuperate."

"Well, *I'm* coming, no matter what you say," George insisted. Nancy gave her friend a grateful look. She'd hoped George would volunteer her help. Nancy's plan would require an extra pair of hands.

Meanwhile, Michael used the odds and ends from his pockets to disconnect the exhaust valve. The limo was still running, though the ignition key had been removed by the driver. Michael opened all the windows to air out the last of the gas and drove them back into town.

Nancy's Mustang and Michael's pickup were the only vehicles left in the parking lot of the Pinnacle Club. The reception was long over. Nancy wondered if there had really been a private supper for the councilman's "special friends."

Could Terry possibly be in on this? Could there be something from his past, something involving the real Michael Mulraney, that was a threat to Terry's career? He was clearly an ambitious man. How far would he go to protect those ambitions?

Nancy didn't mention her suspicions to George. She would be very upset that someone was looking for chinks in her white knight's armor, and Nancy didn't have the time or energy for an argument right then.

Michael took Bess home in his pickup, and George followed Nancy's car in the limo. The long car was part of Nancy's plan.

They parked out of sight from the entrance to the downtown luxury condominium complex. Nancy had driven by it that afternoon to check out where Turner lived. A doorman in a gray uniform sat at a desk just inside the double glass doors which led to the foyer. She and George would have to get past him to the elevators, and that wouldn't be easy.

"We have to distract him," Nancy said to George. "Phase one of Nancy Drew's master plan."

"Let's hope it works," George murmured. "Good luck!" She squeezed Nancy's hand.

The first stage of Nancy's plan involved using her messy appearance to her advantage. She rumpled her hair to look even worse before hurrying up to the building and through the glass doors.

"Somebody jumped into my car at the stoplight," she exclaimed. "I had to jump out to get away! Please—I need a phone."

She'd made that sound pretty convincing, but it was probably her torn stockings that actually convinced the doorman.

He was asking what he could do to help when the second stage of Nancy's plan got underway, right on schedule. George revved the motor of the limo after pulling it across the driveway entrance, just as Nancy had told her to do. The doorman looked toward the street and frowned at the long car. Then he glanced back at Nancy.

"You go ahead and take care of that. I'll wait here," she said with a smile.

The doorman looked toward the limo again. "I'll be right back," he said, and was off down the drive.

So far, so good, thought Nancy. Now all she had to worry about was whether George could make it up the drive without being seen.

A narrow sidewalk ran from the street to the building, bordered by waist-high shrubs. Nancy thought she saw a movement there, then George was out from behind the bushes and through the glass doors in a flash. Her athletic grace came in handy in tight spots like this one.

According to the directory board in the foyer, Turner lived on the fourteenth floor. George and Nancy took the elevator as far as the eleventh and walked the rest of the way, just in case the doorman had returned and was watching the floor indicator over the elevator door to see where they'd gone. It was quite late by now, and Turner's hallway was deserted.

"Are you going to pick the lock?" asked George as they stood in front of his door.

"First I'll see if he's home." Nancy pressed the buzzer. "I shouldn't really break in, but we're talking about murder here."

George had already darted out of view. "What are you going to do if he answers?"

"I'll think of something," said Nancy. She wished she felt as sure of that as she sounded.

There was no answer. Nancy had gambled on that, but the risk had been calculated. If Turner was as much of a party animal as George had said, then he probably wouldn't be home this early on a Friday night.

"That was easy," she said. "Now let's see if the easy way will work a second time."

She fished in her shoulder bag and pulled out a plastic credit card, which she inserted between the door and frame just above the lock. She slid the card down. It was the oldest trick in the book, but Nancy was banking on the fact that this was a doorman building in a well-patrolled, low-crime neighborhood. Maybe Turner hadn't bothered installing fancy locks. A barely audible click confirmed that he had not.

"This may still be our lucky night," said Nancy with a wink at George as the door swung open and they slipped inside.

She took out the flashlight she'd brought from the car and switched it on.

"Wow!" said George as the light beam bounced off expensive furniture and valuable-looking artwork.

"He couldn't possibly pay for this stuff on a political aide's salary, could he?" asked Nancy.

"I heard he doesn't get a regular salary," said George. "His parents pay him. That's how they got the councilman to take him on."

"Which just goes to show that maybe you *should* look a gift horse in the mouth," Nancy murmured with a grin.

Nancy moved away, scanning the walls for entrances to other rooms, then opening them to peer inside. At the third doorway she came across what she'd been looking for.

Books lined the shelves of what appeared to be Turner's study. The bindings looked suspiciously untouched. Nancy suspected Turner wasn't as much of a reader as he wanted people to think.

"The desk is over here," whispered George through the gloom.

Nancy was disappointed to find that none of the drawers was latched. Bad sign. People didn't keep secrets in open drawers, and she was looking for evidence that Turner had a very big secret indeed.

She searched the desk anyway, but she'd been right about locks and secrets. The deep drawer didn't even hold files, only a stack of thick phone books from around the country. Nancy pulled them out and stacked them on top of the desk as she examined each one.

She was about to put them back in the same order she'd found them when she was startled by something. The stack on the desk was noticeably shorter than the depth of the drawer. Yet, when she opened it, the top cover had barely cleared.

She tapped at the inside bottom of the drawer. It sounded hollow all right, and she could see it was inches above the actual base of the desk. She felt around inside.

"Maybe there's a hidden button or something like that to open it," George suggested, peering over Nancy's shoulder.

Nancy nodded, but she had, in fact, decided to try the easy way first. She pulled a nail file from her purse and fitted its thin blade along the side of the false bottom, then levered it upward.

They were in luck that night. Jackpot. Nancy lifted out a pile of manila file folders and leafed quickly through them. Sure enough, the name of Michael Mulraney was printed on one of the tabs.

She was about to open that folder and look inside when she heard the sound she had been dreading ever since they entered the apartment. A key was turning in the main door lock.

Franklin Turner was back!

Nancy took the three top files and stuffed them in her bag, then slid the false drawer bottom back into place and hastily replaced the phone books on top of it. She closed the desk drawer and listened. She could hear Turner moving around the apartment.

George had wedged herself into a corner next to the bookcase, but she wasn't really out of sight. Nancy flipped off the flashlight and crept into the kneehole under the desk. Their one hope was that Turner wouldn't have any reason to come into his study that late at night.

Then, the study door opened, and Nancy heard footsteps walking straight toward her.

It looked as if her lucky streak had run out.

Chapter

Eleven

THEY'D BE CAUGHT the minute he turned on the lamp. He'd see George for sure, and he'd have to step on Nancy to sit down at the desk. She held her breath and didn't make a sound. They'd have to run for it.

But he wasn't walking around the desk to sit down. He'd stopped on the other side. Instead of pressing the button for the desk lamp, he picked up the phone and pushed a button there.

Nancy had noticed the fancy telephone when she was searching the desk. It was the kind with the console that lit up when you lifted the receiver, and there was a row of buttons down the side for presetting numbers you called a lot. Turner must have pushed one of those just then and was waiting for it to ring and be answered.

The minute Turner spoke, Nancy knew her suspicion was right. Turner's was definitely the voice she'd overheard that first night from the copy room at Councilman Terry's office. It was squeaky from tension, just as it had been then.

"Franklin Turner here," he said nervously.

"Don't ask me," he continued after a pause to listen. "I have no idea how they got on to us."

He listened again. "I have no intention of backing out now. There's too much at stake."

Nancy couldn't tell if the person on the other end was urging Turner to back out or warning him not to.

"This girl and her friends were causing more trouble than they were worth."

He paused. "I'm doing my best and will continue to do so. You can be absolutely certain of that," he said, and listened one more time before hanging up without a goodbye.

Nancy was holding her breath, as she made a silent wish that he wouldn't turn the light on now. She could just see his shiny patent leather evening shoes as he stepped forward to search for something on the desk.

What if he looked for one of the missing file folders? She'd only taken three, hoping he wouldn't notice they were gone, but what if he did? Worse yet, she hadn't checked all of the desk drawers. Could there be a gun in one of them?

She was still imagining the unpleasant possibilities when the patent leather shoes turned aside and Turner walked back out of the study, closing the door behind him.

George let out a soft sigh of relief. Nancy unfolded herself from her hiding place and flexed the cramps from her legs. Still, she remained on guard, making a shushing sound in George's direction.

Nancy watched the crack under the study door till the line of light turned dark and she could hear no more movement in the rest of the apartment. Turner had probably gone into the bedroom.

Her eyes had grown accustomed to the dark. A slight shimmer of gray light came through the white drapes which covered the wide window behind the desk. She could make out the shape of the telephone console and reached for it.

The dial tone seemed very loud in the hushed room as she lifted the receiver. Just as she'd guessed, a light came on beneath the array of clear plastic buttons. She could see perfectly well to punch out a number if she wanted, but she didn't do that.

She was interested in the row of buttons down the right side of the console. Those would be the preset numbers. Turner had pressed one of them to make his call, but there were no labels to indicate what they were. And—this Nancy could barely believe—there was no Redial button. If only she could press one, she'd know instantly who Turner had called.

"What are you doing?" George whispered a little frantically as she crept from her corner. "Let's get out of here!"

"In a minute," Nancy whispered back as she pushed the top button in the preset row.

"Who are you calling?" George sounded even more frantic now. "There's a pay phone on the corner!"

Nancy raised a finger to her lips to silence George. Her face was eerily illuminated by the phone light.

A woman's voice answered on the other end of the phone line. "Yes," she said with a refined lift to her tone. Then she waited a moment. "This is the Turner residence," she added, unruffled as could be. "Celia Turner speaking. May I help you?"

Nancy pressed the receiver cradle to disconnect. That must have been Turner's mother. Nancy doubted that was who he'd been speaking to just now.

Nancy punched the next button. The wait for an answer was longer this time, and she heard the phone fumbled and nearly dropped on the other end before a young woman's voice responded with a sleepy "Hello."

Definitely not. Once again, Nancy pressed the cradle.

"What are you doing?" George repeated, more frantic than ever.

"Something important," Nancy whispered as she punched the third button. "I'll only be a couple of minutes longer."

She could feel George's agitation and hoped for a swift answer this time, but that wasn't what she got. The phone rang and rang, but no one picked it up. The same thing happened with the next two buttons. George grew more agitated by the second.

"Markson's Custom Tailoring," came the answer to the next call. "This is a recording. Please, leave your message at the beep."

The voice was even more refined than Mrs. Turner's had been, and with a definite British accent. Nancy smiled ruefully. From what she'd heard about Turner, she wasn't surprised that he thought it necessary to have his tailor on a preset button. She pressed the cradle and held it long enough to disconnect.

As she dialed again, George grabbed her arm. "I don't care how important this is. I want to get out of here right now!"

"Just one more, I promise." Nancy gently peeled George's grip from her arm. The fingers unclenched reluctantly, and Nancy pushed the remaining button.

Three rings followed by a click and a hum. Nancy could tell she'd come up with another recording.

"You've reached 555-8280," said a rather

bored female voice while music played in the background. "State your name, number, and the reason for your call."

As she'd done with Markson's tailoring shop, Nancy hung up before the beep. She silently repeated the number she'd heard to memorize it as she moved quietly away from the desk. She could see just clearly enough through the gloom to avoid falling over furniture as she tiptoed across the thick carpet with George in her wake.

Nancy listened at the door, then turned the knob ever so gently and eased it open. Like the dial tone, even the tiniest noise seemed magnified in the stillness of the apartment. Nancy forced herself to move slowly and carefully though her heart had begun to trip faster with each step. She'd pressed their luck by lingering so long. Now she was very much aware that they had to get out as fast as they could.

Nancy didn't breathe normally again until they were approaching her car. They'd made it out of the apartment, down the service stairs, and through a rear exit without incident. Then they hurried along alleys back to the street.

They kept close to the buildings and away from the streetlights as they scurried toward the car. They were almost there when Nancy pulled her friend abruptly into a doorway.

"Look," she said and gestured toward Turner's apartment complex, which was still visible from where they stood.

The doorman had acted fast. A tow truck had been backed around the semicircular driveway to get it into position in front of the limo. The tow chain stretched taut from the boom on the back of the truck to the bumper of the limo. A loud, metallic rasp shattered the night. George and Nancy watched as the front end of the long, black car was lifted from the ground and tilted steadily upward.

A few minutes later, the limo was angled high enough to be towed. The truck eased forward around the drive, then into the street with the big car suspended behind, only its rear wheels on the ground.

They drove right past the doorway where George and Nancy were hiding. As the truck moved off down the street, Nancy noticed a puff of exhaust smoke trailing from the limo's tailpipe. The big car was still running, its extra-large tank not yet out of gas.

"I wonder why they don't just drive the car away," George commented.

"Maybe it's not legal," said Nancy. "After all, it doesn't belong to them."

"It didn't belong to us, either, and I'm very glad to be rid of it," said George with a shudder.

Nancy didn't have to ask the reason for that shudder. "Why don't you stay at my house tonight?" Nancy asked when they reached the car.

George flashed the first smile Nancy had seen from her in hours.

"That sounds great!" she said, and the gloom lifted.

Nancy was up early the next morning. She crept quietly out of her room, leaving George breathing softly in the other twin bed. An hour later George went out on the wide front porch to find Nancy engrossed in the file folders on her lap.

She flipped the top file closed and gazed out across the peaceful, sycamore-lined street as if she didn't quite recognize where she was.

"There can't be any doubt about it now," she said, more to herself than to George. "Franklin Turner is definitely a blackmailer."

Chapter

Twelve

WHAT'S IN THERE?" asked George, gesturing toward the folders.

"Sad stories," said Nancy, feeling pretty low herself.

"What do you mean?"

"Turner has information on these people about things from their pasts. Things that could cause them trouble now," Nancy explained.

"Like about Michael using someone else's name to get a job?"

Nancy nodded. "None of them are really big offenses, but these aren't big-name people. That's one of the reasons these revelations could be so devastating for them." She couldn't help feeling sorry for them. Although they'd done wrong, Turner's wrong seemed so much worse.

"How do you know Turner was blackmailing them?"

Nancy pulled a page from the top folder. "He made out one of these for each person. It lists the date a note was sent, then the amount asked for and the date it was paid. I'll bet there's a page like this in every one of those files back in his desk too."

George examined the paper. "This amount isn't that big. I thought blackmailers demanded hundreds of thousands."

"I've been thinking about that," said Nancy. "A blackmailer usually gets caught because he gets greedy. He asks for more than the victim can come up with, which sends the victim panicking to the police. Turner was too smart for that." Nancy felt nothing but disgust for his cleverness.

"He also asked for only one payment," she went on. "The blackmailer's second biggest mistake is that he keeps coming back for more until the victim feels like it will never end—"

"And panics and goes to the police," George finished. "Of course, there's no way to prove he wouldn't have gone back for additional payments."

"It doesn't look like it," said Nancy. "These entries begin a year ago, and he hasn't made return visits on any of them yet. But, of course, these are only three out of many." She heaved a sad sigh.

George looked thoughtful. "Do the victims have anything in common?" she asked.

"They all work for the city or were trying to work for the city when Turner went after them."

"I'll bet I know how he did it." George walked over to lean against the porch rail. She looked angry. "His starting this a year ago makes it obvious."

"What do you mean?"

"That's when Councilman Terry assigned Turner to work with the oversight committee." She came back over and sat down beside Nancy again. She still looked angry. "You see, he's good with computers. So he was given the job of checking out people whose names came up before the committee—"

"Because they wanted to work for the city, and the city doesn't want anyone who could bring scandal with them."

"Right."

Nancy shook her head in disgust. "They assigned the most corrupt person of all to find out who's corrupt, and he used the information to line his own pockets."

"I suppose you're right." George sounded discouraged.

"Remember what I said about looking gift horses in the mouth?"

"How could Councilman Terry have known Turner would do something like this?" George rose to her hero's defense.

"He should have run one of those computer checks on him," said Nancy, who was beginning to feel angry herself. "Criminals don't usually start their life of crime at Turner's age. I'd be willing to bet there's a string of petty offenses on his record going back to when he was in diapers."

"Unless he was always tricky enough to keep from getting caught." George looked more discouraged than ever.

"You've got a point," said Nancy.

"So what are you going to do?" asked George. "Take those files to the police?"

"Not just yet," replied Nancy. "Because of the way I got them, I'd like something to back them up in case they can't be used in court. I wish my dad were around so I could check it with him."

"So you need more proof. Do you have a plan?"

Nancy made a face. She really disliked this business. "I'm going to have to go see these people. If I'm lucky, maybe I'll be able to persuade one of them to come clean. But I don't think it's going to be very pleasant."

George looked at the name on the page Nancy had given her earlier. "Marjorie Rothman."

"She's first," said Nancy with a sigh.

"What did she do to get herself on Turner's hit list?"

"She made a mistake when she was very young. She borrowed from the accounts of the business she worked for. She paid back the money, but she still got fired when they found out what she'd been doing. She didn't put any of that on her application to do property appraisals for the city. If she had, it might even have been overlooked."

"If it's such a small thing that she did, why would she pay blackmail over it?"

"Guilt, I guess. She's probably very ashamed of what she did and doesn't want anybody to know. Maybe the amount Turner asked was small enough to make it worth her while to pay and avoid the trouble."

"She's going to have trouble now, isn't she?" George sounded as solemn as Nancy looked.

Nancy stood up slowly. "Yes," she said. "She's going to have trouble now."

Marjorie Rothman's house was small and neat. Carefully tended shrubs bordered the brick path to the stoop. The woman who answered the door was also small and neat.

"May I help you?" she said in a friendly tone.

"Mrs. Rothman, my name is Nancy Drew. I'm here to talk to you about Wyandot Realty," said Nancy.

She'd gotten the name from the file, and mentioning it had exactly the effect she'd anticipated. Mrs. Rothman's already petite form seemed to shrink even smaller as she opened the door and stood aside so Nancy could enter.

"Are you the one who sent that note?"

Marjorie Rothman asked after she'd sat down very primly on the edge of a chintz-covered sofa.

"No," said Nancy. "I'm not the person who blackmailed you, and I'm not here to threaten you now. But I am going to ask you to do something very brave."

"What is that?" asked Mrs. Rothman in a voice as small as she was. Her face was pale against her graying hair.

Nancy had come prepared to use pressure to get the information she needed. Instead, she spoke gently.

"I want you to help me to keep this man from doing the same thing to any more people."

"Was it a man? Do I know him?"

Nancy nodded yes to the first question. "But I don't think you know him."

"Have there been others like me—that he found out things about?"

"Quite a few."

Mrs. Rothman had been staring at the carpet ever since they sat down. "I'm not really very brave," she said, bringing her gaze to meet Nancy's at last. That look told Nancy that Marjorie Rothman was going to help in any way she could.

"My son, Bobby, was only three years old when my husband died," she began.

She told Nancy the whole story, about needing money desperately after her husband had died and left her with a small child to raise. She'd taken some money from the safe at her office in Chicago. She was going to pay it back, but the shortage was discovered before she could. She was fired, and to escape her shame she moved to River Heights. She never was in any trouble again.

Mrs. Rothman seemed relieved once she told her story. She told it even more willingly a second time, downtown for Chief McGinnis and Detective Hicks.

The police brought Franklin Turner in for questioning two hours later. When Chief McGinnis had heard Mrs. Rothman's story and seen the files Nancy had, he'd immediately applied for a search warrant. The minute it came through, he'd sent a team over to Turner's apartment. As soon as they had the evidence they needed, another team went to Councilman Terry's office and picked up their man.

The chief had consented to let Nancy observe the questioning from the next room through one-way glass.

Turner didn't appear to be the least bit upset by the arrest. He smiled arrogantly at the dark glass opposite him, as if he knew he was being watched and didn't care.

Nancy expected him to deny everything. After all, there weren't any witnesses. Mrs. Rothman had never actually seen him, and most likely his other victims hadn't either. He could hardly have missed his three top files between last night and this morning. And he didn't yet know that his home had been searched.

When the police chief strolled into the interrogation room with the rest of the file folders under his arm, though, Turner barely blinked an eye. Nancy was astonished at the way he admitted to the blackmail charges after almost no pressure at all.

"Almost everybody lies on résumés and job applications," he said with a cynical grin. "Some of those lies hide interesting stories. You just have to keep checking the dates and documents till you get to the truth. It's something like being a detective."

He turned his grin toward the mirror across from him. Nancy was certain he knew someone was there.

When asked about Kathy Novello, Turner showed his one and only glimmer of anxiety. "I wasn't there," he said in an agitated tone. Then he seemed to recover his confidence. "I wasn't there," he repeated, darting a smug look at the one-way mirror. "I was in a meeting the evening she was killed. You want witnesses? Ask Bradford Williams. Or Jethro Serkin. They were there too. We were discussing Tim Terry's campaign."

As for being in the copy room the night of Kathy's death, Turner swore he wasn't there either. Nancy hadn't dared tell the police all the details, since she didn't want to betray Michael

Mulraney's confidence. So they didn't question him about either of Michael's "accidents."

He supposedly didn't know anything about the tape in Nancy's car or the rigged limo either. He covered very well and didn't act surprised that she was still alive. "From what I've heard about Ms. Drew," he said, "I imagine she's made an enemy or two in her career."

That was his story, and he stuck to it, cool as could be, no matter how hard they tried to break him down. Nancy could tell that the police were inclined to believe him, but she had some questions they hadn't asked.

Why had he declined his legal right to have a lawyer with him while he was questioned, especially if he intended to confess to the blackmail? And why, since he was so good at stonewalling, did he confess at all? After all, he'd denied everything else.

Nancy put off her pondering when she heard Chief McGinnis ask why someone as well fixed financially as Turner would bother committing petty blackmail.

"Well, there's no such thing as *enough* money," he said with a smirk. "Besides, that nine-to-five stuff is a bore. I needed the stimulation of a challenge." The smirk broadened. "I wanted to see if I could do it."

Looking at his arrogant expression through the glass, Nancy realized that this was the only part of Turner's story that was the whole truth.

He was lying about most everything. She was sure that what he *wasn't* saying was what was really important to this very confusing case. But what was he hiding?

And could she find out in time to save Michael Mulraney?

Chapter

Thirteen

UNFORTUNATELY, CHIEF MCGINNIS didn't see things the way Nancy did.

"Of course we'll check his alibi. But it sounds airtight—and we have no evidence to link him to the Novello girl's death. There's no reason to believe he's not telling the truth," he told Nancy as they walked toward his office.

"You really believe her death was an accident or suicide?" she asked.

"Well," said the chief, "until we get some real proof to the contrary, I'm afraid we'll have to accept that explanation."

Nancy persisted.

"What about the limousine being sabotaged? And the tape in my car? Those weren't coincidences. He must have known about those incidents at least."

"Nancy"—the chief laid a fatherly hand on her shoulder—"I have a lot of respect for your talent. But Turner made one good point. You *have* solved quite a few cases in this town, and I think you have to look at the possibility that you may have made some enemies. We'll investigate, but I think it's more than likely the threats are not related." He gave her a tired smile.

"Right now, we've got a full confession from a blackmailer. He's out of commission, in jail. *If* we come up with anything that links him to these complaints of yours, I'll let you know."

Nancy looked at Chief McGinnis and sighed. "Thanks, Chief," she said, and did her best to smile.

Back at the small, neat house, by the time Nancy finished telling Marjorie Rothman about Turner's confession, the older woman's eyes had brightened considerably.

"All day long I've been afraid and relieved at the same time," she said. "It isn't easy to know that I'll always have to live with everybody knowing what I did." She blew her nose on the crumpled tissue she had been twisting between her fingers.

"I'm sorry I had to be the one to dredge all of this up," said Nancy.

She meant it. This was one "crime" she wished she hadn't uncovered.

"You mustn't feel that way, my dear," said

Mrs. Rothman. "For the first time in years I feel free. I can face life with a clear conscience. You've done me a great service."

"And I have to ask one of you." Nancy leaned forward and looked Mrs. Rothman in the eye. "I need your help."

"I'll do anything I can," said Mrs. Rothman. "What is it you need?" She seemed truly eager to help.

"I have a phone number I need to trace to an address. . . ."

"Of course. Since I'm an appraiser, I use all sorts of directories. It won't be any trouble—just follow me." Mrs. Rothman led Nancy to an immaculately organized study off the living room. She pulled a thick book with a green binding from a shelf over the desk.

"This is what you'll need. River Heights— Telephone Lines Indexed to Residence."

Nancy was relieved when Mrs. Rothman turned discreetly aside to look out the window. Nancy trusted the woman, but even so, people who knew too much seemed to find themselves in dangerous situations.

She scanned the listings and easily located the address corresponding to the phone number on the recording she had reached on Turner's phone.

"Thank you so much," Nancy said. She shook hands warmly as she said goodbye to Mrs. Rothman.

Maybe this phone number would turn out to

be a dead end, but it was all Nancy had to go on. She had to check it out as a last-ditch effort to uncover the truth.

Whatever that may be, Nancy added to herself as she hurried down the shrub-lined path to her car.

Looking at her watch, she was astonished to see that it was seven o'clock. It was too late to do any more today. Besides, she suddenly realized that she was starving. She hadn't eaten since breakfast!

Nancy stopped at a pay phone and called Hannah Gruen. "Where have you been?" the housekeeper asked, her voice full of concern. "Ned called twice. And Bess and George have been sitting here waiting for you to come back for the last hour. They almost had me convinced to call the police! What kind of case are you on, anyway?"

"Oh, Hannah." Nancy laughed. "I'm fine— except that I'm half dead of hunger. I'm on my way home now. I'll tell you all about it when I get there."

"All right," Hannah grumbled. "I'll scrape some dinner together. Just be glad your father's out of town, or we'd have search parties out by now."

"On my way," Nancy repeated, and hung up.

When she got home, she found that Hannah had "scraped together" roast chicken and potatoes, with blueberry pie for dessert. Bess and

George were only too happy to stay when Hannah pressed them, although Bess looked rather pale. "I haven't felt well since last night. A little carbon monoxide poisoning goes a long way toward killing an appetite," she said with a rueful grin.

"I have some news that should put you back on the road to recovery," Nancy promised.

Over the meal, Nancy brought them all up to date, sketching out the details of Turner's confession. She included a description, for George's benefit, of his obnoxious attitude.

"That creep. It makes me sick to think that someone so low could have ruined the lives of such good people," George said. Then she frowned. "Speaking of Turner's victims, I talked to Michael this morning. He's decided to go to the Immigration and Naturalization Service on Monday to turn himself in."

Bess gasped. "That means he's sure to be deported!"

"Yes, but his foreman will handle the business until Michael's brother can get here. The family has applied for and gotten immigration status. They've been on the list for three years, and Michael told me that their green cards came through."

Nancy understood how difficult it must be for Michael to take this step. His family would finally be coming to America, but he wouldn't be there.

"But it's not over yet," Nancy said. "Turner isn't the only one involved. Somehow his blackmail scheme has gotten him involved with Deep Voice. And Deep Voice is part of something bigger. And there's still Kathy's murderer."

"But isn't that Turner?" Bess asked.

"There's been no arrest," Nancy said, staring at her plate.

"I know the mystery isn't solved yet, Nancy, but do you think you'd have time tomorrow to come to a party for the campaign workers?" asked George.

"Sounds like fun. Where's it going to be?"

"Don't know yet. But Jethro Serkin is giving it."

Serkin! Nancy perked up. He was one of the people Turner had named for his alibi. She needed to talk to Jethro Serkin—and here was her chance. "Okay. I'll be there."

"Hey, Nan!" Bess piped up. "You'll never guess who called me this morning for details on last night's fund-raiser. Brenda Carlton! Do you think I should tell her about our adventure afterward?"

Nancy groaned. Brenda Carlton's father owned one of River Heights' biggest newspapers. But that fact didn't make Brenda a born journalist. She wasn't all that good at what she did, but she made up for it by being incredibly aggressive and obnoxious. She also liked to think of herself as a brilliant detective. More than once she had practically blown an important case for Nancy by interfering at the wrong time.

George was grinning. "I know, Bess. Why don't you send her to interview the man of the hour—Franklin Turner? I'm sure he'd have a lot to tell her. In fact, they might just get along really well."

Bess started to giggle. "Oh, George, don't give me any ideas!" she protested.

Nancy laughed too. Bess and George could always take her mind off her troubles.

She decided to forget about the case for the night. She'd take a hot shower, call Ned, get some sleep—and the next day she'd wrap the case up. The answers were all there, waiting for her to unravel. It was only a matter of time.

The next morning, as Nancy parked near the address she'd found in Marjorie Rothman's directory, she wished she'd enlisted her friends' help. She was in front of a downtown commercial high-rise, and she had no way of knowing which office belonged to the phone number from Turner's console.

Inside, she scanned the directory, recognizing some of River Heights' more prestigious law firms and private investment companies. Then she saw something she knew couldn't be a coincidence.

"Serkin, Edwards, Palmer, and Lang, Attorneys-at-Law, Suite 1500," read the listing halfway down the second column.

"Bingo," Nancy whispered.

The fifteenth floor was as deserted as the rest of the building. Someone had accidentally left the front door unlocked. But Nancy didn't doubt that there'd be pretty advanced security for the offices. She'd had some experience picking locks, but even her talents had their limits. A credit card won't do the job here, Nancy told herself, surveying the state-of-the-art office doors.

As it happened, she didn't need to be particularly resourceful after all. The door to Serkin's office was unlocked. Attorneys did work strange hours. Being the daughter of one had taught Nancy that.

She eased the door open and stepped quietly into a spacious reception area. There were no windows, but soft lights illuminated several eighteenth-century paintings on the walls. Plush maroon leather couches were placed at right angles to each other.

She was halfway across the thickly carpeted room when she heard voices. Whoever was working wasn't alone. She'd better do what she'd come for and get out fast.

She had to find out if the phone number from Turner's phone console corresponded to Jethro Serkin's office number. She had a strong suspicion that it did.

Crossing the room to the receptionist's desk, Nancy concentrated on making as little noise as possible. She tuned in to the hum of conversation coming from down the hall. If they heard her, they would stop talking, and that would be her signal to take off.

She leaned over to check the operator's phone bank, but before she could make out the number in the low light, she heard a rumbling bass voice behind her.

"Will this help?"

The desk light snapped on.

Chapter

Fourteen

THERE WAS NO MISTAKING that deep and threatening voice. It was the same one she had overheard in the copy room and again in the limousine.

"I don't believe we've been formally introduced," he said in a tone dripping with silky sarcasm. "I'm Jethro Serkin. By the way, can you see to find what you're snooping for? Could I make it easier for you by turning on more lights?"

Nancy looked down at the number on the phone. It was the same as the one from the recording she'd heard on Franklin Turner's phone. "I can see well enough," she said, trying desperately to keep the fear out of her voice.

"And now that you're here, Nancy Drew, you

might as well be comfortable." Serkin motioned to a tall, broadly built man standing in the doorway that led to an inner office.

"Do whatever it takes, Gus, to make sure she won't budge for a while. I'll be back." He turned to Nancy. "Then you and Gus and I will have a little chat."

Gus led her down a long hallway to a small office and tied her to a very uncomfortable Chippendale straight-back chair.

Nancy could hear Serkin's voice rumbling from the adjoining room. She could tell by the way his comments stopped and started that he was talking on the phone. She strained to hear, but all she could make out were his final words when he raised his voice to say, "Don't worry. She'll stay here."

Gus seemed amused. "Sometimes even the best detectives can find themselves in really tough spots. Looks like it's your turn."

Nancy knew she had to act quickly. Gus picked up a magazine and soon became engrossed. She tried to loosen the rope while he was preoccupied. But just as she was beginning to work the knot free, Serkin emerged from his office. He saw what was happening immediately.

"You idiot." Gus cowered under Serkin's withering stare. "First you lost Mulraney, then you botched the limo rig. Get the chloroform."

Nancy tried to struggle, but Serkin fixed her

with a look. "Don't even think about it," he advised. Then Gus returned and clamped a sweet-smelling cloth over her mouth and nose.

This is it, Nancy thought as she drifted away. My detective days are over.

"Nancy, wake up. Please."

Someone was yelling at her, but she was still too woozy to tell who it could be.

"Nancy. It's me. Michael Mulraney."

Images floated back across her brain. She thought she saw Gus's face. She forced her eyes to open, shaking her head to clear the cloudiness there. A dull throb pulsed at her temples as she remembered where she was. Then she saw Michael sitting across from her, tied to a matching Chippendale chair.

"I got a phone call saying you were in trouble," he explained. "I was to come alone and tell no one or else you'd be killed. That's what they said."

"Well, it's at least partly true. I am definitely in trouble. And now, Michael—"

Nancy didn't get the chance to finish her sentence. The door opened, and Jethro Serkin appeared.

"Did you sleep well? I certainly hope so, because we're all going to a party. And you, my friends, are the guests of honor. Though not, I'm afraid, for long."

Serkin grinned at Nancy and Michael as Gus

got them out of their chairs and shoved them along, still securely bound, out the door and up to the roof. There a helicopter was waiting, its rotor whirring in readiness for whatever journey Serkin had planned. "Where are we going?" asked Nancy.

"Don't worry. You're sure to enjoy yourselves. My friend's lakeside estate is a charming place to throw a lavish bash for hardworking campaign workers."

The pieces clicked together. Tim Terry's voter-registration-drive outing. It looked as if Nancy was going to be there after all. She leaned toward Michael and whispered what little she knew about the event. Serkin turned to look at them.

"You wouldn't be making plans, Nancy, would you?" asked Serkin. "You should be trying to guess what sort of surprise I have planned for you. Or are you too busy enjoying the scenery?"

Nancy had been looking out the window, trying to keep her bearings. They were flying away from River Heights, toward secluded Cedar Lake, where Ned Nickerson's parents kept a summer cottage.

If only Ned were there now!

After a short flight, they landed on a wide, manicured lawn. Serkin hadn't exaggerated about this being a lakeside estate. The house was large as a palace, and under other circumstances Nancy might have agreed that it was also charming.

Gus pushed Nancy and Michael from the helicopter, leading them across the expanse of lawn to a nearby enclosed veranda. Inside, the morning light and soft breeze played on the array of plants and flowers. Unfortunately, Nancy was in no mood to appreciate their beauty.

"What exactly do you have in mind?" she asked. "Why keep us in suspense?"

"You are about to meet a very important man, who also happens to be my boss." Serkin was enjoying his little guessing game.

He turned to greet a tall, distinguished-looking man dressed in tennis clothes who was strolling onto the veranda. He flashed a gold-toothed smile at her.

Nancy bit her lip. Suddenly she could hear Dee Shannon saying, "He never smiled . . ." It all made sense now. But why, oh why, had it taken her so long to figure it out?

When Nancy first saw him at the fund-raiser, Bradford Williams had impressed her as a pleasant, if bland-looking, man. Looking at him now she had a feeling she was going to have to reconsider that evaluation.

"Let me introduce myself, Ms. Drew," he said.

"Don't tell me—let me guess," Nancy said. "Michael Mulraney, I presume."

Williams's eyes flickered, and for a second Nancy had an ugly glimpse of his true character. Then he smiled, and the impression of charm and pleasantness returned. "Impressive!"

He turned to Michael. "My namesake. I'm so very pleased to meet you."

Serkin and Gus stood by as Williams took a seat in a white wicker armchair. As he talked, it felt to Nancy as if the airy and empty space around them had begun to fill with Williams's personality.

"It was a mistake to stir things up the way you have, Ms. Drew. You really should have left Mr. Mulraney—or perhaps I should call him Mr. Dougherty—to fend for himself. Why couldn't you simply back off when we asked you so nicely? Still, a man with my past has to admire such bravery."

Nancy remembered what she'd learned at the pool hall. She was dealing with a professional killer. "Your methods don't seem to have changed too much," she said. "Only now you have other people do the dirty work for you."

"Exactly. And Jethro tried very hard, on my orders, of course, to dispose of you. Usually he's quite good at that."

"But we managed to ruin your plans."

"Not just my plans. My future. Or potentially so. Until Franklin Turner's silly blackmail scheme uncovered the inconvenient presence of a second Michael Mulraney, I had succeeded masterfully with my little masquerade."

"You staged your 'death' very effectively," said Nancy, trying to give the impression she knew the whole story instead of only bits and pieces.

Williams smiled, his gold tooth glinting in the sun.

"Ah, yes. A little plastic surgery, a change of hairstyle, and a move to the big city go a long way," he said cheerfully.

"Why didn't you get your tooth fixed while you were at it?" Nancy asked, curious. "Do you know that people call you 'metal-mouth'?"

"Funny you should ask." Williams chuckled. "You see, this gold tooth has great sentimental value to me. I took my first hit job to make the money for this. I like to say my teeth were killing me."

Serkin roared with laughter. Nancy shuddered. These men were truly evil.

"Now, where were we?" Williams murmured.

Swallowing her fear, Nancy pressed on. "After a year or so you resurfaced and supposedly went into legitimate business. You obviously worked as hard at it as you did at your previous occupation."

"I had important people looking after things for me. It's easy to find that kind of help when you can afford it."

"People like the ones who spotted Franklin Turner when he got too close?" Nancy asked.

"Jethro was on to Franklin from the beginning. Activity in computer files shows up. It showed Franklin up."

"And now he's in jail."

"Franklin has been convinced there are advantages to his present position. He made a stupid mistake, leaving that copy in the machine. Realizing his stupidity, he stopped his petty blackmailing. Now he's realized how crucial it is that he not be stupid again."

"And Kathy Novello? Would you call her stupid also, Mr. Williams?" Keep him talking, she thought.

"You misjudge me if you think I caused that poor young woman's death." Williams leaned back and crossed his legs. "Kathy Novello was simply unlucky. She felt threatened, though Franklin was only trying to find out if she had the missing paper. She fled and apparently fell while running down the fire escape. It was an accident."

He said it so nicely, he almost made his excuses for causing a death sound reasonable.

"Franklin Turner is going to be taken care of," Serkin added. "We won't need to worry about him. Mr. Williams doesn't like loose ends."

Did that mean Franklin was going to be killed? If so, why had he volunteered that confession that Nancy now understood he'd made to protect Williams?

"Franklin will be so grateful to be alive he'll never think of repeating past mistakes." Williams answered Nancy's unspoken question. "And he'll be in Chicago where the exciting new

125

job I have planned for him will quell his need for extracurricular activities as well as his need for funds."

"You're forgetting, Mr. Williams, that there's evidence against him," said Nancy, "and witnesses. Franklin Turner won't be in Chicago. He'll be in prison. Do you think your promises will be enough to keep his mouth shut there?"

"You are clever, Ms. Drew." He laughed. "But one must be crafty as well. That evidence you speak of will disappear. And as for the witnesses, there won't be any—not living witnesses anyway." His smile was more charming than ever.

"Especially not the two of you."

Chapter

Fifteen

HOW ARE YOU planning to dispose of us?" asked Nancy. Keeping up her cool façade was more of a struggle with every second.

"You've no doubt noticed how isolated we are here." Williams gestured toward the dense foliage just beyond the lawn. "I've always appreciated the peace and quiet, and sometimes it suits my business purposes as well. This is one of those times."

"My friends will know something is wrong when they can't get in touch with me." It was already past noon. She had been gone several hours. They were sure to suspect something was up when she wasn't ready for the party.

Williams frowned thoughtfully. "A dedicated worker like Ms. Fayne will attend the worker party. And when she and Ms. Marvin get here they'll understand why they haven't been able to find you this morning." Williams was smiling at his cleverness.

"Jethro has fueled up the cabin cruiser on the lake. When your friends arrive, they will hear that you and Michael went for a short ride. Unfortunately, you had a terrible accident."

This is too neat, Nancy thought. She searched for some way to convince Williams that his plan wouldn't succeed.

"Everyone knows I can handle a boat," she said. "They're sure to think it wasn't an accident."

"But, Nancy, you allowed Michael to pilot the boat. An error in judgment with a fatal result." Williams looked up at Serkin. "That's how it happened. Right?"

Serkin smiled. Gus chewed on a fingernail. Williams stared at her, as if challenging her to think her way out this time.

Michael's temper began to flare. Nancy could tell he'd been trying to keep it under control, but Williams's smug attitude was obviously too much to bear.

"You three will be prime suspects," he fumed. "There's no chance you'll get away with this."

Nancy took his lead. "My father is a very smart man, with friends in the police department. He's coming back to River Heights tonight, and this accident you're planning won't go uninvestigated."

"You must realize by now that I am beyond the reach of your father and his police friends." Williams laughed.

"Mr. Williams is an upstanding businessman," Serkin added. "No one would ever suspect him of any of this."

"Franklin's confession made sure of that," Williams added.

Nancy remembered Chief McGinnis's reluctance. Charging Turner had been enough for him. Without any evidence, McGinnis would see no reason to reopen the case.

Williams went on, "Besides, my day will be spent talking with Councilman Terry about campaign contributions. An airtight alibi, I would say."

With a veranda full of witnesses, Nancy thought. "You seem to have everything worked out," she said.

"Except for one thing," Michael said. "Now that Franklin Turner is in jail, Tim Terry will be watching his campaign for crooks like you. He'll be on guard."

"Terry is more naïve than you might think," said Williams. "Franklin showed us that about him. By the time the councilman realizes he has compromised himself, it will be too late."

Too late for what? Nancy thought. Suddenly

she saw the links that drew Serkin, Williams, and Turner's blackmailing victims together.

"Access to the oversight committee! That's what you're after!" said Nancy. "You want to control the councilman so your companies will get city contracts."

"You're quite the detective after all. River Heights will no doubt mourn your—disappearance."

Nancy glanced at Michael. Solving the mystery hadn't really solved anything. They were still in very serious trouble.

"It's quite simple," Williams concluded. "The real Michael Mulraney never got out of the construction business."

Williams smiled at his little joke, then signaled to Gus. "I think we've chatted long enough. Would you please take our guests down to the dock now?"

Serkin and Williams started down the veranda steps, talking between themselves as they walked away.

When they were halfway across the lawn, Nancy nodded at Michael. It was now or never. The two of them threw themselves at Gus, toppling him to the flagstones. The gun clattered from his hand and slid under a table.

Nancy delivered a deftly aimed kick to his right knee, and he howled in agony. When he tried to struggle to his feet, Michael smacked him down again.

"Good work. Now let's get out of here."

They headed for the opposite end of the veranda. There had to be another way out besides the one Williams and Serkin had taken.

They had obviously heard the commotion. Williams was running back toward the house. "Stop them!" he cried.

Serkin was already up the stairs ahead of him. Nancy and Michael had nearly made it across the veranda when Serkin grabbed Nancy from behind and motioned Michael to halt at gunpoint.

"That was very stupid," said Williams as he joined Serkin. "You take care of them, Jethro. Gus obviously can't get the job done, but I'm sure you can."

Nancy's skin crawled. She was sure he could too. As if to prove her right, Serkin took turns nudging her and Michael with the gun barrel all the way to the dock.

The cruiser was clearly a very rich man's boat, with its sleek modern look and solid teak interiors. Serkin gave them a tour.

"You might as well get a good look," he said as they walked along the starboard side. "After all, it's the last thing you'll ever see."

He pointed out that the cruiser could reach very high speeds. "You'll notice the modern technology here in the bridge. Automatic pilot. Sonar. Radar. Two engines in case one should fail."

How convenient, Nancy thought.

Serkin led them down into the cabin, which was lavishly furnished. There was even a leather sofa facing an entertainment center. Set into the ceiling of the cabin were little round bits of colored glass in a mosaic style reflecting the light above.

Throughout their tour, Nancy searched for a means of escape. She hadn't seen any tools or anything heavy enough to knock out Serkin.

He grabbed the two of them, pushing them into captain's chairs overlooking the boat's port side. "This is an expensive accident that you're going to have," he said as he tied them to the maple chair arms. "Everything on this boat is custom-made. Even these chairs have been designed to withstand high seas. That's why they're bolted to the floor."

Nancy had already noticed.

Serkin finished up by roping their legs to the rungs. "Have a wonderful trip," he said.

Nancy waited until he'd gone up the ladder to the bridge. "We've got to think fast," she said to Michael. "Any chance you're carrying anything sharp?"

"I already thought of that. Gus frisked me when I got to Serkin's office. There's nothing left."

The boat had begun to move. They were leaving shore, heading for a bend in the lake.

"We need to loosen these ropes." Nancy tried to will her heartbeat to slow down. "Move your legs back and forth slowly. Try to get some slack into the knots."

She and Michael struggled for several minutes. The cruiser suddenly took a sharp starboard turn, slowing slightly. Then Nancy heard another engine, less powerful than that of the cruiser, start up and move off into the distance.

The engines of the cruiser were roaring now, and they'd begun to pick up speed. The boat surged forward with a sudden jolt that threw Nancy back in her seat.

The same force had knocked Michael clean off his chair onto the floor. "Hey!" he yelled. His weight had broken the chair. That meant his arms were free. His hands were still tied in front of him, but not as tightly as they had been when the rope was stretched around the chair arms.

"Untie my legs," Nancy cried.

The cruiser was moving faster now, but all Nancy could do was watch while Michael picked at her knots with his tied hands.

At last he had untied her legs. "Hurry, Nancy. Don't wait for me," he gasped as he worked at his own bonds.

Nancy didn't bother answering. She flew out of the chair and stumbled to the ladder. She pulled herself up from rung to rung with her tied hands, then flung herself over the edge of the hatchway onto the bridge.

They were moving very fast now, at full throttle she would guess—breakneck speed straight ahead. She pushed herself up from the deck and stared across the bridge in disbelief.

There was no pilot at the wheel.

Chapter

Sixteen

THEY WERE ALREADY out of sight of Williams's estate, headed like a shot for the other end of the lake. And what lay at the other end was cliffs. Nancy knew that from her previous visits here, even if she hadn't been able to see those cliffs looming ahead each time the slamming prow of the racing cruiser dipped down.

It was obvious now what Williams had planned for them. Serkin had put the cruiser on autopilot—that must have been his dinghy's engine Nancy had heard earlier.

At this speed, the cruiser would come apart like a pile of matchsticks when it hit those rocks, and she and Michael would come apart with it.

Michael had stumbled up beside her and, between buffets of the bow smacking the water then bounding up again, he was pulling at the knots that still held Nancy's wrists.

"The throttle's jammed," she said when he had her free and she'd inspected the mechanism. "We have to get it back to a slower speed."

Her wrists burned where the ropes had been, but she didn't stop to rub them. They struggled with the throttle, but it wouldn't budge.

"Somebody rigged this as skillfully as they rigged that limo," Michael shouted over the roar of the powerful engines. "And look at the wheel!"

Nancy nodded as he pointed at the helm. She'd already seen the chain holding the steering mechanism on its course.

"What are we going to do?" shouted Michael, and Nancy could hear the beginnings of panic in his voice.

They didn't have much choice. "We'll have to swim for it," she shouted back as she headed for the rail.

"No!" he screamed, grabbing her arm. "I can't swim."

Now he tells me! Nancy thought, dismayed. She looked around for life preservers, but there were none. She didn't remember seeing any in the cabin either. Serkin had probably had them removed just in case she and Michael did get loose.

"I'll tow you," she said.

"That won't work."

He was yelling at her, and she could tell that it

wasn't just because of the noise of the engines. He was near full panic now. She had to calm him down.

"I'm a strong swimmer," she shouted. "We'll make it."

She was doing her best to sound reassuring, though she had her doubts that she could actually get them both through the treacherous current to safety.

"I'm telling you it won't work," he insisted. "I lose my head in the water. I'll pull us both down."

Michael's brogue was so thick now that she would have had trouble understanding him even in quieter surroundings. Still, she knew one thing: A panicked person could be deadly in the water. She could knock him out and tow him, but she wasn't sure that would work in this current.

She glanced through the spray-spattered windshield at the rapidly approaching shoreline. Clouds retreated over the looming cliffs. *I will get us out!* she told herself.

"Let's check the engine," she shouted. "Maybe we can stall it somehow."

Serkin had pointed out the engine room during his tour. The door was locked, of course. But Michael flew at it with a force she wouldn't have thought possible for a man of his size.

On his third run, the door splintered and fell backward in response.

Inside, the heat was nearly overpowering.

Steam pulsed from huge pistons, and the roar was deafening. There was no way they could talk to each other in there, not even at shouting volume. Suddenly Michael had Nancy by the arm and was pulling her back outside and toward the bridge deck once more.

"What are you doing?" she protested, but he was hauling her along too forcefully for her to slow their progress much.

"I know a little bit about engines," he shouted once they were far enough from the engine room that she could understand what he was saying. "We couldn't so much as lay a hand on those machines now. They're too hot. They'd sear our skin off in a second. And there weren't any tools around to use either."

Nancy saw immediately the truth of what he was saying and stopped trying to resist as they stumbled up onto the bridge.

"Besides, there are two of them," he went on. "Even if we could shut one engine down, there's no way we could disable *two* in time to keep from hitting those rocks."

The cliffs were closer now. Nancy knew Michael was right.

"We have to think of something else," she hollered, trying not to sound as bereft of hope as she suddenly felt.

"There's no other way," said Michael, looking resigned to his fate. "We have to jump."

"Maybe we can find something that will float," Nancy shouted. "Something less obvious than a life preserver."

Michael looked skeptical, but she'd already pulled herself free of his grasp and was stumbling toward the cabin.

"Check the port side," she shouted. Seeing his confusion, she added, "Around to the left," and pointed at the opposite rail.

He nodded and weaved away.

They were running out of time, and Nancy knew it. A few minutes more and they'd have to jump for it no matter what the risk to either of them. She stared through the hatchway into the cabin, trying desperately to think of a way out of this.

Then she saw it. Why hadn't she thought of that before? She was down the ladder in a flash, falling on the last step and picking herself up, hardly even noticing she'd fallen.

She stumbled to the bench that ran along the cabin wall and began pulling at one of the cushions. Fancy boats were most often furnished with flotation cushions. She hoped with all her heart that this cruiser was no exception.

The ties that held the cushion tore loose, and she staggered toward the ladder with her cumbersome burden. The cushion would lose its awkwardness in the water—unless it wasn't a flotation device at all. In that case, it would waterlog very fast and sink like a boulder. Nancy tried not to think of what would happen if Michael was clutching it at the time.

He had finished his circuit of the portside deck and was back at the hatchway as she emerged and handed the cushion up to him.

"We have to hurry!" she shouted. The cliffs were really close now. "If we're lucky this cushion will float. Then you just hold on tight to it, and we'll get you to shore."

They were at the rail now. She saw the fear flicker in Michael's eyes. Then it was gone, and she knew he was going to jump without further question when she told him to. She admired him so much for that she would have hugged him if there'd been time. Instead, she climbed onto the rail and motioned for him to do the same.

"Jump as far from the boat as you can. Whatever you do, don't freeze up. We're going to make it."

He pulled himself up next to her.

"Wait for my signal," she shouted.

Nancy paused a moment, feeling for the rhythm of the up-and-down movement of the prow as it plowed through the waves. They had to jump when the bow was as high as possible out of the water. That would give them more of an arc to get clear of the boat's churning wake.

A few more seconds—now!

"Jump!" she cried.

The cold September water struck her with a jolting shock. She swallowed water and spray as she was forced beneath the surface by the momentum of her leap. She'd grabbed Michael's arm so they would jump together, but her hold slipped when they hit the water. As she fought her way to the surface, she had no idea whether she would find him there or not.

She broke through into the sunlight and shook the water from her eyes. There he was, about ten feet away. He was holding tight to the cushion, and, sure enough, it was supporting him. Unfortunately, he was still in the cruiser's wake, though Nancy had thrown herself clear. She propelled herself toward him, stroking overarm.

The boat was past them now, roaring off toward the cliffs. Meanwhile, a surge of wave, created by the cruiser's rampage through the water, was headed straight at Nancy and Michael. She grabbed him and stroked one-arm with all her might till she could feel that they were free of the wake. Still, she kept stroking hard as she could.

"Kick!" she hollered at Michael as her own legs whipped up and down beneath the surface.

It wasn't the current she was so intent on escaping now. She didn't look up to see. She didn't have to. She could hear what she'd been dreading. In fact, she was sure everyone for miles must be hearing it too, as the cruiser hit the cliffs with a crash of metal and shattering glass.

Nancy kicked harder still. Maybe two seconds passed, though it seemed much longer.

Then the most dreaded sound of all assaulted the autumn afternoon, as what was left of the cruiser exploded in a gush of flame.

Chapter

Seventeen

A CHUNK OF FLAMING DEBRIS hissed into the water barely two yards away. Nancy waited for the sizzling to stop before reaching for the piece of wreckage as it floated past. She doused it thoroughly to cool it off. Unlike the cushion, this piece of wood was big enough for two.

"Grab on to this with me," she told Michael. "Then let go of the cushion."

Michael had been clinging so tightly to the square of foam and fabric that it took him a moment to give it up. When he had hold of the wreckage at last, he and Nancy began to kick.

The current was strong, but with the floating debris to buoy them up and both of them working together, they would make it to the shore.

By the time Nancy and Michael dragged themselves out of the water and back along the shore to Williams's mansion, the campaign-workers' party was in full swing. The band had set up and was playing rock and roll much too loudly for anyone to have heard the cruiser explode.

The lawn and garden were filled with people. A pleasant breeze fluttered the flowered cloths on the long tables. They were set with dishes that looked far too elegant, in Nancy's opinion, for eating on the lawn.

A chef in a tall, white hat supervised the barbecue area like a captain of a ship. Several cooks of obviously lesser status, wearing much smaller hats, scurried about with heaping platters of smoked turkey, ribs, and chicken to add to those already brimming with corn and salads and baskets of rolls.

From behind some shrubbery, Nancy noticed Jethro Serkin a few tables away. He'd come up to Bradford Williams, who was deep in conversation with Councilman Terry. Serkin appeared to be pretty upset. He pulled Williams aside and whispered something in his ear.

"I wonder what's going on over there," Nancy whispered to Michael.

"It looks like some kind of high-level discussion," he said.

The expression of sudden sorrow on Bradford Williams's face would have convinced anyone but Nancy that he'd just had a terrible shock.

"They're pretending they've just heard about us!" she whispered as the realization hit her.

Then she spotted George and Bess emerging from the crowd. Nancy had a strong suspicion what Williams was intending to say to them. Meanwhile, he couldn't have looked more solemn as he laid a protective hand on George's arm and eased the overflowing plate of food from Bess's hand.

"I think we should go inside," he said in a gentle tone as Nancy moved out of the bushes and close enough to hear. "There's something I have to tell you."

"What's going on?" said George, her eyes widening.

"It would be better if we talked about this privately," said Williams.

"I disagree," said Nancy, stepping out from behind a nearby clutch of partiers. "I think you should say what you have to say right here where everyone can hear. I think they'd all be interested in sharing your sad news, Mr. Williams. Or should I call you Mr. Mulraney?"

George's jaw dropped. "Nancy! What happened to you?" she exclaimed.

"Tell them what's going on," said Nancy, who had not taken her eyes off Williams.

She noticed him falter a moment, almost imperceptibly. Then he composed himself again. He nodded at Serkin, who stepped toward them, slipping his hand inside his jacket.

"Look out. He's got a gun!" shouted Michael as he ran up behind Serkin.

The crowd turned to stare as Michael wrestled Serkin to the ground. Williams took advantage of the distraction and headed across the garden.

"Stop him!" Nancy cried. "Don't let him get away!"

She raced after Williams, shoving some of River Heights' more prominent citizens out of her way as she ran. The bewildered guests obviously had no idea what to do.

By the time Nancy broke free of the crowd, Williams was through the garden and out of sight. Nancy guessed he was heading for his helicopter launch pad. She cut through some shrubbery, ignoring the branches that caught at her soggy clothes. She wasn't about to let him get away now!

As she emerged onto the lawn, she spotted Williams. He was almost to the copter, and he was signaling the pilot to start the engine.

"Nancy, what's going on?" cried George, whose long strides had finally closed the gap between her and Nancy.

"We can't let Williams take off," Nancy shouted over her shoulder. "Call your volunteers!"

George immediately stopped in her tracks. Putting her fingers to her lips, she gave a piercing whistle. "Everybody! Over here!" she screamed.

In a moment a fast-growing crowd was running across the lawn toward the helicopter pad.

Williams had climbed into the helicopter by the time Nancy and her troops reached the launch pad, but he hadn't yet closed the door behind him.

"Grab onto the runner," Nancy shouted as she caught hold of Williams's arm. "This man is a killer—we can't let him get away!"

The youthful volunteers, who had done such a wonderful job of getting potential River Heights voters to register, rose to the challenge once again. They pounced on the nearest of the copter's two runners, pulling the big bird off balance just as it had begun to rise from the ground.

Nancy nearly lost her grip on Williams as the copter tipped and weaved.

"Pull harder on that runner," she urged the still-growing ranks.

More volunteers had arrived and leapt into action.

"Get us out of here, you fool," screamed Williams at the pilot.

The pilot struggled with the controls as George joined Nancy in tugging at Williams's arm.

"He's going for a gun," shouted George as Williams reached for a compartment between the seats.

But before he could latch onto a weapon or anything else, George and Nancy had pulled him from the cockpit. He came out headfirst, nearly taking Nancy with him as he fell. Then he was on the ground with George on top of him and a number of her volunteers following suit.

Nancy heaved a sigh of relief. The real Michael Mulraney had been caught at last.

Two days later Nancy, Bess, and the other "Michael" were at the councilman's office helping George pack up her materials from the voter-registration drive.

"It looks like Tim Terry isn't going to make it to Washington after all," said George mournfully. "In fact, I doubt he'll even be a city councilman after the next election."

"Not when this oversight committee scandal hits the newsstands," said Bess.

Brenda Carlton had already been around asking questions for an article for her father's paper.

"Hiring that creep Turner was a big mistake," Bess went on. "It looks like Mr. Terry is going to pay for it with his career."

"Bess!" Nancy warned.

Michael put his arm around Bess's shoulders and took a more diplomatic tone. "I don't think George wants to talk about the councilman's future right now."

"That's okay," said George. "I can take it. Besides, who knows what Tim Terry's future will be? He's a smart man and a shrewd politician.

He may come out of this better than we think. I do know one thing though."

"What's that?" Nancy asked.

"Whatever happens to him, I'm one person he won't have on his team." George fitted the last stack of flyers into the box she was packing. "My public service is going to be confined to the voter-registration drive from now on. I can be sure that's a good cause."

"My father is glad you took him up on his offer to work out of his office," said Nancy.

"I'm really grateful to him for that," said George. "It means the drive can go on without a hitch." She grinned mischievously. "And now that Bess has some free time, I know she's dying to help."

Bess looked resigned. "Yeah, well, Jeff was cute, but his sole interest in life was being the Video King." Suddenly she brightened. "Hey, isn't this the recruiting season for young lawyers?"

Nancy and George laughed. "I think you finally figured out how to get Bess to do her civic duty," Nancy joked, poking George in the ribs.

Michael lifted the last box onto the hand truck they'd borrowed from the Municipal Building maintenance department.

"I feel like I owe Mr. Drew even more thanks than George does," he said.

"My dad is only too happy to negotiate with

the immigration office for you," said Nancy. She grinned. "Especially since you said you'd speak at the voter-registration rallies. He's very interested in your case. He thinks he may even be able to convince the INS to let you stay in the States."

"Speaking at those rallies is the least I can do. And nobody knows better than I do how much it means to be a citizen of this country, because nobody ever cared more about getting to be one."

"When is your family coming?" Bess interrupted. "I can't wait to meet your brother."

They all laughed.

"That's our Bess," said George.

"It will take a month or so for Jamie and the rest of the Doughertys to make it through the red tape to River Heights," said Nancy. "In the meantime, this is so we won't forget who our first future citizen really is."

She pulled a name tag from her pocket and pinned it on Michael's shirt. She'd found it in a box of supplies left over from the fund-raiser and had written a name on it in big letters that were bright, Irish green.

He looked down at the tag and read aloud with a bit of a brogue and a catch in his voice:

"'Hello. My name is Kevin Dougherty.'"

Nancy's next case:

Superstar Jesse Slade has been missing for three years—until Nancy spots a clue on the videotape of Slade's last concert. She and her friends George and Bess fly to California to find out what really happened to the rock singer.

The first bombshell is that Slade's manager, Tommy Road, vanished at the same time. Posing as a VJ at a rock TV station, Nancy digs deeper into the music scene. Riches and fame are tempting prizes, but can they lead to murder? Nancy uncovers the answer in a deadly sound studio that pumps out killer music. All oldies but baddies . . . in *VANISHING ACT,* Case #34 in The Nancy Drew Files℠.

Health Essentials

Reflexology

Inge Dougans was born in Denmark where she received her reflexology training. In 1983 she started the School of Reflexology and Meridian Therapy and in 1985 she formed the South African Reflexology Society. She gives lectures and workshops on reflexology throughout the UK, Europe and the USA, and runs her own busy practice in South Africa.

Suzanne Ellis was born in South Africa. She obtained an English degree from the University of Natal and has worked as a journalist, documentary scriptwriter and magazine editor. She trained as a reflexologist with Inge Dougans

The Health Essentials Series

There is a growing number of people who find themselves attracted to holistic or alternative therapies and natural approaches to maintaining optimum health and vitality. The *Health Essentials* series is designed to help the newcomer by presenting high quality introductions to all the main complementary health subjects. Each book presents all the essential information on a particular therapy, explaining what it is, how it works and what it can do for the reader. Advice is also given, where possible, on how to begin using the therapy at home, together with comprehensive lists of courses and classes available worldwide.

The *Health Essentials* titles are all written by practising experts in their fields. Exceptionally clear and concise, each text is supported by attractive illustrations.

Series Medical Consultant
Dr John Cosh MD, FRCP

In the same series

Acupuncture by Peter Mole
Alexander Technique, by Richard Brennan
Aromatherapy by Christine Wildwood
Ayurveda by Scott Gerson MD
Chi Kung by James MacRitchie
Chinese Medicine by Tom Williams PhD
Colour Therapy by Pauline Wills
Flower Remedies by Christine Wildwood
Herbal Medicine by Vicki Pitman
Homeopathy by Peter Adams
Iridology by James & Sheelagh Colton
Kinesiology by Ann Holdway
Massage by Stewart Mitchell
Natural Beauty by Sidra Shaukat
Self-Hypnosis by Elaine Sheehan
Shiatsu by Elaine Liechti
Spiritual Healing by Jack Angelo
Vitamin Guide by Hasnain Walji

Health Essentials

REFLEXOLOGY

Foot Massage
for Total Health

Inge Dougans
with
Suzzane Ellis

E L E M E N T
Shaftesbury, Dorset • Rockport, Massachusetts
Melbourne, Victoria

© Element Books Limited 1991
Text © Inge Dougans 1991

First published in Great Britain in 1991 by
Element Books Limited
Shaftesbury, Dorset SP7 8BP

Published in the USA in 1991 by
Element Books, Inc.
PO Box 830, Rockport, MA 01966

Published in Australia in 1991 by
Element Books and distributed by
Penguin Books Australia Ltd.
487 Maroondah Highway,
Ringwood, Victoria 3134

Reprinted January and December 1992
Reprinted 1993
Reprinted March and October 1994
Reprinted May and October 1995
Reprinted 1996

This edition 1997
Reprinted April and June 1997

Cover design and illustration by Max Fairbrother
Design by Nancy Lawrence
Typeset by Selectmove, London
Printed and bound in Great Britain by
Biddles Limited, Guildford & King's Lynn

British Library Cataloguing in Publication
data available

Library of Congress Cataloging in Publication
data available

ISBN 1-86204-045-1

Note from the Publisher

Any information given in any book in the *Health Essentials* series is not intended to be taken as a replacement for medical advice. Any person with a condition requiring medical attention should consult a qualified medical practitioner or suitable therapist.

Contents

I would like to dedicate this book to all the students of reflexology, past, present and future. Without them, this practice could never have evolved into the respected and effective healing art it is today.

Author's special note: Throughout this book, the term 'foot massage' is used as a convenient shorthand to describe Reflexology. However, the authors would stress that this is a convenience term only and is not a proper technical description of the therapy. Reflexology is not massage as understood in the systematic and scientific manipulation of the soft tissues of the body. Reflexology is the application of specific pressures to reflex points in the hands and feet.Nevertheless we feel massage is a useful shorthand justified in this instance for a general understanding of what is involved.

1

What is Reflexology?

REFLEXOLOGY IS A gentle art, a fascinating science and an extremely effective form of therapeutic foot massage. This therapy falls into the realm of 'complementary' medicine. As such, reflexology is considered to be a holistic healing technique which aims to treat the individual as a whole, in order to induce a state of balance and harmony in body, mind and spirit.

Since the time of Hippocrates, health has been defined as a balanced state, and disease an imbalanced state. In modern society, imbalance is the norm. We speed our way through life as if there were no tomorrow, and the demands of the high-speed twentieth century techno-generation are taking their toll on the delicate and intricate human body. A majority of people teeter on the edge of ill-health – in a state of dis-ease and imbalance – and find it difficult to cope with the stresses of day-to-day life. Their potential for perfect health is shrouded by various negative influences. But this potential is in each and every one of us; all it needs as a starting point is the desire to reach a balanced state, which will enable us to enjoy continuous health and vitality. The transition from the state of imbalance to a balanced state requires a gentle and harmless healing process – a process seldom found in the dangerous drugs and radical surgery sometimes so indiscriminately prescribed us by the practitioners of conventional medicine.

Many of the ills of modern man cannot be cured by artificial drugs – drugs more inclined to damage and suppress than to heal. The body heals itself – if given the chance. Because this healing power lies within, we should learn to support and nurture it, not suppress it. Reflexology helps us do this by activating the body's natural healing powers and working to re-establish the equilibrium necessary for normal functioning.

Few people are aware of the fundamental role of feet in health and healing. In fact, few people pay any attention to their feet at all. We tend to torture and neglect them . . . we squeeze them into ill-fitting fashionable shoes, suffocate them in socks and stockings, pound pavements, hike trails and altogether place an inordinate amount of strain on our poor feet. They bear our weight, cope with bad posture and generally take a severe beating on their path through life. Although we may be vaguely aware of the important role they play in carrying us through life, few realize the significant role of our feet in our spiritual and physical well-being.

Our feet connect us to the ground and they are therefore a connection between our earthly and spiritual life. They ground us literally and figuratively. They are our base and foundation and our contact with the earth and the energies that flow through it. And they can also play a major role in attaining and maintaining better health and well-being.

This is because the feet are a perfect microcosm of the body. All the organs, glands and other parts of the body are laid out in the same arrangement on the feet as 'reflections/reflexes' of the body parts. A reflex is an involuntary or unconscious response to a stimulus. In reflexology, when the reflexes on the feet are stimulated, an involuntary response is elicited in organs and glands connected by energy pathways to these specific reflexes. These reflexes, when correctly stimulated, can have a profound influence on our state of health.

This microcosmic representation of body parts is also evident in the iris of the eye, in the ear and on the hands. These representations of body parts are, however, easiest to locate on the feet, where they cover a larger area and are more specific; this makes them easy to work with. The feet are also particularly sensitive, due to the abundance of nerve endings present.

Nerves conduct electrical impulses. Imagine these impulses as channels of energy which connect the feet to the rest of the body. When pressure is applied to certain points on the feet, electro-chemical nerve impulses are activated, forming a 'message'. This message passes through 'afferent neurons' (neurons conveying messages to the centre) to a ganglion (a collection of nerve cells and fibres which form an independent nerve centre outside the spinal cord and the brain). The message then passes from the ganglion via 'efferent neurons' (conveying messages out from the centre to the periphery) to the specific organ, which will then respond. The nerve impulses initiated by pressing reflex areas on the feet might possibly link into the autonomic nervous system, which is primarily concerned with the involuntary action of internal organs, muscles and glands.

The goal of reflexology is to trigger the return to homoeostasis – a state of equilibrium or balance. The most important step towards achieving this is to reduce tension and induce relaxation. Relaxation is the first step to normalization. When the body is relaxed, circulation can flow unimpeded and supply nutrients and oxygen necessary to the cells, and the body organs can return to a normal state and function efficiently.

Professional massage of the reflex areas on the feet serves to establish which parts of the body are out of balance and therefore not working efficiently. Treatment can then be given to correct these imbalances and thus return the body to good working order. Not only is this form of therapy useful for treating ill-health, but it is also effective in maintaining good health and preventing illness. With reflex massage health problems can be detected early and treatment given to prevent serious symptoms from developing.

One of the most important benefits of reflexology is its efficacy in inducing a state of relaxation. Stress – a major problem of the twentieth century – is directly responsible for a multitude of modern diseases and disorders. Constant exposure to stress gradually erodes the body's immune system, and the end result is disease. Some estimates indicate that up to 90 per cent of modern diseases are a direct result of prolonged exposure to stress. Because reflexology reduces the negative effects of stress and helps the body normalize, it helps ward off the potential of more lethal disease.

HOW IT ALL BEGAN

Foot massage is not new to the human race. There is strong evidence that a form of foot therapy, similar to what we call reflexology today, has been practised for centuries by many diverse cultures around the world.

Exactly where it all began is still somewhat elusive. As yet, there is no conclusive proof that modern reflexology had its roots in ancient China, but the main school of thought claims that it originated in the East at about the same time as acupuncture. To quote Dr W. Fitzgerald in his book *Zone Therapy*:

A form of treatment by means of pressure points was known in India and China some 5000 years ago. This knowledge appears to have been lost and forgotten; perhaps it was set aside in favour of acupuncture which emerged as a stronger growth from the same root.

This view is also taken by Dr Franz Wagner (*Reflex Zone Massage*):

The ancient Chinese developed the technique of acupressure, the roots of which lie in the knowledge of reflex zones and the relationships between them. Today the most highly developed and perhaps strongest branch of this ancient form of therapy is acupuncture. In massaging the reflex zones of the feet we are massaging tissue, and we are working along the meridians of acupuncture.

Historically, the Chinese were way ahead of Westerners in understanding the holistic functioning of the human body and its relationship to external natural forces. Thousands of years ago they developed the idea that different parts of the body represent different contacts with the outside world: the head connects us to heaven; with our hands we contact each other by touching and working together; the nipples are the contact that binds us with nourishment to the world; the genitals carry new life that can be born into the world; the anus connects us to the world through the cycle of matter and the feet connect us to the earth through movement.

The Chinese were also aware of the importance of feet in treating disease. In AD 1017, Dr Wang Wei had a human figure cast in bronze on which were marked those points on the body important for acupuncture. When this knowledge was put into practice in treating the sick, the practitioner positioned the needles in the appropriate areas of the body and then applied deep pressure therapy on the soles of the inside and outside edge of both feet. Concentrated pressure was then applied on the big toe. The feet were used in conjunction with the acupuncture needles to channel extra energy through the body. Dr Wei said that the feet were the most sensitive part of the body and contained great energizing areas.

There can therefore be little doubt that a strong connection exists between reflexology and acupuncture. They are certainly based on similar ideas. Both are considered meridian therapies, which propose that energy lines link the hands and feet to various body parts. However, while acupuncture went from strength to strength in the East, reflexology was, for some unknown reason, disregarded. It has only recently re-emerged in the West. Acupuncture, despite its popularity in the East, was an unknown art in the West until introduced into western medicine in 1883, by Dutch physician Ten Tyne. Until the introduction of acupuncture to the West, western medicine did not acknowledge the meridian energy system – a system which plays a vital role in my approach to reflexology.

Apart from the Chinese, other ancient cultures also prac-tised foot massage as a form of therapeutic and preventative medicine. The oldest documentation depicting the practice of reflexology was discovered in Egypt. This, a pictograph, is dated around 2500–2330 BC. It was found at Saqqara in the tomb of an Egyptian physician, Ankmahor. The scene in the pictograph depicts two darker skinned men 'working' on the feet of two men with lighter skin. Apparently the heiroglyphic above the scene reads: Patient: 'Do not hurt me.' Practitioner: 'I shall act so you praise me.'

Another theory claims that foot reflex therapy was passed down to the American Indians by the Incas. One American Indian tribe – the Cherokee Indians of North Carolina – can attest that they have, for centuries, acknowledged the importance of feet in maintaining physical, mental and spiritual balance. According to Jenny Wallace, a therapist from this clan:

In my tribe working on the feet is a very important healing art and is part of a sacred ceremony. The feet walk upon the earth and through this your spirit is connected to the universe. Our feet are our contact with the earth and the energies that flow through it.

Reflexology may have remained the property of these ancient and exotic cultures and been lost to the West had it not been for the enquiring medical minds in Europe and America in the late nineteenth and early twentieth centuries.

The Germans began to look at physiological reflex action in the late 1890s and early 1900s. They began to examine the treatment of disease by massage and developed techniques that became known as reflex massage. It is generally believed that Dr Alfons Cornelius was probably the first to apply massage to 'reflex zones'. The story goes that in 1893, Cornelius suffered an infection. In the course of his convalescence he received a daily massage. At the spa he noticed how effective the massages of one particular medical officer were. The man worked longer on areas that he found painful. This concept inspired Cornelius, who, after examining himself, instructed his masseur to work only on the painful areas. His pain quickly disappeared and in four weeks he had completely recovered. This led him to pursue the use of pressure in his own medical practice. He published his manuscript *Druckpunkte* or *Pressure Points* in 1902. However, American Dr William Fitzgerald is the person who deserves most credit for establishing the basis of modern reflexology with his 'discovery' of zones and his techniques known as 'zone therapy'.

ZONE THERAPY

Dr William Fitzgerald, regarded as the founder of zone therapy, was born in Connecticut, USA, in 1872. He graduated in medicine from the University of Vermont and spent two and a half years working at the Boston City Hospital. He also practised at hospitals in Vienna, and London. While working in Vienna, he probably came into contact with the work of Dr H. Bressler, who was investigating the possibility of treating organs with pressure points. Fitzgerald noticed that, when treating different patients for the same disorder with a minor operation, some would feel considerable pain while others would feel very little. His investigations revealed that those who experienced little pain were actually producing an anaesthetic effect on themselves by applying pressure to areas of their bodies. Intrigued by this, he continued his research into this phenomenon while he was working as Head Physician at the Hospital for Diseases of the Ear, Nose and Throat in Hartford, Connecticut, testing out many of his theories on patients. He found that if pressure was applied to the fingers, it would create an anaesthetic effect on the hand, arm and shoulder, right up to the jaw, face, ear and nose. He applied the pressure using tight bands of elastic on the middle section of each finger or with small clamps which he placed on the tips. He was able to carry out minor surgical operations just using this pressure technique. By exerting this pressure on a specific part of the body he learned to predict which other parts of the body would be affected.

Developing this work further, he systemized the body into zones. He established ten equal longitudinal zones running the length of the body from the top of the head to the tips of the toes. The number ten corresponds to the fingers and toes. Each finger and toe falls into one zone. To establish the zone divisions, imagine a line drawn through the centre of the body with five zones on either side of this line. The thumb and big toe fall into zone one and the small finger and toe both fall into zone five. These zones are of equal width and extend right through the body from front to back. The theory is that parts of the body found within a certain zone will be linked to one another by the energy flow within the zone and can therefore affect one another.

Fitzgerald and his colleague Dr Edwin Bowers were so enthusiastic about their discoveries that they developed a unique method of convincing colleagues of the validity of their theory. They would apply pressure to the sceptical person's hand, then stick a pin in the area of the face anaesthetized by the pressure. This was rather a dramatic way to prove a point, but it worked! In 1915, Bowers wrote the article that first publicly described this treatment which they had named 'zone therapy'. This was published in *Everybody's*

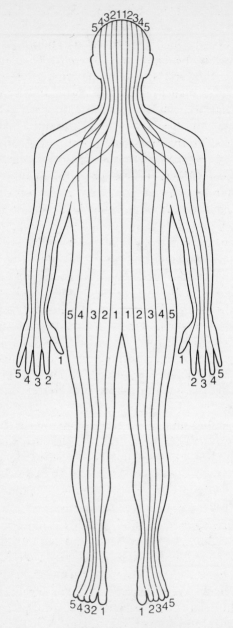

Fig. 1. The zones

Magazine and entitled 'To Stop That Toothache Squeeze Your Toe!'

In 1917, the combined work of Dr Fitzgerald and Dr Bowers was published in the book *Zone Therapy*. Diagrams of the zones of the feet and the corresponding division of the ten zones of the body appeared in the first edition of this book. The reflex areas, so crucial to modern reflexology, were not singled out for any special attention by Fitzgerald.

Fitzgerald and his theories were not enthusiastically received by the medical profession, but one physician believed in this work – Dr Joseph Riley. This was most auspicious, as it was Riley's research assistant Eunice Ingham who was destined to make the greatest contribution to modern reflexology.

Eunice Ingham (1879–1974) should probably be referred to as the Mother of Modern Reflexology. It was as a result of her untiring research and dedication that reflexology finally came into its own. She separated the work on the reflexes of the feet from zone therapy in general. Ingham had been using zone therapy in her work but began to feel more strongly that the feet should be specific targets for the therapy, because of their highly sensitive nature. She charted the feet in relation to the zones and their effects on the rest of the anatomy, until finally she had evolved on the feet themselves a 'map' of the entire body. So successful were her findings, and so effective her treatments, that her reputation soon spread. She took her work to the public and non-medical community as she realized that lay people could learn the proper reflexology techniques to help themselves, their families and friends. She was called on to speak at conventions and shared her knowledge with chiropodists, masseurs and physiotherapists, naturopaths and osteopaths. For over thirty years Eunice Ingham travelled America teaching her method through books, charts and seminars to thousands of people in and out of the medical profession. Her two books *Stories The Feet Can Tell* (1938) and *Stories The Feet Have Told* (1951) were probably the first books written on the subject. Today her legacy continues under the direction of her nephew Dwight Byers who runs the International Institute of Reflexology in St Petersburg.

Zone therapy is without doubt the basis of modern reflexology and most reflexologists use this as a useful adjunct to

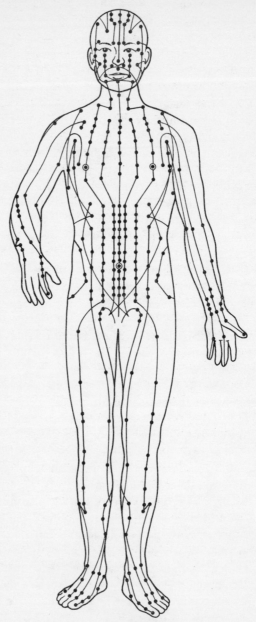

Fig. 2. The meridians

reflexology. However, it is my belief that the Chinese meridian system is, in fact, the vital link between the feet and the rest of the body.

The question as to the relationship between reflexology, acupuncture, shiatsu and acupressure is often asked. According to acupuncture, the body has twelve pairs of meridians or pathways. These form the single energy system and maintain the health of the organism. Meridians are pathways through which the energy of the universe circulates throughout the body organs and keeps the universe and the body in harmony. The acupuncturist believes that illness or pain occurs when the pathways become blocked, disrupting the energy flow and breaking the body's harmony. The Chinese, in acupuncture, developed the use of needles to unblock these pathways. In shiatsu, the Japanese use direct thumb and finger pressure on the acupuncture points to achieve similar results. In reflexology, finger pressure unblocks the sections of meridians found in the feet.

To date, most reflexologists have believed in the energy lines of the zone system. Although this theory has stood many reflexologists in good stead and contributed greatly to the development of modern reflexology, I personally do not adhere to this theory. I believe that the effects elicited by massaging the feet are caused by stimulation of the six main meridians that run through the feet. Fitzgerald recognized the energy connection between the feet and other body parts, and without his pioneering work, reflexology might not be where it is today. But as the eastern concept of energy systems was not recognized in the West at the time of his research, the connection with the meridians was not understood. I am convinced that the energy channels linking the feet to the other body parts are the meridians described by the Chinese in acupuncture, and not the zones described by Dr Fitzgerald. This book, therefore, differs from previous reflexology books, because we now move away from the theory of zone therapy and into the realm of meridian therapy.

2

What Can Reflexology Do For You?

R EFLEXOLOGY IS A holistic therapy and as such, aims to treat the body as a whole, endeavouring to get to the root cause of disease and treat this – not the symptom. For best results the participation of the patient is required. In all holistic therapies, much emphasis is placed on taking responsibility for your own state of health. In orthodox medicine, the tendency is to hand over responsibility to the doctor and expect him to cure all ills. This is a bit of a tall order. Dis-ease is a direct result of your own thoughts and actions. In order to change this, you have to take a long hard look at yourself – something many people don't find easy. It is usually far more simple to place the responsibility and blame outside yourself. This attitude however, will rarely facilitate a true cure.

People venturing into the field of complementary medicine must understand that there is no such thing as an instant cure. Becoming well requires a healing process – a process which often not only affects the body, but the mind as well, bringing to the awareness the overwhelming effects that attitude, lifestyle and diet have on health. Once this is accepted, it becomes obvious that in order to achieve perfect health and well-being, we must be prepared to make an effort to substitute good habits for bad.

It is also imperative to be willing to 'let go' of disease. A reflexology practitioner will be compassionate, caring and dedicated to the client's welfare, but no practitioner can decide for the client that he/she is going to get well. That, the client has to do for himself. Many people hang on to disease as a psychological security blanket. We discover at a very early age that illness elicits sympathy and attention and all too often this conditioning stays with us into adulthood, and becomes a hard habit to break. A genuine desire for health and willingness to let go of disease is of vital importance to any healing process.

Reflexology is not a magic panacea or any kind of instant short-cut. The role of reflexology is to facilitate healing. The reflexologist doesn't cure – only the body cures. What reflexology does is work with the subtle energy flows which revitalize the body so that its own natural healing capacity can get to work. The specific techniques for applying pressure to the feet create channels for healing energy to circulate to all parts of the body.

The human body is a magnificent machine. Thousands of parts work together to keep the body functioning at optimum levels. Unfortunately, the negative effects of attitudes, lifestyle and diet throw the body out of sync, causing malfunctions in various parts. If one part ceases to function efficiently, the whole suffers. Then the minor aches, pains and general fatigue that are often forerunners of more serious complaints begin to manifest. The analogy of a car – a very good example – is often used. To get maximum response from your car, you have to keep it in good working order – if one part is out of order, the performance of the car suffers, and it has to go to the garage for a tune-up or you trade it in for a new one. Reflexology can be considered a body tune-up. And as you can't trade your body in for a new one, it makes good sense to look after the one you have!

So, what exactly can reflexology do for you? By far the most important benefit of reflexology is its ability to reduce stress and induce deep relaxation. When in a relaxed state, the body has the opportunity to heal itself and function more efficiently. Another positive effect is improved circulation. This in turn cleanses the body of toxins and impurities. Improved nerve supply, revitalized energy and overall body balancing are further positive effects.

As stress is one of the greatest problems in this last decade of the twentieth century, and the prime instigator of numerous more deadly diseases, it is in the role of stress reduction that reflexology can be of most benefit.

REFLEXOLOGY VERSUS THE STRESS SYNDROME

Stress is difficult to avoid. It is an integral part of modern life. The days when the stress syndrome was only associated with high-powered business executives are long gone. Today, young children, women, men and the elderly are all subject to varying degrees of stress. Survival in twentieth century society is stressful – traffic, television, noise, job pressure, family problems, financial problems; and global problems such as wars, famines, disease, environmental imbalances, pollution – the list is endless. Few escape the consequences of stress. The increasing number of people with high blood pressure, heart attacks and strokes is evidence of this – and these are only the more obvious stress-related diseases. Other symptoms are more nebulous. Long-term symptoms of constant exposure to stress are fatigue, anxiety and depression. The nervous system becomes so drained and depleted that the only physical reaction is fatigue.

Not all stress is negative. It can be immensely stimulating. An athlete or performer subjects himself to the stress which is part of achieving and experiencing life's ultimate sensations. The human body is equipped to cope with this kind of short-term stress. But long-term, constant exposure to stress is devastating. Persistent daily stresses gradually erode the body's immune system and disrupt the body's delicate chemical and electrical balance. The end result is mental and physical disease.

The stress reaction is a primitive response to a threatening or dangerous situation. It is commonly referred to as the 'fight-or-flight' syndrome. When confronted with a situation we perceive as threatening, the sympathetic nervous system activates involuntary responses designed to activate all the major systems of the body.

When the body prepares for 'fight-or-flight', it does so with short-term goals in mind. Fuel is released in the form of glucose or stored blood sugar. More blood is sent to the muscles. Air passages relax and a sense of stimulation is produced. The

14

adrenal glands release adrenaline and noradrenaline into the blood stream. These two hormones mimic the actions of nervous stimulation in a number of organs in the body. The heart rate increases, blood vessels dilate in some areas and constrict in others, the rate of respiration increases and most digestive activities slow down or stop altogether. Digestion and excretion are not high priorities, so adrenaline causes vascular constriction which reduces the flow of blood to these areas. By all this we are prepared for a short burst of heightened activity.

In modern society many influences can trigger this response. Most of these cannot be handled with a short burst of activity. So the body's response is repressed. Often stress situations are continuous, so stress responses are semi-permanently on red alert – a situation which cannot be maintained for too long without the body suffering from extreme exhaustion. The stress build-up eventually explodes internally and knocks our systems out of balance.

Long-term adrenal stimulation with no discharge of energy will deplete essential minerals and vitamins from the system, for example Vitamins B and C, which are vital to the functioning of the immune system. This will result in lowered resistance and increased susceptibility to diseases directly related to a lowered immune system – such as ME and AIDS. Long-term adrenal build-up can also affect blood pressure and cause a build-up of fatty substances on blood vessel walls, as well as damage the functioning of the digestive system.

Stress affects different people in different ways and to varying degrees. One person may exhibit cardiovascular problems, another gastrointestinal upset, anorexia, palpitations, sweating or headaches – to mention but a few of the myriad of bodily reactions to stress. The cardiovascular and digestive systems are obvious candidates for the ill-effects of stress – high blood pressure, ulcers, indigestion and the like. Stress can also be linked to infectious diseases. When the body is busy with the effects of residual stress, it cannot organize an effective defence against invading organisms. It is a vicious cycle.

Reflexology helps alleviate the effects of stress by inducing deep relaxation, and thereby allowing the nervous system to function normally and free the body to seek its own homoeostasis. Tension is relaxed, vascular constriction reduced and blood and nerve supply flow more freely, allowing oxygen and nutrients to make their way to where they are needed. Reflexology is a powerful antidote to stress. A relaxed balanced body can heal itself and reflexology is a guaranteed method of relaxing the body and balancing the biological systems.

Reflexology Improves Circulation

One of Eunice Ingham's favourite sayings was 'Circulation is life. Stagnation is death.' Every practitioner acknowledges the importance of good circulation. If the smallest fraction of circulation is cut off from one or more parts of the body, the effects soon become evident as a variety of aches and pains.

Blood carries oxygen and nutrients to the cells and removes waste products and toxins from the cells. During this process blood vessels contract and relax so their resilience is most important for proper functioning. Stress and tension tighten up the cardiovascular system and restrict blood flow. Circulation becomes sluggish, causing high or low blood pressure.

High blood pressure can cause numerous problems – for example arteriosclerosis or hardening of the arteries. The increased pressure forces materials into the walls of the arteries. These materials build up, coating the insides. Blood flow is reduced, which signals a hormone in the kidneys to be released and the pressure is further increased. The heart, brain and kidneys could be affected.

Reduced blood flow to the organs inhibits the oxygen supply and nutrients to the cells. Without oxygen, cells die. Without the proper nutrients, cells fail to function efficiently. The glands and organs begin to malfunction and lose their balancing qualities; this could cause them to overreact or underreact.

A good example of the body's balancing act is the pancreas. One of its jobs is to maintain the balance of glucose, or blood sugar. This is achieved with the hormone insulin, which activates the body cells to take up the glucose from the blood. Without insulin, the glucose is not consumed or is stored improperly. It accumulates in the blood, causing the dangerous condition diabetes. If there is an excess of insulin produced, the opposite effect occurs. When insulin removes glucose from the blood, the storage of glucose in the form of glycogen is increased at the expense of the blood. Low blood sugar/hypoglycaemia is the result. The balancing act has been upset. Glands and organs depend on equilibrium, and on the blood circulation to bring the needed elements.

With improved circulation, the body is cleansed of toxins and impurities. If the body's built-in cleansing systems – the lymphatic and excretory systems – become blocked or function improperly, toxins and waste matter build up. The increased state of relaxation facilitated by reflexology allows the body systems – including the excretory systems – to function efficiently and waste is properly eliminated. By reducing stress and tension, reflexology allows the cardiovascular vessels to conduct the flow of blood naturally and easily.

Reflexology Improves Nerve Function

The organs and glands contribute to the overall well-being of the body – each making contributions to maintaining an efficient, fully operated mechanism. But all receive their instructions from the most intricate of all networks, the nerves. These cord-like structures, comprised of a collection of nerve fibres, convey impulses between a part of the central nervous system and other regions of the body. Problems can often be caused by tension putting pressure on a vital nerve plexus or even a single nerve structure supplying a vital organ. As tension is eased, pressure on the nerves and vessels is relaxed, thus improving the flow of blood and its supply of oxygen and nutrients to all parts of the body.

Every part of the body is operated by messages carried back and forth along neural pathways. Stimulation of sensory nerve endings sends information to the spinal cord and brain. The brain and spinal cord send instructions to the organs and muscles. The neural pathways are both living tissue and electrical channels and can be impinged upon or polluted by many factors. When neural pathways are impaired nerve function is impeded – messages are delivered slowly and unreliably, or not at all, and body processes operate at less than optimum levels. Reflexology, by stimulating the thousands of nerve endings in the feet, encourages the opening and clearing of neural pathways.

Reflexology Revitalizes Energy and Rebalances the Whole System

The body is a dynamic energy field; energy circulates throughout the body. For optimum functioning, energy must flow unimpeded and the yin and yang energy currents must complement each other. Reflexology opens up these energy pathways, energizing the physical, emotional and mental aspects of the body. When the body is 'out of balance', it is not functioning efficiently. We are all easily thrown off balance by stress, attitudes, lifestyle and diet. Reflexology helps return the body to a dynamic state of balance.

WHO CAN BENEFIT FROM REFLEXOLOGY?

Reflexology doesn't discriminate. There are no boundaries or limitations. People of any race, age, colour or creed, men, women, teenagers, children, babies and the elderly – all can enjoy the positive benefits reflexology has to offer. As reflexology can do no harm, the only restrictions are those determined by the clients' pain threshold and their reactions to massage. Elderly people with no specific complaint will benefit from a couple of courses of treatment a year to keep the bodily functions toned and for a sense of well-being. Results are also good with children and babies because they are more relaxed and supple and because their bodies are highly receptive to therapeutic stimuli.

Reflexologists Don't . . .

Reflexologists don't practise medicine. According to the law, only licensed physicians are allowed to do that. Reflexologists *never* diagnose a disease, treat for a specific condition, prescribe or adjust medication. They do not treat specific diseases although they help eliminate problems caused by specific diseases. By bringing the body back into a state of balance, treatment can combat a number of disorders. Tender reflexes indicate which parts of the body are congested. This 'diagnosis' is only of parts of the body 'out of balance' and not specific, named disorders.

The Reflexology Treatment

A reflexology treatment should always be a most pleasant experience. A client may be tense and apprehensive on the first visit, but any good practitioner will always make an effort to relax the client and give full, undivided attention. The practitioner will require a thorough medical history in as much detail as possible, as all problems, not only those specifically causing trouble at the time, are relevant in ascertaining a complete health picture of the client.

Many people are embarrassed about their feet. When visiting a reflexologist, any insecurity regarding the state of your feet should be forgotten. To a reflexologist, your feet represent your body and they tell a thousand stories about the state of the body. Every nick and crevice holds a key to the nature of the problem. And reflexology is the key to relieving these.

Comfort is the first prerequisite in the treatment so correct positioning is important. The client will be seated comfortably, preferably on a soft treatment couch with the head and upper part of the body upright – the head and neck well supported, so the client and reflexologist have eye contact. The lower legs will be well supported with the feet in a comfortable position. Shoes and stockings must be removed and tight garments should be loosened so as not to hinder circulation.

The practitioner begins by disinfecting the feet and the first physical contact is usually a gentle stroking movement, before the practitioner proceeds with a general examination of the feet. As every individual is different, so too are their feet, which reveal a variety of characteristics peculiar to that particular person.

Temperature, static build-up, muscle tone and tissue tone and skin condition are all noted as the therapist tries to get as comprehensive a view of the client as possible. Cold, bluish or reddish feet indicate poor circulation. Feet that perspire indicate a glandular imbalance. Dry skin could indicate poor circulation. Callouses, corns, bunions and the like, and their possible links, will also be noted. (Further information on this in Chapter 3.) Care must be taken with infectious areas as they could spread to other areas of the foot and to the practitioner. These should be covered with a plaster or cotton wool before they are worked on. Working on varicose veins should be avoided as it could further damage the veins. Swelling and puffiness, especially around the ankles, can relate to internal problems. Tense feet may indicate tension in the body, and limp feet may indicate poor muscle tone.

What the Reflexology Treatment Feels Like

In one word – wonderful. Calming, comforting and exhilarating. It is certainly not ticklish, since the massage technique is too firm to tickle. The foot massage technique is different to other forms of massage. The thumb is the most important working 'tool' used to apply pressure to the reflex areas – each of which is about the size of a pinhead. The foot is always well supported and the pressure firm but not agonizing.

Sensations vary on different parts of the feet, depending on the functioning of the related body parts. Congested areas will be sensitive – the more sensitive it is, the more congested it is. The sensations range from the feeling of something sharp (like a piece of glass) being pressed into the foot to a dull ache, discomfort, tightness or just firm pressure. Sensitivity varies from person to person. For example, some people may be relatively unhealthy and have insensitive reflexes, while others may be reasonably healthy and have tender reflexes. This also varies from treatment to treatment, depending on factors such as stress, mood and time of day. In many cases, a client may feel little or no tenderness at all during the first treatment. This does not necessarily mean no areas are congested. It more often than not indicates an energy blockage in the feet which needs to be freed. The feet usually become more sensitive with subsequent treatments.

As treatment progresses, tenderness should diminish. The treatment should never be painful or cause the client any discomfort. The practitioner will adjust pressure to suit the client. No matter what the sensations, treatment is always effective and should leave the client feeling light, tingly and thoroughly pampered.

Reactions to Reflexology Treatment

People differ, so do reactions. On the whole, reactions immediately after a reflexology treatment are largely pleasant – calm and relaxed or energized and rejuvenated. However, there is some bad with the good. Reflexology activates the body's healing power, so some form of reaction is inevitable as the body rids itself of toxins. This is referred to as a 'healing crisis' and is usually a cleansing process. The severity of reactions depends on the degree of imbalance, but should never be too radical. The most common phrase following a first treatment is 'I have never slept so well!'

Most common reactions are cleansing reactions which manifest in the eliminating systems of the body – the kidneys, bowels, skin and lungs. The following reactions are not unusual:

– increased urination as the kidneys are stimulated to produce more urine, which may also be darker and stronger smelling due to the toxic content
– flatulence and more frequent bowel movements
– aggravated skin conditions, particularly those that have been suppressed; increased perspiration and pimples
– improved skin tone and tissue texture due to improved circulation
– increased secretions of the mucous membranes in the nose, mouth and bronchi
– disrupted sleep patterns – either deeper or more disturbed sleep
– dizziness or nausea
– a temporary outbreak of a disease which has been suppressed
– increased discharge from the vagina in women
– feverishness
– tiredness

Whatever the reactions, however, they are a necessary part of the healing process and will pass. It is a good idea to drink a lot of water (preferably boiled) to help flush the toxins out as fast as possible.

Length of a Reflexology Treatment

The length of treatment and number of sessions will vary depending on the client and the condition – for example, the patient's constitution, the history and nature of his illness, his age, the ability of his body to react to the treatments, his way of life and his attitude to the treatment.

The first treatment is investigative and exploratory and should take about an hour. Following treatments would be thirty to forty minutes. If the session is too short, insufficient stimulus is provided for the body to mobilize its own healing powers; if it is too long, there is a danger of overstimulating which can cause excessive elimination and discomfort.

An effect is often experienced immediately after the first treatment. Generally results are apparent after three to four treatments – either complete or considerable improvement. Disorders present for a long time take longer to correct than those present for a short time. A course of treatments is recommended for all conditions (even if one session appears to have corrected the problem) to balance the body totally and prevent a recurrence of the disorder. The course should be eight to twelve treatments once or twice a week. For optimum results two sessions a week are recommended until there is an improvement, then the frequency can gradually be reduced.

If there is no reaction after several sessions, the body could be unreceptive, due to external factors, such as heavy medication or psychological attitude, which are blocking the therapeutic impulses. As long as reactions are positive there is value in continuing the treatment.

In cases of severe illness such as cancer, multiple sclerosis or paralysis, reflexology may not remove the cause of the disease, but it can significantly improve the patient's general condition as it helps relieve pain; activates the excretory organs; stimulates the respiratory system and helps the patient achieve better control of bladder and bowels.

PREVENTATIVE THERAPY

Health-threatening dangers lurk around every corner of our modern environment: polluted land, air and water, contaminated and irradiated food, a completely contaminated environment. Add to this the stress of our day-to-day lives – bad diet, attitudes and lifestyle – and we have a potentially lethal cocktail designed to attract disease. Most people wait until disease rears its ugly head before they seek help. But it makes far more sense to listen to the body's warning signals and take action early. Apart from caring for the body by eating more sensibly, exercising and calming the mind and body through relaxation and meditation techniques, occasional visits to a reflexologist as extra 'maintenance' can be of enormous benefit to all.

Preventative therapy is useful for people who have completed a course of treatment and want to continue it to avoid any problems re-emerging, as well as for those who may not have any acute symptoms but realize the need for preventative action. Treatments at regular intervals can assist the body in maintaining a balanced state, and prevent the possibility of slight imbalances from becoming troublesome. It is possible to detect imbalances in the early stages and prevent more serious problems occurring. The intervals between treatments will vary from person to person and may involve weeks or months. For best results, treatment should be applied in the correct manner by a trained therapist, but it can also be beneficial for clients to work on certain reflexes themselves between sessions, to act as a boost to the treatment. To quote Avi Grinberg in *Holistic Reflexology*:

The truly successful treatment is not the one that saves the person from a condition that is in its advanced stage, but is one that prevents its development into a serious or chronic condition.

Healing is always a possibility. There are many components of healing beyond the physical. So with reflexology, even though we may be working on the physical level, we still need to be quite conscious of the mental, emotional and spiritual levels. Healing usually occurs when these three elements are recognized. There needs to be a balance between the body and its environment, the physical, emotional and mental conditions. Clients need to be in balance with the individuals and relationships in their lives – relationships at school, work, or during leisure time. All these things need to be balanced and then healing can occur.

Rest, a change of environment, or most importantly, a change in attitude can allow this balance to be restored. Often we do not get the rest we would like, or cannot change our environment, but a change in attitude can have astounding benefits.

This change in attitude is very important. Many people feel the need to talk during a session. By talking about what is happening in their lives, they can sometimes come to a new understanding of their problems. Or perhaps the reflexologist can suggest a different perspective or approach to a problem in a non-judgmental way. This helps the client relax and see that a change in attitude is possible. This new attitude may allow clients to make changes in their environment and this in turn will help the body to function in a state of balance or homoeostasis – the major goal of reflexology.

3

Meridians

MERIDIANS AND REFLEXOLOGY

The concept of energy channels is the central point around which the practices of reflexology and acupuncture are based. Both are based on the premise that vital energy is channelled along various lines throughout the body. In acupuncture, the lines are known as meridians; in reflexology, zones. Both ascertain that disease is caused by blockages in energy lines, and treatment involves clearing out these obstructions by stimulating various points along the lines. In acupuncture, points situated all over the body are stimulated by needles. Reflexology concentrates only on reflex areas and sections of meridians found on the feet which are stimulated by a specific massage technique.

The similarity between the two therapies seems to be more than just coincidence. When Dr Fitzgerald developed the zone theory in the early 1900s, the Chinese concept of meridians was completely unknown in the West. Fitzgerald's 'discovery' of the existence of energy lines was undoubtedly a breakthrough and an invaluable contribution to the re-emergence of reflexology in the West. But it seems very likely and also a logical assumption that the energy lines Fitzgerald stumbled upon were, in fact, the meridians understood by the Chinese for thousands of years.

Closer study of the meridians reveals that the six main meridians are found in the feet, specifically the toes. Thus, massaging the feet is, in actual fact, stimulating and clearing congestions in the meridians. When congestions are cleared, energy is able to flow freely and the body is able to achieve a state of balance.

The six main meridians are those which actually penetrate the major body organs – the liver, spleen/pancreas, stomach, gall bladder, bladder and kidney. The other six meridians – lung, large intestine, pericardium/circulation, Three E/endocrine, small intestine and heart – are situated in the arms and do not actually penetrate specific organs. However, as the meridian cycle is one continuous energy flow, the six meridians which do not penetrate organs are indirectly stimulated when the main meridians are worked on. This is due to the fact that the organs related to these meridians are found along the six main meridians. For example, the lung meridian runs along the arm down to the thumb, but the lung itself is penetrated by the stomach meridian, and therefore congestions would be indirectly affected by stimulating the stomach meridian.

Meridians have a long and authentic history. The Chinese discovered the meridian system approximately 3000 years ago. The fact that this system has been used successfully all this time, and is going from strength to strength, particularly in the West, is proof of its efficacy. It is a logical progression to now incorporate meridians into the realm of reflexology in order to advance and enhance this holistic health therapy.

An understanding of meridians can help reflexologists to understand the disease pathway more comprehensively. A basic knowledge of meridians can be of enormous benefit in pinpointing problems. If, for example, pain, irritation or any other condition does not improve satisfactorily through treatment of the reflex area, one should observe the meridian which traverses the part of the body in question, and treat the reflex area of the organ related to that meridian. The meridians can be used simply and effectively for a better understanding of conditions. For example, a client has arthritis in the little finger, tennis elbow, fibrositis in the shoulder muscles, infection in the lymph glands of the throat, trigeminal neuralgia and hearing diseases. One need simply look at the small intestine meridian which starts in the little finger and ends just in front of the ear and passes the locations of all the above disorders. Could this mean that the small intestine disorder could aggravate or even cause these problems? Clinical results of balancing the meridians certainly indicate this.

WHAT ARE MERIDIANS?

All life and matter is energy operating at various frequencies. This energy, known as ch'i or life-force, is what keeps us alive. The Chinese discovered that this ch'i circulates in the body along 'meridians', similar to the blood, nerve and lymphatic circuits. This vital life-force controls the workings of the main organs and systems of the body. It circulates from one organ to another. For each organ to maintain a perfect state of health, the ch'i energy must be able to flow freely along the meridians. If this is balanced, it is impossible to be ill in body, mind or spirit. All illness is a result of an imbalance in the energy flow.

Meridians are located throughout the body. They have been described as containing a free-flowing, colourless, non-cellular liquid which may be partly actuated by the heart (*Handbook of Acupressure II*, by Iona Marsaa-Teergurden). Meridians have been measured and mapped by modern technological methods, electronically, thermatically and radioactively. With practice they can be felt. There are specific acupuncture points along the meridians. These points are electromagnetic in character and consist of small oval cells called Bonham Corpuscles which surround the capillaries in the skin, the blood vessels and the organs throughout the body. There are some five hundred points which are most frequently used. They are stimulated in a definite sequence depending on the action required. Meridians are named by the live functions with which they seem to associate. In most cases, this name is the same as that of many of the gross organs we are familiar with.

The Chinese maintain that the ch'i circulates in the meridians twenty-five times a day and twenty-five times a night. In a sense, there is only one single meridian which goes right round the entire body, but many different meridians are described according to their positions and functions. There are twelve main meridians which are bilateral (paired) resulting in twenty-four separate pathways. Each meridian is connected and related to a specific organ from which it gets its name. It is also connected to a partner meridian and organ with which it has a specific relationship. The partner meridians each consist of a yin and a yang meridian/organ and come under the dominance of one of the five elements.

The twelve main meridians control the lungs, large intestine, stomach, spleen/pancreas, heart, small intestine, bladder, kidney, pericardium, 'triple warmer', gall-bladder and liver. Within our bodies the yang organs are those which are hollow and involved in absorption and discharge such as the stomach and bladder; the yin organs are the dense, blood-filled organs such as the heart, which regulate the body. There is constant interaction between yin and yang forces and, if the yin/yang balance between the organs is interrupted, the flow of ch'i throughout the body will be affected and we will fall ill.

The acupuncturist balances this ch'i with needles, and sometimes laser equipment. In shiatsu, the same effect is achieved utilizing finger pressure. In the VacuFlex Reflexology System (described later in the book) rubber cups are used. These cups which suction on to the body are strategically placed on a particular meridian and thereby balance the energy flow.

The Meridian Cycle

Meridians are classified yin or yang on the basis of the direction in which they flow on the surface of the body. Meridians interconnect deep within the torso and have an internal branch and a surface branch. The section worked on is the surface branch which is accessible to touch techniques. Yang energy flows from the sun and yang meridians run from the fingers to the face, or from the face to the feet. Yin energy from the earth flows from the feet to the torso and from the torso along the inside (yin side) of the arms to the fingertips. Since the meridian flow is actually one long continuous unbroken flow, the energy flows in one definite direction and from one meridian to another in a well-determined order. Because there is no beginning or end to this flow, the order of the meridian is represented as a wheel. As we go round this wheel following the meridian line, the flow follows this order of the body:

– from torso to fingertips – along the inside of the arm = yin.
– from fingertips to face – along the outside/back of the arm = yang.
– from face to feet – along the outside of the leg = yang.
– from feet to torso – along the inside of the leg = yin.

The Chinese Clock/Midday-Midnight Law

The Chinese recognized a twenty-four hour movement of energy referred to as the Chinese Clock. This 'clock' is a twenty-four hour cycle which divides the day and night into two-hour periods. Each one of these is associated with a surge of energy in one of the organs and its meridian. For example, between the hours of 3 and 5 am, the lungs receive their daily booster. The cycle begins with the lungs and for this reason it is said that these are the hours when it is most suitable to be born.

The Chinese believe that the best time for stimulating a particular organ is at the two-hour period when its energy is 'full'. Alternatively, it should be sedated at the opposite period of the day or night. For example the lungs should be stimulated between 3 and 5 am and sedated between 3 and 5 pm. The opposite treatment should be applied at the opposite time on the clock. The organ maximum energy periods are included in the detailed section on meridians.

The Five Elements

Meridian therapy and acupuncture can be more clearly understood in the light of the Chinese belief that five elements comprise the world, and that everything on earth essentially falls into the category of one or more of these elements.

The five elements are generated and destroyed according to a law of cyclical interaction: fire produces earth, earth produces metal, metal finds water, water produces wood and wood becomes fire. By substituting for each element a corresponding yin organ, for example, we see that the heart (fire) aids or reinforces the action of the spleen/pancreas (earth); the spleen/pancreas the lungs (metal); the lungs the kidneys (water); the kidneys the liver (wood) and the liver the heart.

Conversely, just as fire melts metal, metal cuts down wood, wood covers earth, earth absorbs water and water puts out fire, so the diseased or malfunctioning heart adversely affects the action of the lungs, the lungs affect the liver, the liver affects the spleen/pancreas, and the spleen/pancreas affects the kidneys and the kidneys affect the heart. So, to the Chinese, the nourishing and inhibiting cycle relates not only to the construction and working of the universe, but to the human body as well.

From another aspect, the mind fuels the body with negative or positive thoughts. Negative thoughts breed destructive elements. Destructive elements create tension and constrictions of circulation. Disease manifests in tense, sluggish areas of the body. The organs become diseased and fail to function. Our thinking becomes even more disturbed and negative. Pain permeates most of our days which causes us to become more and more dissociated from nature. Our vital energy becomes weaker and weaker until eventually we die and go back to the earth.

Each of the five elements is assigned at least one yin and one yang organ. They are identified with the five elements in the following manner:

Fire: yin – heart, pericardium (circulation)
    yang – small intestine, triple warmer
Earth: yin – spleen/pancreas
    yang – stomach
Metal: yin – lungs
    yang – large intestine
Water: yin – kidneys
    yang – bladder
Wood: yin – liver
    yang – gall bladder

Symptoms/Signs to Note Along Meridians

Before we look into the meridians and their symptoms, we will take a brief look at the disorders and congestions which can occur along the meridians and indicate where problems may lie. These may take the form of skin disorders, warts, birthmarks, lumps, nail problems and the like.

If a person has skin problems, it may be obvious that the lung and large intestine are the root cause, but note must be taken of exactly where the problem manifests on the body; down the legs, for example, or on the back. Often these will occur parallel to each other. For example, someone with psoriasis may have it on the outer side of the leg (gall bladder meridian) and down the back (bladder meridian).

Look at the nails for white spots, ridges, problems with the root of the nails or any other nail defects. Ridges often indicate high acidity, and if you take note on which meridian it manifests, you will see where the congestion occurs – for example, if it is on the thumb, the acidity is congesting the lung meridian. If there are white spots on the nails, these indicate a deficiency. As the nail takes approximately three months to grow, divide the nail into segments. The centre, for example, indicates approximately six weeks. One can thereby ascertain the approximate period when the deficiency occurred and relate it to the situation at the time – for example, the person may have been on a sugar binge or through a great deal of stress which caused the deficiency. Always note these signs, and pinpoint the meridian on which they appear in order to trace the problem organ.

MERIDIANS

Lung Meridian
Yin meridian
Partner meridian – Large Intestine – Yang
Element – Metal
Organ Maximum Energy Period – 3 am to 5 am

The lungs and large intestine control elimination; the former carbon dioxide, the latter solid residue. As these meridians are partnered, they can directly affect each other – for example chest problems can be accompanied by constipation and vice versa.

The lungs regulate respiration. They are responsible for taking ch'i from the air and for regulating the states of ch'i in the body. Healthy lungs and regular even respiration ensure that ch'i enters and leaves the body smoothly. An imbalance results in symptoms such as asthma, coughs and various forms of chest congestion. Respiratory functions affect all the rhythms of the body including the blood flow.

The lungs are called the 'tender' organ because they are the most easily influenced by environmental factors and are involved with regulating sweat secretion which increases resistance to external environmental influences.

Large Intestine Meridian
Yang meridian
Partner Meridian – Lung – Yin
Element – Metal
Organ Maximum Energy Period – 5 am to 7 am

'The large intestine forms the lower part of the digestive tract and is in charge of transporting, transforming and eliminating surplus matter. If these wastes are not eliminated regularly, it can have a toxic effect on the entire system. Thus *mental* constipation – toxic thoughts and feelings – are often associated with this meridian, in addition to *physical* constipation or diarrhoea,' to quote from Iona Marsaa-Teegurden's '*Acupressure Handbook*'.

The *Nei Ching* refers to the large intestine as the generator of evolution and change – and as being integral to the well-being of the whole body. The important function of elimination of waste material is vital to the maintenance of health. If waste is not effectively excreted, the rest of the system has to cope with an additional load of toxic waste and this will cause disharmony throughout the body. An imbalance in the large intestine can result in abdominal pain, diarrhoea, constipation, bloatedness, swelling, acne and boils, headaches and stuffy nose.

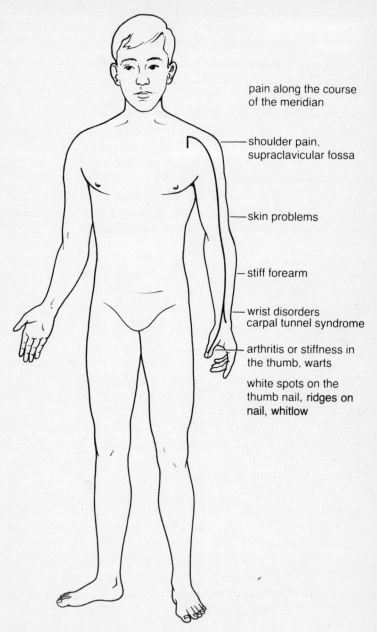

pain along the course
of the meridian

shoulder pain,
supraclavicular fossa

skin problems

stiff forearm

wrist disorders
carpal tunnel syndrome

arthritis or stiffness in
the thumb, warts

white spots on the
thumb nail, ridges on
nail, whitlow

Fig.3. The lung meridian

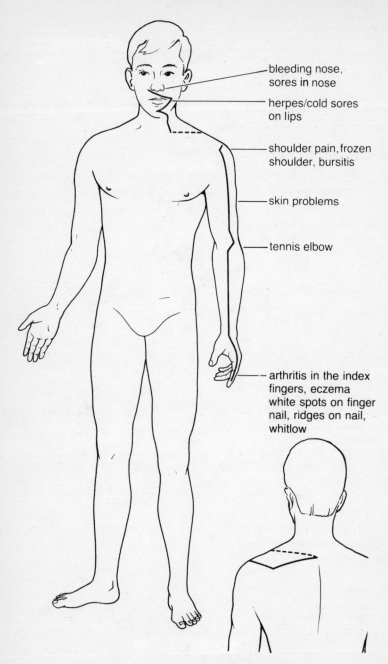

Fig. 4. The large intestine (colon) meridian

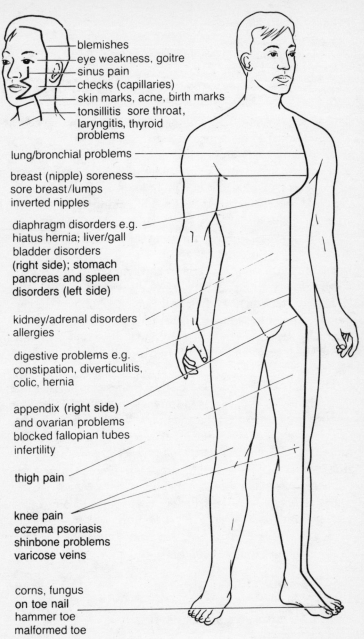

blemishes
eye weakness, goitre
sinus pain
checks (capillaries)
skin marks, acne, birth marks
tonsillitis sore throat,
laryngitis, thyroid
problems

lung/bronchial problems

breast (nipple) soreness
sore breast/lumps
inverted nipples

diaphragm disorders e.g.
hiatus hernia; liver/gall
bladder disorders
(right side); stomach
pancreas and spleen
disorders (left side)

kidney/adrenal disorders
allergies

digestive problems e.g.
constipation, diverticulitis,
colic, hernia

appendix (right side)
and ovarian problems
blocked fallopian tubes
infertility

thigh pain

knee pain
eczema psoriasis
shinbone problems
varicose veins

corns, fungus
on toe nail
hammer toe
malformed toe

Fig. 5. The stomach meridian

Stomach Meridian
Yang Meridian
Partner Meridian – Spleen/Pancreas – Yin
Element – Earth
Organ Maximum Energy Period – 7 am to 9 am

The functions and activities of the stomach and spleen are closely related. The stomach controls digestion – it receives nourishment, integrates it and passes on the 'pure' food energy to be distributed by the spleen. The spleen then transforms it into the raw material for ch'i and blood. If the stomach does not hold and digest food, the spleen cannot transform it and transport its essence. They are interdependent meridians.

According to Chinese philosophy, the stomach is related to appetite, digestion and transport of food and liquid, but the ruler of food transport and energy consumption is the stomach's partner, the spleen/pancreas.

The two meridians of the earth element work together more closely than any of the others to stabilize the individual. The earth element represents harmony and if there is no harmony in the stomach, pancreas and spleen, this will affect all the other organs.

The stomach is referred to by the Chinese as the 'sea of food and fluid' as it governs digestion and is responsible for 'receiving' and 'ripening' ingested food and fluids. Without the nourishing activities of the stomach the other organs in the body could not function. The stomach is *central* physically and functionally; thus, according to Oriental therapists *any problem in the stomach is quickly reflected in the other organs.*

If this organ is out of balance, whatever is taken in, be it physical or psychic food, will not be utilized correctly. Energy depletion – lethargy, weakness and debilitation are symptoms warning us that the function of this organ is impaired.

Spleen/Pancreas Meridian
Yin Meridian
Partner Meridian – Stomach – Yang
Element – Earth
Organ Maximum Energy Period – 9 am to 11 am

A traditional saying that combines the meaning of several references in the *Nei Ching* states that 'the spleen rules transformation and transportation'. It is the crucial link in the process by which food is transformed into ch'i and blood. If this process of food transformation is not activated nourishment and ch'i are not available for the muscles so they become weak and the lips and mouth become pale and dry. The spleen is traditionally referred to as the 'foundation of postnatal existence'. If the spleen is imbalanced the whole body or some part of it may develop deficient ch'i or deficient blood.

Physiologically, the pancreas has considerable control over the body's nourishment, since its secretions help digest all the main kinds of food: proteins, fats and starch.

According to the Chinese, 'The spleen governs the blood'; it helps create blood and keeps it flowing in its proper paths. It therefore also influences menstruation. The spleen destroys spent red blood cells and forms antibodies which neutralize poisonous bacteria, thus influencing immunity to infection. Another important function of this meridian has to do with the transformation of liquids; the classics say that oedema (swelling from retention of excess fluids) is related to the spleen.

Heart Meridian
Yin Meridian
Partner Meridian – Small Intestine – Yang
Element – Fire
Organ Maximum Energy Period – 11 am to 1 pm

The heart and small intestine meridians are coupled; the *Nei Ching* explains their relationship: 'The heart controls the blood and unites with the small intestine. If the heart becomes heated, the heat will converge in the small intestine, producing blood in the urine.'

The classics say, 'The heart rules the blood and blood vessels.' It regulates the blood flow, so when the heart is functioning properly, the blood flows smoothly. If the heart is strong, the body will be healthy and the emotions orderly; if it is weak, all the other meridians will be disturbed.

It is also said that the heart rules the spirit. So, when the heart's blood and ch'i are harmonious, spirit is nourished and

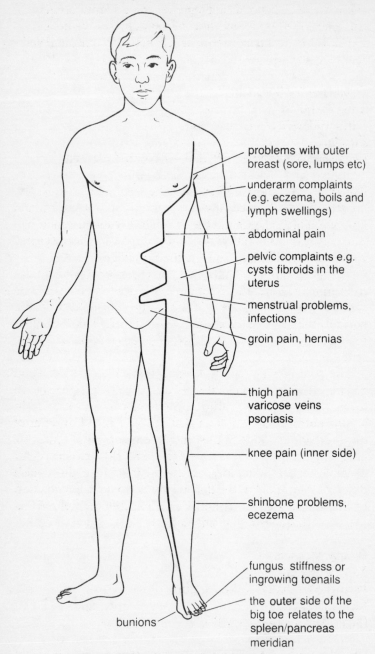

problems with outer
breast (sore, lumps etc)

underarm complaints
(e.g. eczema, boils and
lymph swellings)

abdominal pain

pelvic complaints e.g.
cysts fibroids in the
uterus

menstrual problems,
infections

groin pain, hernias

thigh pain
varicose veins
psoriasis

knee pain (inner side)

shinbone problems,
ecezema

fungus stiffness or
ingrowing toenails

the outer side of the
big toe relates to the
spleen/pancreas
meridian

bunions

Fig. 6. The spleen/pancreas meridian

the individual responds appropriately to the environment. If this is impaired symptoms like insomnia, excessive dreaming, forgetfulness, hysteria, irrational behaviour, insanity and delirium may manifest.

Small Intestine Meridian
Yang Meridian
Partner Meridian – Heart – Yin
Element – Fire
Organ Maximum Energy Period – 1 pm to 3 pm

The small intestine meridian rules the separation of the 'pure' and the 'impure'. It continues the process of separation and absorption of food begun in the stomach. Because the meridian is in charge of assimilation this flow has considerable influence over body nourishment and body-mind vitality.

The small intestine influences the functioning of the large intestine both directly and indirectly. In addition to passing solid residue on to the large intestine, the small intestine also controls the proportion of liquid to solid matter in the faeces, reabsorbing some liquids for the body's use and passing some on to be eliminated.

The 'sorting out' process – keeping that which has value and passing on waste to where it can be removed – happens on all levels, both physiological and psychological, for example in sorting out the 'rubbish' from that which is useful in terms of ideas, emotions and thoughts. If this function is not operating efficiently symptoms that express this confusion may arise – for example hearing difficulties, such as the inability to distinguish different sounds. Thus the flow relates not only to assimilation of foodstuffs but also to assimilation of experience, feelings and ideas and to spiritual nourishment.

Bladder Meridian
Yang Meridian
Partner Meridian – Kidney – Yin
Element – Water
Organ Maximum Energy Period – 3 pm to 5 pm

The partnership of the kidney and bladder meridians is one of

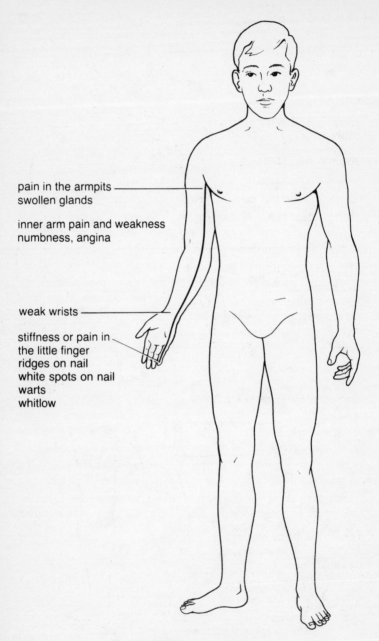

pain in the armpits
swollen glands

inner arm pain and weakness
numbness, angina

weak wrists

stiffness or pain in
the little finger
ridges on nail
white spots on nail
warts
whitlow

Fig.7. The heart meridian

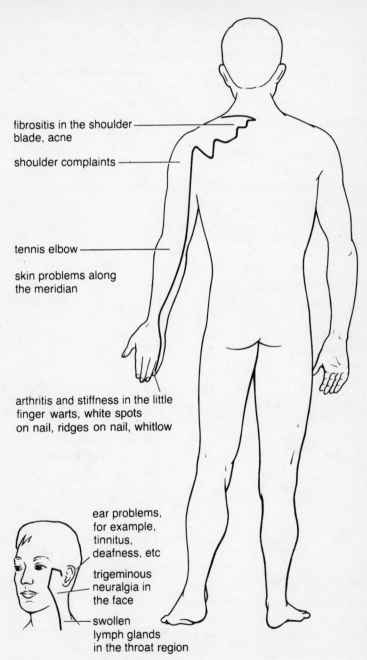

fibrositis in the shoulder
blade, acne

shoulder complaints

tennis elbow

skin problems along
the meridian

arthritis and stiffness in the little
finger warts, white spots
on nail, ridges on nail, whitlow

ear problems,
for example,
tinnitus,
deafness, etc

trigeminous
neuralgia in
the face

swollen
lymph glands
in the throat region

Fig. 8. The small intestine meridian

the most obvious and means that the bladder meridian has a role in stimulating and regulating the kidneys.

The function of the bladder is to receive and excrete urine produced in the kidneys, and the meridian is therefore in charge of maintaining normal fluid levels in the body. It is also coupled with the function of the kidney in helping to store the vital essence (see below). The bladder is essential to life because if it is not functioning, the rest of the system becomes poisoned and stressed beyond endurance.

The bladder meridian strongly affects the spinal cord and nerves and it is most effective to release the tensions along its route.

Kidney Meridian
Yin Meridian
Partner Meridian – Bladder – Yang
Element – Water
Organ Maximum Energy Period – 5 pm to 7 pm

The *Nei Ching* states: 'When the kidneys are deficient . . . the spirit becomes easily provoked.'

'The kidneys store the Jing' and rule birth, development and maturation. Jing is the substance – a vital essence – that is the source of life and individual development. It has the potential for differentiation into yin and yang and therefore produces life. The body and all the organs need Jing to thrive, and because the kidneys store Jing, they bestow this potential for life activity. They have therefore a special relationship with the other organs because the yin and yang, or life activity of each organ ultimately depends on the yin and yang of the kidneys.

The kidneys regulate the amount of water in the body. Fluid is essential to life. The flow of the fluid enables waste material to be collected and excreted in the form of urine. Enormous amounts of blood flow through the kidneys to be purified. If the blood does not flow as it should symptoms such as high blood pressure or hypertension may result and there may be a build-up of toxic substances that the body would be unable to deal with.

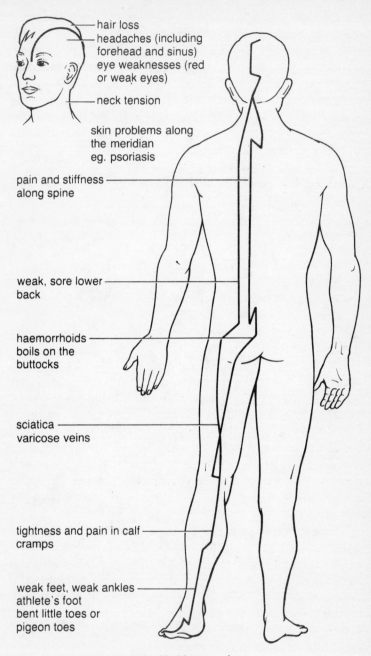

hair loss
headaches (including forehead and sinus) eye weaknesses (red or weak eyes)

neck tension

skin problems along the meridian eg. psoriasis

pain and stiffness along spine

weak, sore lower back

haemorrhoids boils on the buttocks

sciatica varicose veins

tightness and pain in calf cramps

weak feet, weak ankles athlete's foot bent little toes or pigeon toes

Fig. 9. The bladder meridian

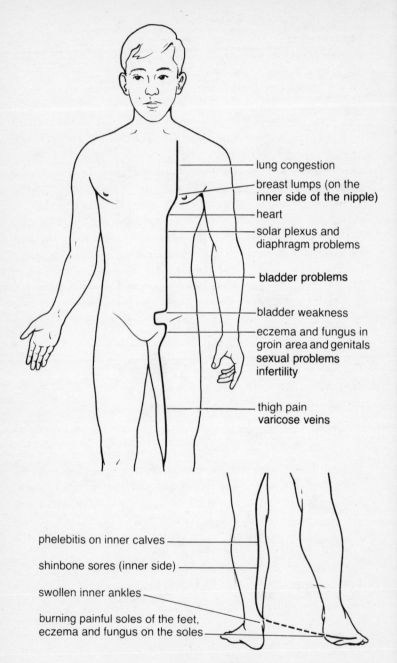

lung congestion

breast lumps (on the inner side of the nipple)

heart

solar plexus and diaphragm problems

bladder problems

bladder weakness

eczema and fungus in groin area and genitals
sexual problems
infertility

thigh pain
varicose veins

phelebitis on inner calves

shinbone sores (inner side)

swollen inner ankles

burning painful soles of the feet, eczema and fungus on the soles

Fig. 10. The kidney meridian

Circulation/Pericardium Meridian
Yin Meridian
Partner Meridian – Endocrine/Triple Warmer/ Three E – Yang
Element – Fire
Organ Maximum Energy Period – 7 pm to 9 pm

The pericardium and triple warmer are coupled meridians and both have protective functions. The pericardium protects the heart – the ruler – and the triple warmer protects the other nine meridians. The condition of either affects the other; if the triple warmer is imbalanced, the organs are deprived of proper nourishment and revolt against the heart; if the pericardium is weak, the heart will be attacked and the nourishing activities of the triple warmer will be less effective.

One main function of this meridian is to protect the heart – physically as well as energetically. The pericardium is a fibrous sac enclosing a slippery lubricated membrane which prevents friction as the heart beats. Stresses and shocks first affect the pericardium and do not penetrate the heart unless the pericardium is weakened.

Triple Warmer/Endocrine/Three E Meridian
Yang Meridian
Partner Meridian – Pericardium – Yin
Element – Fire
Organ Maximum Energy Period – 9 pm to 11 pm

The triple warmer meridian governs the cycle of ch'i transformation. This is the partner of the circulation meridian and thus works closely with it. Though there is no anatomical organ that correlates with the triple warmer, the Chinese believe that all the organs in the body are guarded by it and that heat is controlled by this function.

The three 'heaters' or 'warmers' correspond to divisions of the torso; the upper warmer to the thoracic cavity; the middle warmer to the abdominal cavity; the lower warmer to the pelvic cavity. This meridian governs activities involving all the organs; it unites the respiratory, digestive and excretory functions into an energetic whole. It may be related to the hypothalamus, the link between the nervous system and

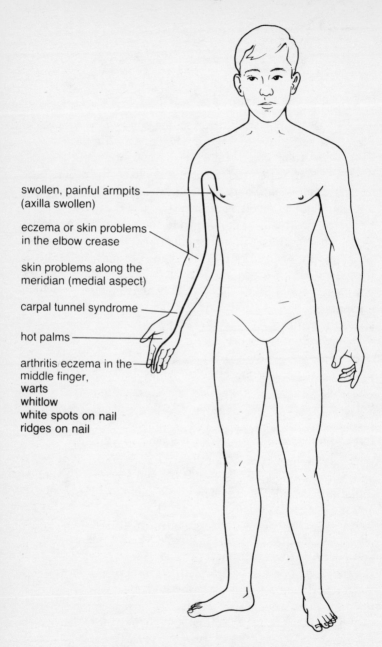

swollen, painful armpits
(axilla swollen)

eczema or skin problems
in the elbow crease

skin problems along the
meridian (medial aspect)

carpal tunnel syndrome

hot palms

arthritis eczema in the
middle finger,
warts
whitlow
white spots on nail
ridges on nail

Fig. 11. The circulation/pericardium meridian

endocrine glands. Its functions include:

1. Regulation of the autonomic nervous system and thus of the heart and abdominal organs especially in their response to emotion.
2. Control of the pituitary gland (which regulates output of all the endocrine glands).
3. Regulation of body temperature, appetite and thirst.
4. Control of emotions and moods – the urges of pleasure and displeasure which influence social relations.

This meridian, like its partner, has several names, as it is tied to numerous organs. In English it is called the triple warmer, in Chinese *sanjiao* which means three body cavity – signifying the division of the body into three sections. The burner of the upper section, the breast cavity, is the lungs; the middle burner in the diaphragm section is the spleen/pancreas; the burners of the lower pelvic section are the kidneys.

Gall Bladder Meridian
Yang Meridian
Partner Meridian – Liver – Yin
Element – Wood
Organ Maximum Energy Period – 11 pm to 1 am

It is essential to note that the Chinese think about the organs as functions operating on all levels of the body-mind . . . 'the liver has the functions of a military leader who excels in his strategic planning; the gall bladder occupies the position of an important and upright official who excels through his decisions and judgment' (Nei Ching).

According to the Ancients the attitudes of all the other organs originate in the energy of the gall bladder. It is different from the other hollow organs in that all the others transport 'impure' or foreign matter – food, liquids and the waste products thereof. Only the gall bladder transports 'pure' liquids exclusively, in that it stores and concentrates bile.

This meridian is one of the most well-travelled meridians, traversing almost the entire body except the arms. It zigzags throughout the head in a pattern which, in times of stress and

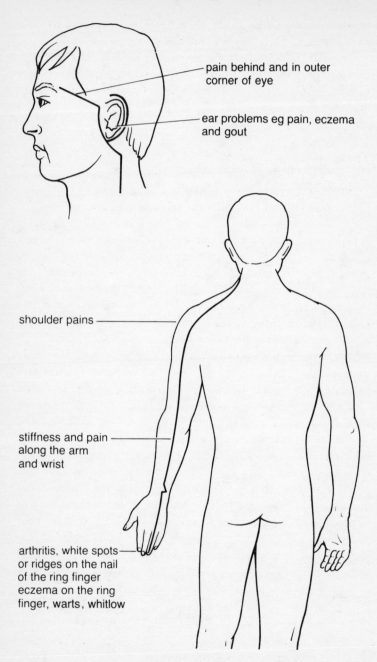

pain behind and in outer corner of eye

ear problems eg pain, eczema and gout

shoulder pains

stiffness and pain along the arm and wrist

arthritis, white spots or ridges on the nail of the ring finger eczema on the ring finger, warts, whitlow

Fig. 12. The triple warmer/endocrine/three E meridian

tension, becomes like a vice and is therefore important in cases of headaches, neck tension and 'uptightness'.

The *Nei Ching* says that the gall bladder rules decision making, thus anger and rash decisions may be due to an excess of gall bladder ch'i, while indecision and timidity may be a sign of gall bladder disharmony and weakness.

Liver Meridian
Yin Meridian
Partner Meridian – Gall Bladder – Yang
Element – Wood
Organ Maximum Energy Period – 1 am to 3 am

'The liver rules flowing and spreading' according to the Chinese classics. The liver or liver ch'i is responsible for the smooth movement of bodily substances and for the regularity of body activities. It moves the ch'i and blood in all directions, sending them to every part of the body. The *Nei Ching* metaphorically calls the liver 'the general of an army' because it maintains evenness and harmony of movement throughout the body.

The liver is the primary centre of metabolism. Not only does it secrete bile, synthesize proteins, neutralize toxins and regulate blood sugar levels, it also stores glycogen (starch), changes it back into glucose (sugar) and releases it when needed. Since the brain does not store any glucose, the liver's steady supply is crucial to life, and this is why the Chinese saw the liver as vital to conscious and unconscious thought processes.

The liver meridian helps control the functions of the nervous system and is very important for psychological problems such as depression and anger. Motivation – the will to become 'that self which one truly is' . . . is associated with balance of this meridian along with a sense of well-being and a reasonable temperament.

CASE HISTORIES

A reflexologist is a therapist who, by stimulating reflexes in the feet, encourages the body to heal itself. In most

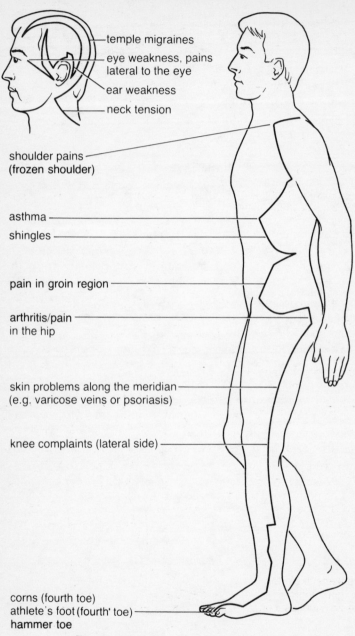

temple migraines

eye weakness, pains
lateral to the eye

ear weakness

neck tension

shoulder pains
(frozen shoulder)

asthma

shingles

pain in groin region

arthritis/pain
in the hip

skin problems along the meridian
(e.g. varicose veins or psoriasis)

knee complaints (lateral side)

corns (fourth toe)
athlete's foot (fourth' toe)
hammer toe

Fig. 13. *The gall bladder meridian*

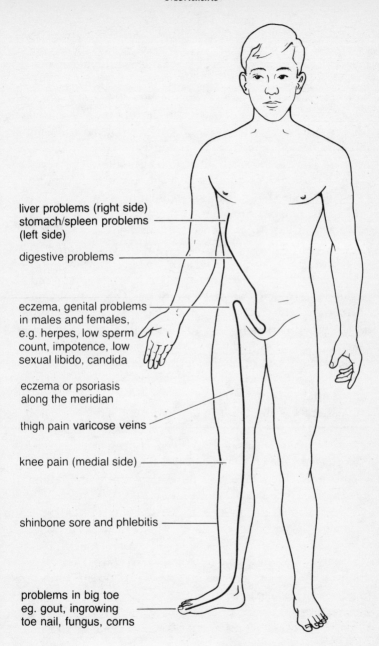

liver problems (right side)
stomach/spleen problems
(left side)

digestive problems

eczema, genital problems
in males and females,
e.g. herpes, low sperm
count, impotence, low
sexual libido, candida

eczema or psoriasis
along the meridian

thigh pain **varicose veins**

knee pain (medial side)

shinbone sore and phlebitis

problems in big toe
eg. gout, ingrowing
toe nail, fungus, corns

Fig. 14. *The liver meridian*

countries reflexologists are not allowed to diagnose any specific condition. In my work as a teacher and practitioner I have found it important that a client understands the nature of their complaints so that they are more willing to cooperate with any advice. In order to understand the complaint the practitioner requires a detailed case history of all symptoms, not only those causing the most severe problems at the time of consultation. The complaints can then be related to the meridians in order to ascertain which organs are out of balance. Instead of using the symptoms to diagnose a medical condition one must understand them in accordance with the Chinese philosophy of blockage in energy flow.

Study of the path of the twelve meridians shows that the stomach meridian penetrates all the major organs in the body as well as passing through all the reflexes of the major organs in the feet. This is therefore the dominant meridian and it is often the root cause of congestions. This will obviously affect the partner meridian, the spleen/pancreas, as well as all the other meridians. This root congestion will manifest as different symptoms in different people, but in ninety percent of problems, the stomach and its meridian are involved.

In the case histories where there are problems with the arms and hands these relate to the lung, large intestine, circulation/pericardium, triple warmer/endocrine, small intestine and heart meridians. None of these meridians penetrate any of the major organs, but a problem with an organ can cause a blockage in the ch'i energy in the arms and hands resulting in uncomfortable symptoms – for example the painful thumbs mentioned in the first two case histories.

It is of vital importance to do a complete reflexology treatment in each case, no matter what the symptoms, rather than to work only on the isolated reflexes one may think are congested. Weakness may be expressed in congestions of ch'i energy at any point along a meridian, not just in the actual organs. For example in the case histories relating to the large intestine meridian the main symptoms were manifest in problems on the arms and face, yet the cause was a large intestine imbalance. The kidney and bladder meridians are partner meridians and the main symptoms which indicate imbalance in these organs are headaches, weak eyes, neck tension and back problems and, to some degree, sciatica and leg problems. Dis-ease in the liver and gall bladder meridians often manifest as migraines, gout, nausea, gall stones, frozen shoulder, hip and leg complaints and sexual problems.

The following case histories have all been effectively treated with the reflexology techniques described in this book in Chapter 6. The techniques clear the congestions in the meridians allowing the energy to flow freely and the body to reach a state of balance. Each case history has been described so that the reader can relate the most painful symptoms to blockages along specific meridians but, as previously mentioned, one will inevitably find numerous symptoms relating to the stomach, spleen and pancreas and their meridians. Therefore a change in diet and lifestyle will always have positive results.

Lung Meridian (See illustration p. 33)
Female: Age – 30s
Symptoms: The main reason the client came for treatment was severe pain in a 'nerve' in both thumbs. Other symptoms noted: feels a 'total mess' – allergies; skin problems; rashes on her face and scalp; frequently blocked nose; headaches (forehead and neck); wine makes her nauseous; discontinued contraceptive pills three to four months previously – periods are now regular but heavy and painful; suffers slight constipation.

On studying the case history, one notices obvious symptoms related to the stomach, spleen/pancreas and their meridians – such as allergies, rashes on her face, heavy and painful periods and slight constipation. But the reason she sought treatment was due to the problem with her thumbs which indicates a blockage in the ch'i energy of the lung meridian.

Female: Age – 60s
Symptoms: The main problem, extremely painful thumbs, had been previously diagnosed as arthritis. Other symptoms include bronchial problems; 'nervous' throat – she is constantly clearing her throat; and chronic constipation.

Large callouses on the lung and bronchi reflexes of her feet indicate problems in the respiratory system, while the pain in her thumbs verifies this.

As mentioned in the introduction, problems with the stomach, spleen/pancreas and their meridians are often the root cause and this also applied in this case. Reference to the stomach meridian shows that the pathway includes the bronchi, lung, throat and large intestine. But the main congestion in the ch'i energy is related to the lung meridian.

Large Intestine (Colon) Meridian (See illustration p. 34)
Female: Age – 38
Symptoms: As a teenager she had a wart on her right index finger. She suffered from cold sores on the lips and inside the nose four times a year for which treatment was required. Constipation; nervous stomach which would progress into painful colic if left unattended. Colds invariably developed into chest problems and occasionally pneumonia. As soon as she disrupts her diet she develops fever blisters on her lips and sores in her nose, and the wart scar becomes sore and itchy. These are all symptoms found along the large intestine meridian and when the sores erupt they are warning signals of overloading this organ.

Again none of the meridians in the arm and face penetrate any major organs. But organs related to the meridians in the arms – in this case the large intestine – are penetrated by the stomach and other meridians and the cause will therefore usually be found in one or more of the major organs and their meridians.

Female: Age – mid 50s
Symptoms: Pain in upper right arm from forearm to index finger. The arm sometimes goes into spasm. This condition has existed for three years. Neck tension; constipation (takes laxatives regularly); slow digestion; had a hiatus hernia; meningitis as a child; one short leg; backache.
Previous Operations: Appendectomy and an operation for endometriosis.

As in the previous case, the main problems were with her arms which indicate congestions along the large intestine meridian. However, one still needs to study and stimulate all other organs and their meridians.

Stomach Meridian (See illustration p.35)
Female: Age – 55
Symptoms: The reason she sought treatment was a continuous laryingitis problem which had occured six times in one year. Other symptoms noted include fatigue, constipation and tension headaches.
Previous Operations: Appendectomy; hysterectomy; lump-ectomy from breast under nipple.

These symptoms all run along the stomach meridian except the tension headaches which relate to the bladder meridian. The hysterectomy can be seen as caused by a combination of meridians – the stomach and the spleen/pancreas.

This is a classic example of a ch'i energy imbalance along the stomach meridian. Over the years symptoms have been dealt with by operations and medication. However, the main cause, an imbalance in the acid/alkaline intake in food, had not been considered.

Female: Age – 30s
Symptoms: The client's main concerns were a constant 'burning' stomach, the bad condition of her nails and dry hair. Other symptoms noted include fatigue, slight constipation, regular menstrual cycle but heavy and painful with sore breasts and backache. Generally has very bad teeth.
Previous Operations: Tonsillectomy; wisdom teeth extracted.

The 'burning stomach' was a sure sign of an acid condition. Her food intake consisted mainly of diet coke, coffee, cheese, bread and pasta and she ate very few vegetables. It is therefore understandable that the stomach and its meridian are the cause, but other symptoms have manifested as well to indicate the congestion. The hair, nails and fatigue can be related to the thyroid (on the stomach meridian). The large intestine (constipation) and teeth are also on the stomach meridian. The breasts were sore on the sides (pancreas meridian) and this links with the heavy cycle.

Spleen/Pancreas Meridian (See illustration p.38)
Female: Age – 40s
Symptoms: Daily headaches; constipation; sweet tooth; regular menstrual cycle but heavy with slight cramps.
Previous Operations: Bunion removed: lumpectomy on right breast.

The client's main problem was daily headaches which indicate an imbalance on the bladder meridian. I considered this case to be more of a problem with the spleen/pancreas and its meridian as the other symptoms and operations noted were largely on the spleen/pancreas meridian. However, the effect of the imbalance was manifest in the form of headaches.

Female: Age – late 20s.
Symptoms: Chronic skin problems on the face; system feels 'burny'; constipation; headaches; painful menstruation until she started taking contraceptive pills three months previously.
Previous Operations: Bunions removed.

This is a combination of problems along the stomach and spleen/pancreas meridians. The bunion problem was an early indication of an imbalance in the pancreas, but as the cause was not treated, the problems moved on to the stomach and resulted in skin and digestive problems. The headaches are due to congestions on the bladder meridian.

Heart Meridian (See illustration p.40)
Female: Age – 62
Symptoms: Medical diagnosis of a weak heart – has an 'extra tick'; pain in little finger on the left hand; aching muscles on the left side of the body specifically the left shoulder which can last up to three to four weeks; middle-ear imbalance. (Refer to illustration of the heart meridian and its partner the small intestine – pages 40 and 41.) Other symptoms noted: constipation; nausea which continues at times for up to three weeks; instant migraines after eating cheese or chocolate; high blood pressure; problems with menstrual cycle – still has periods despite her age and had cramps which stopped when she started taking contraceptive pills.
Previous Operations: Appendectomy; bunion removal twenty

years before; three cysts removed from the breast (on the pancreas meridian).

Although there are numerous problems relating to the heart meridian, I believe the main cause is on the stomach and spleen/pancreas meridians – obvious in the problems with the menstrual cycle, three cysts, bunions and appendectomy. The liver and gall bladder are also penetrated by the stomach meridian which could produce the symptoms of nausea and migraines. Note also that the kidneys are on the stomach meridian and the heart is on the kidney meridian. To take care of a weak heart, one should not overload the kidneys. This can be prevented by ensuring correct acid/alkaline balance in food intake.

Small Intestine Meridian (See illustration p.41)
Female: Age – early 30s
Symptoms: Severe neck, back and shoulder problems – pinched sensation from shoulder down the arm and at one point she lost all feeling in her arm; weak stomach – often experiences cramps after meals; weakness in throat; tennis elbow; at the age of six had a hernia in the groin; at age five suffered a severe ear infection which caused balance problems.

Problems along the small intestine meridian are obvious in the symptoms on the shoulder, neck/arm, elbow, ears and throat. Again remember that meridians in the arms do not penetrate any major organs and one would have to look for the cause on one of the main meridians and the related organs. The weak stomach and cramps after meals indicate a stomach imbalance. But the ch'i energy congestions are mainly located along the arm, shoulder, neck, ears and throat.

Female: Age – late 30s
Symptoms: The client was recommended by her doctor to try reflexology for the very painful trigenimous neuralgia in her face. After ten years of medical treatment, the only further relief they could offer was to sever the nerve in the face which would cause paralysis on one side. Other symptoms noted: Bloated painful colon with constipation and diarrhoea; bleeding gums; heavy menstrual cycle which lasts over eight

days; was on excessive medication – nine painkillers a day plus sleeping tablets.

The first problem to solve would be the constipation. The neuralgia is obviously a symptom of an imbalance of the small intestine and its meridian. A side-effect of the medication is constipation so it is a vicious circle.

Bladder Meridian (See illustration p.43)
Female: Age – 40s
Symptoms: Headaches in the crown, forehead and neck region; backaches; constantly tired; high blood pressure; was a bedwetter.
Previous Operations: Ureter stretched; hysterectomy; operations on both knees with the result that she cannot bend her knees at all.

The headaches and backaches can be traced to the bladder meridian while all the operations are situated on the stomach and spleen/pancreas meridians.

Male: Age – 50s
Symptoms: Daily migraines which run from the back of the head over the crown; generally feels stressed at work and at home; doesn't sleep well – has to relieve himself three to four times a night; fatigue.
Previous Operations: Appendectomy; tonsillectomy; prostate operation.

The appendix and tonsils are on the stomach meridian, whereas the prostate is on the spleen/pancreas meridian. Feeling stressed, bad sleep patterns and fatigue are the result of an imbalance on the stomach and spleen/pancreas meridians. The effects – headaches and weak bladder – are found on the bladder meridian.

Kidney Meridian (See illustration p.44)
Male: Age – mid 60s
Symptoms: General bad circulation; painful calves; tingling burning sensation on the feet; has to get up every night to urinate.
Previous Operations: Three bypass operations; lumpectomy on the elbow.

Reference to the kidney meridian shows that the heart is situated on its pathway. The burning area on the feet was around the kidney reflexes. Furthermore, five plantar warts were situated on the heart reflex of his foot. The lump on the elbow can be traced to the heart meridian. Problems with the calf muscles relate to the partner meridian, the bladder.

Circulation/Pericardium Meridian (See illustration p.46)
I have only seen case histories along the pericardium meridian as symptoms within larger case histories. Lesser symptoms such as eczema, psoriasis, pains in the armpits, carpal tunnel syndrome and arthritis in the middle finger have all been periphery problems of imbalances along the stomach, spleen/pancreas or kidney meridians. Other symptoms which are a result of an imbalance along the pericardium meridian are heart disease; disturbances in heart rhythm; mental disorders such as fear, nervousness and schizophrenia; car sickness and nausea.

Triple Warmer/Endocrine/Three E Meridian (See illustration p.48)
Female: Age – early 30s
Symptoms: Severe eczema on both ring fingers – cannot wear rings; prolapsed uterus – doctor recommended a hysterectomy after a difficult birth.
Previous Operations: Tonsillectomy; appendectomy; lumpectomy on breast around nipple area.

All the symptoms and operations are a result of imbalances along the stomach and spleen/pancreas meridians. The effects of the imbalances have manifest as severe eczema on the ring fingers – the endocrine meridian.

Female: Age – early 40s.
Symptoms: Pains around the ears – diagnosed by her GP as gout – had been so severe she was not able to wash or comb her hair or lie on her ear, particularly during menstruation or ovulation; menstrual cycle problems; sore breasts; weakness in the throat.

This client drank red wine with her meals every evening which affected the endocrine meridian so severely that it resulted in gout. Menstrual cycle problems relate to the spleen/pancreas meridian and the sore breast and weakness in the throat relate to its partner the stomach meridian.

Gall Bladder Meridian (See illustration p.50)
Female: Age – 50s
Symptoms: Depression and nervousness; pain in the right knee extending up to the hip joint – mainly affecting her during the night; acidic burning urine; previous kidney problems; headaches on the temple and top of the head; pain around the ears; heavy menstruation although at menopause age; hot flushes; slight constipation.

The client came for treatment for depression and nervousness. This can sometimes be seen as an imbalance in the pancreas and therefore tied in with the spleen/pancreas and stomach and their meridians. The other symptoms noted – headaches, pain around the ears and pain in the knee relate to the gall bladder meridian. The previous kidney problems, acidic burning urine, heavy menstruation, hot flushes and slight constipation can also be related to the stomach and spleen/pancreas and their meridians.

Female: Age – 50s
Symptoms: Severe lower back pain; leg pains on lateral side; constipation; nausea (cannot tolerate rich foods); allergic to painkillers; hyperventilates; very acidic; sore gums; regular menstrual cycle but painful and heavy.

Previous Operations: Gall stones removed twenty years before.

The leg pains are on the gall bladder meridian but the acidity, constipation, problems with gall stones and sore gums are all on the stomach meridian.

Liver Meridian (See illustration p.51)
Female: Age – 50s
Symptoms: Low libido since hysterectomy two years previously; skin problems; weak bladder; eyes have weakened since a bladder repair operation.

The libido and hysterectomy are related to an imbalance on the liver meridian, but the hysterectomy could be related to the spleen/pancreas. Notice the link between the eyes and the bladder.

Female: Age – 60s
Symptoms: Gout in big toe; occasional nausea; medial knee pains; neck calcified; loose stomach; irregular menstrual cycle when younger which was heavy and painful; had difficulty becoming pregnant; occasional hot flushes.
Previous Operations: Appendectomy; ovarian cysts removed.

The gout and knee pains are on the liver meridian. The irregular menstrual cycle is related to the pancreas while the partner meridian – the stomach – is evident in the operations.

4

Mapping The Feet

UNDERSTANDING THE STRUCTURE of the feet in relation to the body is the first and most important step to understanding reflexology. It is, in fact, very simple, as the feet are a perfect microcosm or mini-map of the whole body and all the organs and body parts are reflected on the feet in almost the same arrangement as in the body. These reflexes are found on the soles, tops and along the inside and outside of the feet and their positions follow a logical anatomical pattern similar to that of the body.

MAPPING THE REFLEXES ON THE FEET

The body itself can be considered as divided horizontally into four parts: the head and neck area; the thoracic area from the shoulders to the diaphragm; the abdominal area from the diaphragm to the pelvic area, and the pelvis. These areas can be clearly delineated on the feet and provide a precise picture of the body as it is reflected on the feet. We will therefore examine the situation of body organs in horizontal divisions, as this facilitates easy study and reference. It also fits in more accurately with the massage technique I teach, which is easier to understand if it is studied together with the meridians.

The sections described above are also clearly visible in the foot structure:

1. The head and neck area = the toes
2. The thoracic area = the ball of the foot
3. The abdominal area = the arch
4. The pelvic area = the heel
5. The reproductive area = the ankle:
6. The spine = the inner foot
7. The outer body = the outer foot
8. Breast area and special circulation points = the tops of the feet.

The Head and Neck Area – The Toes

The toes incorporate reflexes to all parts of the body found above the shoulder girdle. If you imagine the two big toes as two half heads with a common neck the positions of the reflexes are placed very logically. Obviously some reflexes overlap as they do in the body. Each big toe contains reflex points for the pituitary gland, pineal gland, hypothalamus, brain, temples, teeth, the seven cervical (neck) vertebrae, sinuses, mastoid, tonsils, nose, mouth and other face reflexes as well as part of the eustachian tubes.

The other four toes on each foot contain reflex points for the eyes, ears, teeth, sinuses, lachrymal glands (tear ducts), speech centre, upper lymph system, collar bone (shoulder girdle), eustachian tubes, 'chronic' eye and ear problems.

The Head and the Brain
Reflexes of the head and the brain are on the pads of the big toes from the tip behind the nail down over the metatarsal bone; reflexes for the sides of the head and brain are on the sides of the big toes. On the top of the toes are the face reflexes including the mouth, nose, teeth and tonsils. At the base of the big toe are the neck reflexes.

The Sinuses
The sinuses are cavities within the skull bones situated above and to the sides of the nose in the cheekbones behind the

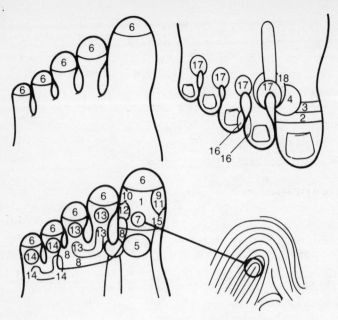

1	Brain	11	Hypothalamus
2	Mouth	12	Mastoid
3	Nose	13	Eyes
4	Tonsils	14	Ears
5	Neck	15	Cervical spine (C1–C7)
6	Sinus, Teeth and Top of Head	16	Lachrymal glands (tearducts)
7	Pituitary gland		
8	Eustachian gland	17	Upper lymph system
9	Pineal gland	18	Speech centre
10	Temples		

Fig. 15. The head and neck area

eyebrows. They communicate with the nasal cavities through small openings. They act as protection for the eyes and the brain and give resonance to the voice.

The reflexes are situated on the tips of all the toes.

The Pituitary Gland

This gland, known also as the 'master gland', is considered the most important gland in the body as it controls the functions of all the endocrine glands. About the size and shape of a cherry, the pituitary gland is attached to the base of the brain. Numerous hormones are produced by this gland – these influence growth, sexual development, metabolism, pregnancy, mineral and sugar contents of the blood, fluid retention and energy levels.

The reflex point is found on both feet where the whorl of the toe print converges into a central point. It is usually situated on the inner side of the toe and often requires a little searching. More often than not, this reflex is found to be off-centre. Since the hormonal system is extremely sensitive and easily thrown off-balance, this reflex is usually very tender.

The Hypothalamus

A number of bodily activities are controlled by this part of the brain. It regulates the autonomic nervous system and controls emotional reactions, appetite, body temperature and sleep.

The hypothalamus reflex areas are found on both feet on the outer side and top of the big toe – the same reflex point as the pineal gland.

The Pineal Gland

The pineal gland is a small gland situated within the hypo-thalamus section of the brain. Its functions are not completely understood, but it is known to stimulate the cells in the skin to produce the black pigment melanin. It is thought to play a part in mood and circadian rhythms, and is sometimes referred to as the psychic 'third eye'.

The reflexes are on both feet on the outer tip of the big toes – the same as the hypothalamus reflex.

The Teeth

The reflexes to the teeth are exactly distributed over the ten toes: incisors (1) on the big toe: incisors and canine teeth (2, 3) on the second toe: premolars (4, 5) on the third toe: molars (6, 7) on the fourth toe: wisdom teeth (8) on the fifth toe. These reflexes are in the same position as the sinus reflexes.

The Eyes

The eyes are important sensory organs – the organs of sight. The retina receives impressions of images via the pupils and the lens. The optic nerve conveys the impressions from the receptors in the eye to the visual area of the cerebral cortex where they are interpreted.

These reflexes are on both feet on the cushions of the second and third toes and may extend slightly down the toes. Reflexes for chronic eye conditions are on the 'shelf' at the base of these two toes.

The Ears

The ear is the organ of hearing. It is a highly complex system of cavities, bones and membranes, constructed in such a way that sound waves in the atmosphere are caught up and transmitted to the hearing centre in the temporal lobe of the cerebral cortex. The ear also plays a part in maintaining balance.

The reflexes are situated on both feet on the cushions of the fourth and fifth toes and may extend slightly down the toes. The reflexes for the eustachian tubes extend from the inner side of the big toe along the base of the second and third toes to the fourth toe. Reflexes for chronic ear conditions are found on the 'shelf' at the base of these two toes – the same section as the eustachian tubes. The mastoid – the part of the skull behind the ear which contains the air spaces that communicate with the ear – is also treated on these reflexes.

The Tonsils

These are paired organs composed of lymphatic tissue and thought to be involved in defence of this area. The reflexes are found on both feet – on the top of the foot at the base of the big toe near the web between the big and second toes.

The Lymph System

The lymphatic system forms a subsidiary or secondary circulatory system. It is a network of lymphatic vessels situated throughout the body which acts to drain tissue fluid surrounding the cells in the body. Lymph nodes filter the lymph to prevent infection passing into the blood stream and add lymphocytes which are important for the formation of antibodies and immunological reactions. The main sites of the lymph nodes are in the neck, armpit, thorax, abdomen, groin, pelvis and behind the knee.

On the front of the foot, the webs between the toes are the

reflexes for the drainage of the lymphatics in the neck/chest region of the body. Lymph reflexes for the groin area are tied in with the reproductive system and are found in the same area as the reflexes for the fallopian tubes and vas deferens described later in this chapter. These reflexes run across the top of the foot from the inner ankle bone to the outer ankle bone and incorporate the six main meridians. Congestions in the groin can be traced to a specific meridian and its organ depending on where lumps are situated – proving the significance of the meridians.

The Thoracic Area – The Ball of the Foot

This section of the foot corresponds with the thoracic area in the body from the shoulder girdle to the diaphragm. Several vital reflexes are situated here: the heart, lungs, oesophagus, trachea, bronchi, thyroid and thymus glands, diaphragm and solar plexus.

The Lungs

The lungs are cone-shaped, spongy organs in the thorax which lie on either side of the heart. It is here that the process of respiration takes place – the exchange of oxygen for carbon dioxide. The main air passage of the respiratory system found in the thorax is the trachea (windpipe) which divides into the bronchi to enter the left and right lungs.

The lung reflexes are found on the soles of both feet from the second toe (stomach meridian) to just past the fourth toe (gall bladder meridian). Reflexes of the trachea and bronchi are found below the big toe and second toes (stomach and liver meridians) connected to the lung reflex. These same reflexes are also found in similar positions on the tops of the feet.

The Heart

The heart is a hollow, cone-shaped, muscular organ which lies in the chest on the left side of the body in a space between the lungs. It acts as a pump circulating blood throughout the body. Efficient functioning of the heart is essential to allow good blood circulation throughout the body, which is necessary for efficient transport of gases, foods and waste products. The chest area also contains other major vessels leading to and from the heart – the vena cavae, aorta and other arteries and veins.

The reflex to the heart is situated on the sole of the left foot only – on the kidney meridian above the diaphragm level.

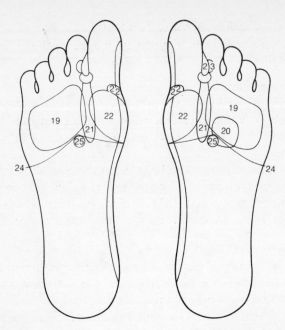

19 Lungs
20 Heart
21 Oesophagus, Trachea, Bronchi,
   Thymus gland
22 Thyroid, Parathyroid

23 Thyroid–helper reflex
   (stomach meridian)
24 Diaphragm
25 Solar Plexus

Fig. 16. The thoracic area

The Thymus Gland, Oesophagus, Trachea and Bronchi
The thymus gland is situated in the thoracic cavity. It is quite large in childhood, reaches maximum size at ten to twelve years, then slowly regresses and has almost disappeared in adult life. It is involved in the immune system. Its only known function is the formation of lymphocytes.

The oesophagus is the gullet – a muscular tube passing from the pharynx down through the chest, and joining the stomach below the diaphragm. Food and fluid are propelled through it by peristalsis.

The trachea is the windpipe. It passes down from the larynx into the throat, where it divides into two main bronchi.

The bronchi are the two main divisions of the trachea which enter the lungs.

All these reflexes are found on both feet in the same area –
on the soles of the feet in a vertical line between the first and
second toes.

The Thyroid Gland

The thyroid gland is located in the neck. It controls the rate of
metabolism, which is necessary for normal mental and physical
development and maintains the correct amount of calcium in
the blood.

This reflex is situated on both feet at the base of the big toe,
down around the ball and into the groove below the bone. The
most important part is the section along the bone. There is also
a 'helper' reflex on the second toe – the stomach meridian.

The Parathyroid Glands

These are four small glands situated around the thyroid gland.
Their main function is to maintain the correct amount of
calcium and phosphorus in the blood and bones.

The reflex is situated on both feet at the base of the big toe
on the outer side.

The Diaphragm

The diaphragm, one of the muscles of respiration, is a
large, dome-shaped wall which separates the thorax from the
abdomen. It is the most important muscle for breathing.

This reflex is situated on the soles of both feet, and extends
across all six meridians at the base of the ball of the foot
separating the ball from the arch.

The Solar Plexus

The solar plexus is a network of sympathetic nerve ganglia
in the abdomen and is the nerve supply to the abdominal
organs below the diaphragm. It is sometimes referred to as
the 'abdominal brain' or the 'nerve switchboard' and is situated
behind the stomach and in front of the diaphragm.

The reflex is at the same level as the reflex to the diaphragm
located at a specific point in the centre of the diaphragm reflex.
This point is visible on the foot as the apex of the arch that
runs across the base of the ball of the foot. This reflex is most
useful for inducing a relaxed state. It can relieve stress and
nervousness, aid deep regular breathing and restore calm.

The Abdominal Area – The Arch of the Foot

The arch of the foot is clearly visible on the sole – the raised area which extends from the base of the ball to the beginning of the heel. It is divided into two parts: the upper part corresponds to the section of the body from the diaphragm to the waistline; the lower part corresponds to the section of the body from the waistline to the pelvic area.

Reflexes above the waistline: liver, gall bladder, stomach, pancreas, duodenum, spleen, adrenals and kidneys.

The Liver
The liver is the largest and most complex organ/gland in the body. It controls many of the chemical processes and has many functions. These include: processing nutrients from the blood, storing fats, sugars and proteins until the body needs them; detoxifying the blood and manufacturing bile for fat digestion; storing sugars in the form of glycogen to be used when the body needs an increased supply of energy; and the storage and metabolism of fats and proteins.

This reflex is found on the sole of the right foot only, below the diaphragm level, extending from the pancreas meridian on the inside of the foot to below the little toe. It ends just above the waistline.

The Gall Bladder
This is a small, muscular, pear-shaped sac attached to the under-surface of the liver. Its function is to excrete bile for food digestion.

The gall bladder reflex is on the sole of the right foot only, embedded within the liver reflex beneath and between the third and fourth toes.

The Stomach
The stomach is a large muscular bag which lies below the diaphragm mainly to the left side of the body. Food passes from the mouth down the oesophagus into the stomach where it is churned up and mixed with gastric juices and enzymes to start the digestive process.

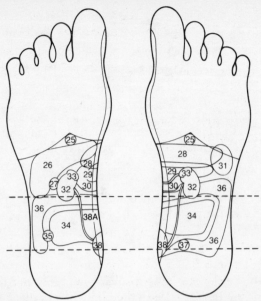

<table>
<tr><td>above the waistline</td><td>below the waistline</td></tr>
</table>

above the waistline	below the waistline
26 Liver	34 Small intestine
27 Gall bladder	35 Ileo-caecal valve, appendix
28 Stomach	36 Ascending, Transverse,
29 Pancreas	Descending and Sigmoid
30 Duodenum	Colon
31 Spleen	37 Rectum/Anus
32 Kidneys	38 Bladder
33 Adrenals	38A Ureter

Fig. 17. The abdominal area

The reflexes are found on the soles of both feet – extending from the big toe to the second toe on the right foot and the big toe to the outer edge of the fourth toe on the left foot. Horizontally they are situated just below the diaphragm level.

The Pancreas

The pancreas is a large glandular structure in the abdomen. It is both an endocrine and exocrine gland secreting insulin and digestive juices. It is probably best known for its function as an endocrine gland and for the production of the hormones insulin and glucagon which are important in the control of sugar metabolism.

The reflexes are situated on the soles of both feet – more on the left foot than the right foot – below the stomach and above the waistline. On the right foot it extends into just below the big toe, and on the left foot as far as the fourth toe.

The Duodenum

This is the first, C-shaped part of the small intestine, about 20 to 25 centimetres long. It extends from the pyloric sphincter of the stomach to the jejunum. Pancreatic and common bile ducts open into it, releasing secretions responsible for the breakdown of food.

The reflexes are on the soles of both feet immediately below the pancreas, touching the waistline and extending inwards to the second toe.

The Spleen

The spleen is a large, very vascular, gland-like but ductless organ found on the left side of the body behind the stomach. It plays an important part in the immune system, and is part of the lymphatic system. It contains lymphatic tissue which manufactures the white blood cells, breaks down old red blood corpuscles and filters the lymph of toxins.

The reflex is found on the outer side of the left foot (opposite the liver reflex on the right foot), beneath the fourth toe (gall bladder meridian), just below the diaphragm line in line with the stomach reflex.

The Kidneys

The kidneys are part of the main excretory system of the body – the urinary system – which collectively refers to the kidneys, ureter tubes, urethra and bladder. They are two bean-shaped organs which filter toxins from the blood, produce urine and regulate the retention of important minerals and water.

The reflexes are found on the soles of both feet positioned just above the waistline on the kidney and stomach meridians, just below the stomach reflex. The right kidney is positioned slightly lower than the left kidney.

The Adrenal Glands

These are two triangular endocrine glands situated on the

upper tip of each kidney. As part of the endocrine system they perform numerous vital functions. The adrenal glands are divided into two distinct regions, the cortex and medulla. The adrenal cortex produces steroid hormones which regulate carbohydrate metabolism and have anti-allergic and anti-inflammatory properties. The cortex also produces hormones which control the reabsorption of sodium and water in the kidneys, as well as the secretion of potassium and the sex hormones testosterone and oestrogen.

The adrenal medulla produces adrenaline and noradrenaline which work in conjunction with the sympathetic nervous system. The output of adrenaline is increased at times of anxiety and stress and is responsible for organ changes in the 'fight-or-flight' situation.

The reflexes are situated on the soles of both feet on top of the kidney reflexes.

The Abdominal Area – The Arch of the Foot

Now we come to the lower part of the arch of the foot, which corresponds to the section of the body from the waistline to the pelvic area (diagram, page 71).
Reflexes below the waistline: small intestine, ileo-caecal valve, appendix, large intestine, adrenals, kidneys, ureters, bladder.

The Small Intestine
This is a muscular tube about 6 to 7 metres in length. It is the main area of the digestive tract where absorption takes place. It leads from the pyloric sphincter of the stomach to the caecum of the large intestine and lies in a coiled position in the abdominal cavity surrounded by the large intestine. The small intestine is divided into three sections – the duodenum, jejunum and the ileum.

The reflex is situated on the soles of both feet, under the large intestine reflex just below the waistline to the end of the arch extending across to below the fourth toe.

The Ileo-Caecal Valve
This valve is situated where the small intestine and large intestine join; it therefore controls the passage of contents of

the small intestine through to the large intestine. It prevents backflow of faecal matter from the large intestine and controls mucous secretions.

The reflex is found on the sole of the right foot below and between the third and fourth toes just above the level of the pelvic floor.

The Appendix

The appendix is a worm-like tube about 9 to 10 centimetres in length with a blind end projecting downwards from the caecum of the large intestine in the lower right part of the abdominal cavity. Located directly below the ileo-caecal valve, it helps lubricate the large intestine, is rich in lymphoid tissue and secretes antibodies.

The reflex is situated only on the sole of the right foot, in the same area as the ileo-caecal valve.

The Large Intestine

This is a tube about 1.5 metres in length. It starts on the right side of the body at the caecum (ileo-caecal valve) and goes up the right side to below the liver where it bends to the left (hepatic flexure) and passes across the abdomen as the transverse colon. At the left side of the abdomen, it bends down below the spleen (splenic flexure) to become the descending colon which passes down the left side of the abdomen. It then turns towards the midline and takes the shape of a double S-shaped bend known as the sigmoid flexure. This leads into the rectum which in turn leads to the anus.

When the residue of food reaches the large intestine it is in fluid form. The function of the large intestine is to remove some of the water and salts by absorption and to convert the waste matter into faeces ready for excretion.

The reflexes are found on the soles of both feet. On the right foot this begins just below the reflex for the ileo-caecal valve and extends upwards (ascending colon), then turns just below the liver reflex to become the transverse colon which extends across the entire foot. It continues across to the left foot and turns just below the spleen reflex to become the descending colon. Just above the pelvic floor it turns again into the sigmoid colon which ends at the reflex of the rectum/anus.

The Ureters

Ureter tubes are muscular tubes about 30 centimetres in length which connect the kidneys and bladder and function as a passageway for urine. There are two tubes, one from each kidney, which pass downwards through the abdomen into the pelvis where they enter the bladder.

The reflexes are situated on the soles of both feet linking the kidney reflexes to the bladder reflexes which are situated on the inner side of the instep. The ureter reflex can often be seen as distinct lines running across the arch.

The Bladder

The bladder is an elastic muscular sac situated in the centre of the pelvis. Urine for excretion passes from the kidneys down the ureters and is stored in the bladder until it is eliminated via the urethra.

The reflexes are found on both feet on the side of the foot below the inner ankle bone on the heel line. This reflex is often clearly visible as a puffy area.

The Pelvic Area – The Heel of the Foot

Few organs are represented here, but this area is of vital importance as all six main meridians traverse the pelvic section of the heel. As a result, many congestions here can be traced to meridians and their organs.

The Sciatic Nerve

This is the largest nerve in the body. It arises from the sacral plexus of nerves formed by the lower lumbar and upper sacral spinal nerves. It runs from the buttocks down the back of the thigh to divide just above the knee into two main branches which supply the lower leg. The sciatic nerve and reflex are found on the soles of both feet – in a band about a third of the way down the pad of the heel extending right across the foot.

The Reproductive Area – The Ankle

The outer ankle contains the ovaries/testes reflexes, and the inner ankle contains the uterus, prostate, vagina and penis

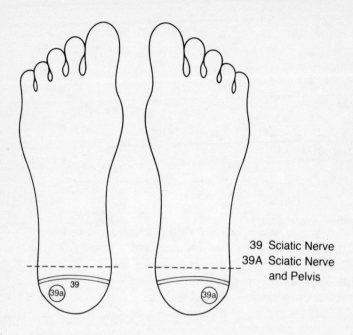

39 Sciatic Nerve
39A Sciatic Nerve
and Pelvis

Fig. 18. The pelvic area

reflexes. The reflex points for the fallopian tubes, lymph drainage area in the groin, vas deferens and seminal vesicles are found in a narrow band running below the outer ankle bone across the top of the foot to the inner ankle bone. The kidney/bladder meridian is situated on both sides up the back of the ankle.

The Ovaries
These are the female gonads or sex glands. They are small, almond-shaped glands about 2 to 3 centimetres long. There are two ovaries – one on each side of the uterus. These are part of the female reproductive system and produce ova as well as the hormones oestrogen and progesterone.

The reflexes are found on both feet on the outer side, midway between the ankle bone and the back of the heel – the right ovary on the right foot, the left ovary on the left foot. The helper area is the heel due to the presence of the meridians.

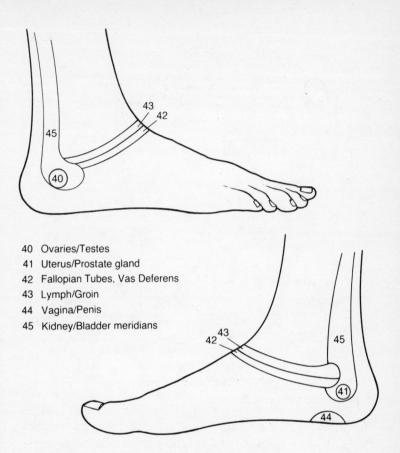

40 Ovaries/Testes
41 Uterus/Prostate gland
42 Fallopian Tubes, Vas Deferens
43 Lymph/Groin
44 Vagina/Penis
45 Kidney/Bladder meridians

Fig. 19. The reproductive area

The Testes

The testes are the male reproductive glands which produce spermatozoa and the male hormone testosterone. There are two testes suspended outside the body in the scrotum – a sac of thin, dark-coloured skin which lies behind the penis.

The reflexes are found on males in the same area as the ovaries in females, that is, midway between the outer ankle bone and the heel. The helper area is the heel.

The Uterus

The uterus is a hollow, pear-shaped organ about 10 centimetres long situated in the centre of the pelvic cavity in females. Its function is the nourishment and protection of the foetus during pregnancy and its expulsion at term.

The reflex points are located on both feet on the inside of the ankles, midway on a diagonal line between the ankle bone and the back of the heel. The helper area is the heel.

The Prostate Gland

This gland lies at the base of the bladder and surrounds the urethra. It produces the thin lubricating fluid which forms part of the semen to aid the transport of sperm cells.

Reflexes are found on both feet in the same place as the uterus reflex on females – midway in a diagonal line between the inner ankle bone and the heel. Again, the heel is the helper area.

The Fallopian Tubes

In females these two tubes, about 10 to 14 centimetres in length, connect the ovaries with the cavity of the uterus. Their function is to conduct the ova expelled from the ovaries during ovulation down the tube to the uterus.

The reflexes are found on both feet. They run across the top of the foot linking the reflex of the uterus to the reflex of the ovaries. This area is usually massaged in conjunction with the reflexes of the ovaries and uterus.

The Seminal Vesicles/Vas Deferens

The seminal vesicles lie next to the prostate and store semen. The vas deferens are a pair of excretory ducts which convey semen from the testes through the prostate and into the urethra.

The reflexes are located in the same area as the fallopian tubes in females – across the top of the foot from one ankle bone to the other, linking the prostate and testes reflexes.

The Spine – The Inner Foot

The inside of each foot is naturally curved to correspond to the spine.

The Spine

The spine, also known as the backbone or vertebral column, is the central support of the body. It carries the weight of the body and is an important axis of movement. The spine is made up of thirty-three vertebrae. The structure of the bones is arranged in such a way as to give the spine four curves. The spine is divided into four sections from top to bottom: seven cervical vertebrae (including the first two, axis and atlas) = the neck; twelve thoracic vertebrae = the back; five lumbar vertebrae = the loin; five sacral vertebrae = the pelvis; four/five coccycal vertebrae = the tail. The vertebrae of the sacrum and coccyx are fused to form two immobile bones. Vertebrae are joined by

15 Spine

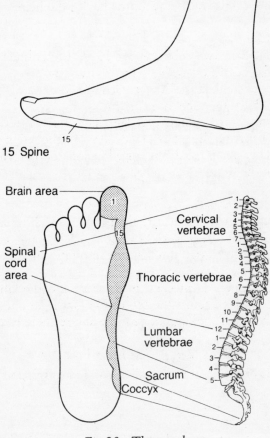

Fig. 20. The vertebrae

discs of cartilage and are held in place by ligaments.

The spinal column encloses the spinal cord, the central channel of the nervous system, which is a continuation of the brain stem. It carries the nerves from the brain to all parts of the body. Associated with each vertebra is a spinal nerve. These nerves arise from the spinal cord and affect the level of the body at which they arise – that is, the thoracic nerves affect the thorax, and the lumbar nerves the lower abdomen and legs.

The reflex zones run along the inner side of both feet – half the spine represented on each foot. The cervical vertebrae reflex runs from the base of the big toe nail to the base of the toe (between the first and second joints of the big toe). The thoracic reflex runs along the ball of the foot below the big toe (shoulder to waistline), the arch from the waistline to pelvic line corresponds to the lumbar region and the heel line to the base of the heel to the sacrum/coccyx.

The Outer Foot – The Outer Body

The outer edge of the foot corresponds to the outer part of the body – the joints, ligaments and surrounding muscles. From the base of the toe to the diaphragm line = shoulder and upper arm; diaphragm line to waistline = elbow, forearm, wrist and hand; waistline to end of heel = leg, knee and hip.

The Knee
The knee joint joins the upper and lower leg and facilitates flexibility of the lower limb.

Reflexes are found on both feet on the outer side just below the bony projection of the fifth metatarsal which is usually quite prominent on the side of the foot. Again, remember the six meridians run through the knee, so by pinpointing the exact location of the knee pain, one can relate it to a specific meridian and locate the problematic organ.

The Hip
The hip joint is where the thigh bone (femur) meets the pelvis.

The reflex is found on both feet extending towards the toe in front of the knee reflex. It covers a half moon shape, moving

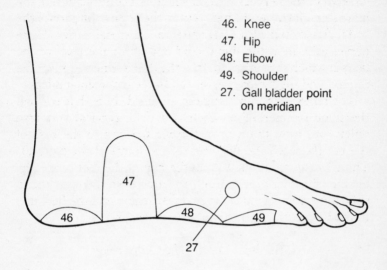

46. Knee
47. Hip
48. Elbow
49. Shoulder
27. Gall bladder point on meridian

Fig. 21. The outer foot

out from the line along the side of the foot and up in line with one fourth toe and the gall bladder meridian. A number of hip problems may be gall bladder related, as the gall bladder meridian passes directly through the hip.

The Elbow and Shoulder

The elbow is the joint between the upper arm and the forearm. It is formed by the humerus above and the radius and ulna below. The shoulder joint is where the bone of the upper arm (humerus) meets the shoulder blade (scapula).

The reflexes to the elbow are situated on both feet on the outer side along the arch and the ball. The shoulder and the surrounding muscles are found on both feet at the base of the fifth toe covering the sole, outer side and top.

The Top of the Foot – The Breast Area and Circulation Points

Reflexes found on the top of the foot include the circulation and breast. Most of the reflexes represented on the soles are also found on the tops of the feet in the meridians.

The Breast
Here it is important to look at the meridians. If there are breast problems, note exactly where these are situated so as to identify the meridian that runs through the affected section of the breast and thereby the problem organ.

Special Circulation Points
These points are to stimulate the heart, circulation and body temperature. These are found on the top and soles of both feet at the web between the second and third toes. As these are points on the stomach meridian, they have an effect on the thyroid which in turn affects body temperature, heart and circulation.

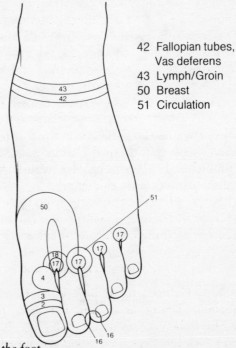

42 Fallopian tubes,
    Vas deferens
43 Lymph/Groin
50 Breast
51 Circulation

Fig. 22. The top of the foot

5

Reading The Feet

THERE IS an overriding tendency to blame foot problems and deformities such as corns, callouses and bunions on ill-fitting shoes. This is part of the problem – but only part. Problem areas on the feet relate to problem areas in the body. Which is the cause and which the effect is questionable. It is a 'chicken or egg' situation. Congestions along a meridian will disrupt the body's equilibrium – be they internal or external. If the problem is internal, the reflex area and the relevant meridian will be particularly sensitive to excess pressure and friction and more susceptible to the formations of corns and callouses. However, these external problems cause congestions along the meridians in the same way as internal congestions. If these are not dealt with they have an adverse effect on body parts along the whole meridian creating an imbalance throughout the body.

With the combination of reflexes and meridians, we can now look at these problems in a different light and unravel the tales they have to tell about the state of the body as a whole. The areas where the problems manifest are particularly significant when integrating the concept of meridians.

Bunions (Hallux valgus)

A bunion (Hallux valgus) is a prominence of the head of the metatarsal bone at its junction with the big toe. It is caused by inflammation and swelling of the bursa (bursitis) at that joint. The bursa is a pocket of fluid enclosed in fibrous

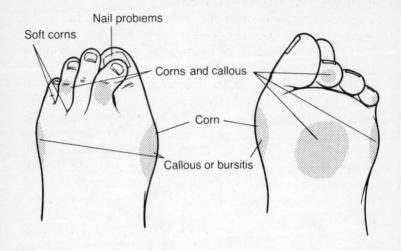

Soft corns

Nail problems

Corns and callous

Corn

Callous or bursitis

*Fig.23. Hammer second toe and other common
foot problems*

tissue which surrounds the joints and serves to protect them from friction. In this condition the metatarsal joint becomes enlarged and is therefore subject to pressure and friction from shoes which further aggravates the problem and damages the skin.

As the bunion develops, the big toe moves sideways constricting and displacing the other toes – particularly the second toe which is forced out of alignment into a position on top of the big toe. This is known as a hammer toe and it may, in time, become permanently bent. Its position above the other toes makes it prone to corns and callouses on the top of the toe due mainly to pressure from shoes.

The constriction of the toes can also affect the little toe – forcing it towards the middle of the foot and causing a 'bunionette' on the outer side at the base of the little toe.

What Meridians Reveal About Bunions

Two important meridians are found on the big toe – the spleen/pancreas meridian on the outer side and the liver meridian on the inner side towards the second toe. Bunions are situated on the pancreas meridian and the thyroid reflex. The internal branch of the spleen/pancreas meridian runs through the thyroid, further indicating their close relationship. Most people with bunions also have problems along the spleen/pancreas meridian or pancreatic disorders, for example, problems related to sugar metabolism like a sweet tooth; cravings for stimulants like tea, coffee, cigarettes and alchohol, and constant hunger. They may suffer from depression due to the fact that the thyroid is affected. Many people who have had bunions removed or repaired at an early age often develop thyroid problems in later life. Or vice versa – people with thyroid problems often develop bunions. This is because the underlying causes of the symptom – the pancreas and thyroid imbalances – have not been corrected.

Once a bunion has developed in an adult foot it cannot be realigned or straightened without surgery. No exercise or manipulation will push it back. By understanding the connection with the meridians, we can understand the cause of the problem – a pancreas imbalance – and set about rectifying that. This problem is most effectively rectified by a change of diet. Pain caused by bunions can be significantly alleviated with reflexology treatments and a change of diet.

Corns and Callouses

Callouses

Repeated pressure and friction on the skin will cause it to thicken as a means of protection. Foot callouses are quite common as the skin on the feet is subject to a great deal of pressure – particularly from ill-fitting shoes. If this thickening is aggravated by consistent pressure, the build-up of skin will lead to pain and discomfort. Callouses are especially visible on the tops of the toes and soles of the feet. They are easily removed by a chiropodist but will recur if the reason for their formation is not dealt with.

Corns

Corns usually develop on the joints of the toes which, due to their relative prominence, are particularly sensitive to pressure from shoes. At the focal point of this pressure, the skin hardens and thickens. A corn – basically a concentrated area of hard skin – forms in the middle of the area of thickening where the pressure is greatest. Corns also develop on the soles of the feet in areas of excessive pressure. The stabbing pain which is often characteristic of corns is caused by the hard skin exerting secondary pressure onto the sensitive tissue and nerve endings beneath it.

Meridians and Corns and Callouses

Corns and callouses usually develop on the tops of the toes. It is important to note exactly where these appear and establish on which meridian they are manifest and in turn which organs are out of balance. For example, the stomach meridian runs along the second and third toes, and problems here indicate congestions along the stomach meridian. Symptoms such as acidity, gastritis, ulcers, appendix and tonsil trouble, sinus, skin problems and breast problems are often found in people with problems on the second and third toes.

The second and third toes are also often longer than the first toe. This can indicate a genetic weakness in the stomach, often inherited, but can also be due to dietary deficiencies during the embryonic period which have caused stomach weakness. If the weakness is genetic, care should always be taken with diet – for example, avoiding excessively acid foods.

Some people have a long callous under the second toe. This relates to the bronchi/throat reflex area. If there is a deep groove in the skin it could also relate to a weakness in the throat, and the person may have a tendency to suffer from throat, tonsil and bronchial problems. The stomach meridian traverses through the throat area – tonsils, thyroid and the throat itself. The stomach meridian is on top of the second toe while the throat and bronchial reflexes are on the soles between the first and second toes. Moving down, the meridian runs underneath the bone region – the thyroid. Many people have a groove or hard callous around the bone which, again, can be related to an imbalance in the thyroid region; often due to an imbalance in the spleen/pancreas and stomach meridians, as these two are very closely related. Hard skin over the lung reflex is also a common problem. This can indicate a weak chest. The stomach meridian also runs through the lung area and the gall bladder meridian enters the lung area from the side.

As you can see, it is important to take careful note of where corns and callouses form and refer them to the meridians in order to understand the root cause of the problem.

Athlete's Foot

Athlete's foot is a fungal infection which usually manifests on the skin between the toes. This is the most common site of infection as the moist, warm conditions stimulate the fungus to multiply. The fungus thrives on keratin – a protein found in the outer layers of the skin. A major symptom of this condition is itching. If this is accompanied by loose scaley skin surrounding patches of pink, exposed skin, it is a definite sign of infection.

Occasionally a fissure – a split in the skin – may occur at the base of the toes. If this is deep, there could be a problem with bleeding. It could also be infected with bacteria and become inflamed if not taken care of. According to medical belief athlete's foot is very easily transmitted to others, particularly where there is communal bathing.

Meridians and Athlete's Foot

Again, it is important to take note of exactly where on the foot the problem is. Athlete's foot will most often manifest in between the fourth and fifth toes – the bladder meridian – and can therefore be related to the bladder. If between the third and fourth toe, it would be related to the gall bladder meridian.

Toenail Troubles

Ingrowing Toenail

As anyone who suffers from this problem knows, it can be extremely painful and uncomfortable. Interestingly, those most often affected by this condition are young people in their teens and twenties. It usually occurs on the big toe when the side of the nail penetrates the skin of the nail groove and becomes embedded in the soft skin tissue. If the wound is hampered in its efforts to heal, it produces granulation tissue which accumulates on the side and top of the nail. This tissue bleeds very easily. Ingrowing toenails can be caused by cutting the nail too short or cutting down the sides of the nail. Thin brittle nails and moist skin will increase susceptibility to this problem.

Involuted Toenail

An involuted toenail, if not correctly tended, can develop into an ingrowing toenail. This condition occurs when the normal curve of the toenail is so exaggerated that it produces pain down the side of the nail. The exaggerated curve can also encourage the development of corns and callouses on the sides of the nail which will increase discomfort. It is difficult to cut this type of nail, but cutting down the sides must be avoided, as this will result in the new nail growth forcing its way through the soft skin at the side of the nail, causing an ingrowing toenail.

Thickened Toenail

A toenail will thicken if the nail cell production centre is damaged. This can happen if the nail is persistently rubbed against a shoe over a prolonged period, or if the toenail has sustained injury in an accident. Unfortunately, this condition is irreversible. A further complication arises as the nail grows – the new growth curves – and is uncomfortable and unsightly. This curvature is known as a ram's-horn nail. Many elderly people are afflicted by this problem.

Fungal Infection of the Toenail

Fungal infection of the toenail often accompanies athlete's foot. The fungus penetrates the nail causing it to thicken. If the condition deteriorates, the colour and texture of the nail will also be affected, becoming darker and 'crumbly'.

Meridians and Toenail Troubles

With all toenail troubles, it is imperative that meridians are taken into account. Take, for example, ingrowing toenails. This problem is often found in young people and situated on the big toe – the spleen/pancreas meridian mentioned earlier. These people usually have a diet high in sugar, junk food, alcohol, cigarettes – and many of their problems can be related to sugar metabolism or pancreatic disorders. They could suffer from severe migraines or headaches. Remember that the big toe is also the head reflex. Over the years, I have seen many cases of clients suffering from headaches who also had ingrown toenails. Check the section on meridians, and note which meridians run through the area of the foot where the physical deformities and problems are found, in order to ascertain which organ is faulty and needs correcting.

Plantar Digital Neuritis

Neuritis is the inflammation of a nerve, with pain, tenderness and loss of function. This particular form of neuritis affects the toes, usually the fourth toe. The pain usually begins at the web between the third and fourth toes and shoots up into the fourth toe. The sensations experienced in the toe may vary from slight numbness to intense pain, depending on how severely the nerve is affected. The discomfort can be alleviated by massaging the toe. This problem usually occurs in women.

Meridians and Plantar Digital Neuritis

The gall bladder meridian is found on the fourth toe, where this problem is most common. Plantar digital neuritis is found in many women, and I have witnessed numerous cases where women have this problem around premenstrual time when they often crave chocolates, caffeine and other stimulants. The condition can therefore be related to overloading of the gall bladder meridian. Often symptoms will indicate other gall bladder related problems. This can also be associated with hip trouble – and can possibly be seen as a puffy area in line with the fourth toe close to the ankle. The gall bladder meridian runs through the hip region, and swelling here may indicate congestions along the gall bladder meridian.

Flat Feet

Flat feet (Pes planus) can be caused by numerous factors. They are usually inherited, but may also develop due to weakness in the joints or 'overloading' the feet, or they may be the result of a long illness. In childhood this condition can occur if growth is too rapid, or if the child is malnourished or overweight. The weaker the foot, the greater the possibility of this condition developing. Apart from causing an unattractive style of walking, flat feet can also affect the spine.

In flat feet the arch of the foot is flattened and sinks. This causes overstretching and weakness of both muscles and tendons and places a strain on the bone structure. Another problem is that the nerves and blood vessels, which are usually protected from contact with the ground by the shape of the arch, are now subject to pressure and their condition will deteriorate affecting the reflexes in this area.

The Highly Arched Foot

The highly arched foot is usually stiff which limits manouvre-ability and therefore prevents efficient functioning of the foot. Due to the exaggerated height of the arch, the toes will not have correct contact with the ground when standing. The unnatural shape and position of the toes makes them particularly susceptible to external pressures and therefore prone to corns and callouses. This condition may be inherited or could be the result of nerve and muscle imbalance. It is often seen in the neurological conditions poliomyelitis and spina bifida.

As a reflexologist, I would see the problem of flat feet as related to a rigid spine, indicating that the person is not very supple and could also be inclined to lower back problems. A highly curved arch or curved spine reflex also indicates a spinal problem, and this can cause problems with the upper part of the body – the lung area. If you press your fist against the lung reflex of the foot and gently press the foot back into a normal position, you will see the spinal reflex 'correcting' itself, and can therefore deduce that the client has a tendency to lower back problems, neck tension, congestions in the lung area and, as the toes are often also affected, problems along the meridians found in the toes.

The Heel

As the heel is subject to immense stress and bears a great deal of body weight it has the extra protection of a thick layer of fatty tissue under the heel bone.

Heel Callous
This is formed when areas of skin around the edge of the heel become thicker than usual to protect it from aggravating pressure and friction. It can develop into a painful condition if not dealt with.

Heel Fissure
A heel fissure develops when the skin on the edge of the heel splits. This is usually due to the fact that the skin is excessively dry and is being pinched by ill-fitting shoes. If the fissure is deep, pain and bleeding can occur.

Reflexes/Meridians and Heel Problems
The heel is the pelvic reflex, and problems here will often indicate prostate problems in men and uterus problems in women. Many women have deep cracks in their heel just prior to a hysterectomy and these often heal naturally after a hysterectomy. Any other reproductive problems in men and women – infertility, heavy bleeding and discomfort – can be related to imbalances in the pelvic region. All six main meridians run through this area and organs and meridians can be stimulated by massage here.

6

Techniques

THE BODY IS reflected on the feet in a three-dimensional form. In the body, the organs overlap each other; therefore the reflex areas do the same on the feet. Many organs are minute and not reflected on the charts, but all are worked on in the step-by-step treatment sequence. In the massage technique I teach, treatment always includes both feet. The reflex areas of both left and right feet are alternately massaged from toes to heel.

Many of the reflexology books available teach the 'thumb walking' technique and propose working one foot completely before moving on to the next. The main objective of the reflexologist is to stimulate the reflexes of the feet by massage. As any technique which achieves this result is equally effective, it is the prerogative of each individual practitioner to choose which technique works best for them. I have found in my years of practice and teaching that the techniques illustrated here have proven their worth for both practitioner and patient.

The most important aspect of this specific treatment procedure is that BOTH FEET ARE WORKED THROUGH ALTERNATELY FROM TOP TO TOE. This facilitates a natural flow in the procedure. One foot represents half a body, and as many organs are paired and found on both sides of the body, it would be wrong to complete one foot at a time. This would mean that only half the organ had been stimulated. The theory behind alternating feet is to stimulate each organ completely before moving on to the next. In this way each body part is worked as a unit even though half is on the left foot and half on the right. To execute effective reflexology massage techniques, familiarity with techniques and grips is a necessity.

Holding the Foot

Standard Support Grip (Figure 24)

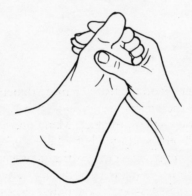

Fig. 24.

The first priority is to learn proper support or the pressure techniques will never be mastered correctly. The hands perform complementary functions throughout the treatment. While one hand presses, the other braces and supports or pushes the foot towards the pressure. To simplify things, the hand applying pressure will be referred to as the 'working hand' and the other hand the 'supporting hand'. Neither hand should ever be idle.

There is one main support technique. This is referred to as the *standard support grip* (Figure 24). Take the foot in the support hand, either from the inside or the outside – the web of the hand between the thumb and the index finger touching the side of the foot with the four fingers on top of the foot and the thumb on the sole. The support hand must always stay close to the working hand. Whichever grip you use on whatever reflex, always keep the foot bent slightly towards you and never in a tight grip with the toes bent backwards.

Pressure Techniques
The Rotating Thumb Technique (Figure 25)

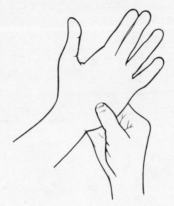

Fig. 25.

This is the most important technique to master, as it is used to apply pressure to most of the reflexes throughout the treatment procedure. It is combined with finger techniques.

Before working on the feet, exercise the 'rotating thumb' technique on the palm of your hand. It helps to visualize the object being worked on (hand or foot) as divided into small squares, all of which must be systematically stimulated. As you work, move from square to square, apply pressure and rotation to each square. The movement of the thumb from point to point must be small, moving along progressively, leaving no space between the points covered by the thumb tip.

For this exercise, place the four fingers of the working hand on the back of the hand to be worked on, keeping the thumb free to work on the palm. Bend the thumb from the first joint to between a 75 and 90 degree angle – the angle must ensure that the thumb nail doesn't dig into the flesh. This is the standard position of the 'rotating thumb'. The contact point is the tip of the thumb. Apply firm pressure with the tip of the thumb to the point to be worked on, and rotate the thumb, clockwise or anticlockwise. Keep the firm pressure constant and *stay on the square*. Two to three rotations are sufficient. Lift the thumb, move to the next point and repeat the procedure. The basic movement is: press in, rotate, lift, move. The choice to increase the amount of pressure or number of rotations depends on the practitioner and patient.

Observe the movement of the thumb on the working hand. The most visible rotation must be at the second thumb joint – where the metacarpals of the hand join the phalanges of the thumb. Two basic tenets for ease in executing this technique are to keep the thumb bent and the shoulders down. There should be very little strain on the arm muscles, elbows, neck and shoulders.

Furthermore, you will notice how much more pressure can be applied with the thumb in a bent position as opposed to a flat thumb. Ensure that the distance between the thumb and fist is sufficient to allow for easy rotation movements – approximately 2 centimetres apart. By exercising the correct technique, the treatment procedure should not be at all strenuous for the practitioner. Practise this thumb rotating technique on your hand until you feel completely comfortable with it. Also ensure that you exercise the thumbs on both hands to enable you to work efficiently with either thumb, as it is important to be able to switch hands during the treatment sequence.

Finger Techniques (Figures 26-28)
1. Hands are placed on either side of the foot with the thumbs on the sole and four fingers on top. The index and third fingers are the working tools, the third finger usually placed on top of the index finger to create extra leverage. This is used on the fallopian tubes/vas deferens and lymphatic reflexes which run

Fig. 26.

from the outside ankle bone along the top of the foot at the ankle joint to the inside ankle bone. With the fingers, press in, rotate, lift and move as with the 'rotating thumb', moving point by point up both sides until the fingers meet at the centre on top of the foot. (Figure 26)

2. This is used on the sides and tops of the toes. Place the index finger on one side and thumb on the other side of the

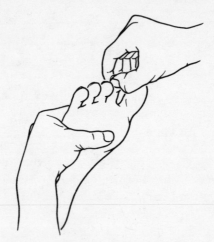

Fig. 27.

toe to be worked on. 'Rub' the toe, moving the fingers gently back and forth in opposite directions. (Figure 27)

3. Use both hands. Place the hands on either side of the foot, thumbs on the sole forming the support and four fingers on top.

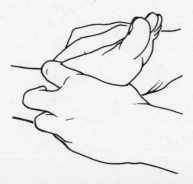

Fig. 28.

The eight fingers are the working tools. Starting from the ankle joint, exert deep, smooth pressure with the fingers massaging down the foot towards the toes – slowly and gently, but with firm pressure. Repeat this procedure a few times. Improvize a bit, but massage well. Also use a criss-cross movement with the thumbs on the sole of the foot. This is usually part of the winding down stage of the treatment which culminates in the solar plexus breathing technique. Cream or oil can be used at this stage to facilitate easy movement. (Figure 28)

Pinch Technique (Figure 29)

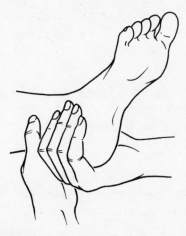

Fig. 29.

The support hand cups the foot at the ankle, while the working hand locates the tendon at the back of the heel and moves up and down the tendon pinching this tendon gently between the thumb and index finger. This is used to stimulate the kidney and bladder meridian.

Knead Technique (Figure 30)

This is a relatively easy technique, much like kneading bread. It is used mainly on the heel area which is usually rather tough, and therefore needs more pressure for effective stimulation. Cup the ankle in the palm of the support hand, keeping the heel area free. Make a fist with the working hand, then use

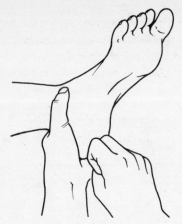

Fig. 30.

the knuckles of the second joint of the fingers to 'knead' the heel as you would dough. This is used for working reflexes in the heel – the sciatic reflex and nerve and the reproductive reflexes.

These are the main basic finger and thumb techniques used in the treatment procedure. As one of the main benefits of reflexology is the relaxation aspect, it is important to become familiar with a few basic relaxation techniques.

Relaxation Techniques

1. Achilles Tendon Stretch (Figure 31)
Cup the heel of one foot so that it rests in the palm of the hand. Grasp the top of the foot near the toes in the standard support

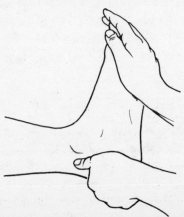

Fig. 31.

grip. Pull the top of the foot towards you, allowing the heel to move backwards, then reverse the procedure, pulling the heel towards you and pushing the top of the foot backwards so that the bottom of the foot stretches out. Repeat this two or three times.

2. Ankle Rotation (Figure 32)

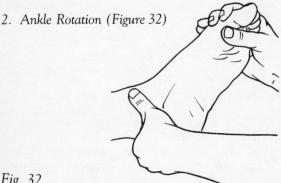

Fig. 32.

Cup the back of the ankle of the right foot in the palm of the left (support) hand, with the thumb on the outside of the ankle and the fingers on the inside. Ensure a firm but not tight grasp. Working with the right hand from the inside of the foot, grasp the foot at the base of the big toe in the standard support grip. Hold the foot with equal pressure. Use the hand holding the ankle joint as a pivot, and rotate the foot with the right hand in 360 degree circles, first clockwise a few times then anticlockwise. Work the other foot the same way alternating hands accordingly. Do not force the foot into exaggerated circles, manoeuvre it slowly and gently only as far as is comfortable for the client. This movement must be carried out smoothly and affects the entire area of the hip joint and tailbone, relaxes the anus and surrounding area and affects all the lower back muscles.

3. Side to Side (Figure 33)
This method of vigorously shaking the foot helps circulation, eases tenderness, and relaxes ankle and calf muscles. Place both palms on either side of the foot just above the ankles. Keep the hands as relaxed and loose as possible. Do not force the foot to rotate further than is comfortable for the subject.

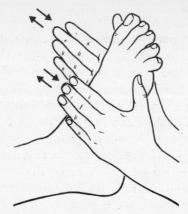

Fig. 33.

Roll the foot from side to side by gently moving it back and forth between your hands which move in opposite directions from each other. Move the hands gradually up the sides of the feet until the entire foot is worked. This is usually executed slowly to release tension, relax the edges of the ankle and calf and stimulate the whole foot.

4. *Loosen Ankles (Figure 34)*

Hook the base of both palms above the back sides of the heel so that the palms cover the ankle bones. The ankle joint serves as the pivot point. Move the hands rapidly backwards and forwards in opposite directions to each other, keeping the hands hooked beneath the ankle bones. The foot will shake from side to side when this movement is properly executed.

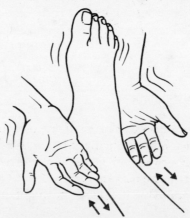

Fig. 34.

5. The Spinal Twist (Figure 35)

Grasp the foot from the inside of the instep with both hands, fingers on top, thumbs on the sole – the web between the thumb and the index finger on the spinal reflex. The index fingers of each hand should be touching. When working the right foot, the right hand starting position will be at the ankle joint on the top of the foot and vice versa on the left foot. The hand close to the ankle will provide the support. The hand nearest the toes will execute the twisting action. The two hands should be used as a unit, keeping all the fingers together and the two hands touching at all times. Keeping the support hand very steady, twist the working hand up and down. The support hand must remain completely stationary. Then move both hands forward slightly and repeat the twisting action.

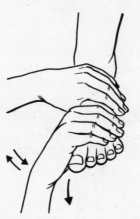

Fig. 35.

Continue this movement (grip, twist, reposition, grip, twist, reposition) until you reach the neck reflex area at the base of the big toe. Do not twist both hands at the same time. Repeat this on both feet. If the person is tense it may be necessary to repeat a few times. This is a very effective tension reducer, enjoyed by most.

6. *Wringing the Foot (Figure 36)*

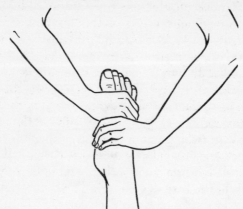

Fig. 36.

This is similar to the spinal twist, except both hands move in the wringing motion. Grab the foot in both hands as you would a wet towel and wring gently, each hand twisting in opposite directions. Your elbows should fly up and move when you do this. Move the hands gradually up the foot to 'wring' the entire foot..

7. *Rotate All Toes (Figure 37)*
The principle here is the same as the ankle rotation. It is a relaxation technique which not only increases flexibility of the toes, but releases tension and loosens muscles in the neck and shoulder line. The big toe is most important here. It represents half of the head area. The head joins the body as the toe joins

Fig. 37.

the foot, so the area joining the toe to the foot corresponds to the neck. To execute this procedure begin with the big toe and work through all the toes of one foot before moving on to the other foot. Hold the foot with the support hand in the standard support grip. With the thumb and fingers of the support hand, firmly hold the base of the toe you are going to rotate. With the working hand grasp the toe close to the base joint (metatarsal/phalange joint), with the thumb below, index and third finger on top. Now gently 'lift' the toe in its joint with a slight upward pull, and rotate in 360 degree circles, clockwise and anticlockwise a few times. Movements must be gentle but firm, the support hand stabilizing each toe individually at the base as it is worked on.

8. *Solar Plexus (Figure 38)*

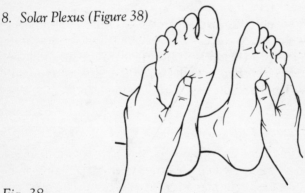

Fig. 38.

The solar plexus is referred to as the 'nerve switchboard' of the body, as it is the main storage area for stress. Applying pressure to this reflex will always bring about a feeling of relaxation. To locate the solar plexus reflex, grasp the top of the foot at the metatarsal area and squeeze gently. A depression will appear on the sole of the foot at the centre of the diaphragm line – the centre of the base of the ball of the foot. This is the solar plexus reflex. This technique is applied to both feet simultaneously. Pressure applied to this reflex is usually used as a relaxation technique to complete the treatment but can be used at any time during treatment if necessary.

Take the left foot in the right hand and the right foot in the left hand, fingers on top, thumbs below – from the outside of the foot. Place the tips of the thumbs on the solar plexus reflex. Ask the subject to inhale slowly as you press in on this point and exhale as you release pressure. Do not lose contact with the foot. Repeat this exercise a few times.

Grips

The following are descriptions of the specific 'hand-holds' (or hand positions) used in the practice of reflexology. They facilitate comfortable and effective execution of the thumb and finger pressure techniques.

Grip A (Figure 39)

Make a clenched fist with the working hand keeping the thumb free. The fist of the working hand will provide additional support on the sole of the foot. The 'rotating thumb' technique is used to exert pressure on the reflex points. The support hand is in the standard support position close to the working hand. With Grip A the left hand is usually the support hand and the right hand the worker.

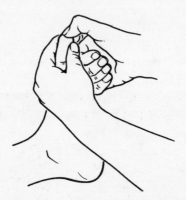

Fig. 39.

Reflexes worked with Grip A
Sinuses
Chronic eyes and ears
Bronchia, lungs, heart

Grip B (Figure 40)

Here the support hand holds the foot in the standard support grip close to the toes. With the working hand, clasp the foot from above. Place the fingers on the top of the feet pointing towards the ankle. The thumb is then positioned to work under the toes.

Fig. 40.

Reflexes worked with Grip B
Pituitary gland
Brain matter
Eyes and ears

Grip C (Figure 41)

This is an alternative grip with which to locate and stimulate the pituitary gland if you have trouble with Grip B. Bend the

Fig. 41.

index finger at the second joint and use this as you would the thumb, find the reflex, press in, rotate clockwise and anticlockwise a few times then release pressure when you feel the reflex has been sufficiently stimulated.

Reflexes worked with Grip C
Pituitary gland

Grip D (Figure 42)
Here the left hand is the support hand and the right hand the working hand on both feet. 'Cup' the arch of the foot in the palm of the support hand. The thumb of the working hand provides extra support on the sole of the foot on the thoracic reflexes, and the index finger is responsible for the rotations on the top of the foot. Place the third finger on top of the index finger to enable you to exert greater pressure on the lymphatic reflexes. With the thumb on the sole and fingers on top, reach between the toes till the web between the thumb and index finger touches the web between the big and second toe. Reach as far down the top of the foot as possible with the fingers and, using the rotation movement as you would with the thumb, work point by point towards the webs. When you get to the webs, apply a tight, pinching pressure on the webs as these are the most active lymphatic reflexes. Repeat this between each toe, using the grooves between the metatarsal bones as guidelines. Repeat this procedure on both feet.

Fig. 42.

Reflexes worked with Grip D
Upper lymphatics

Grip E (Figure 43)
In this grip the elbows move out and up into the air to facilitate the angle necessary to get right into the thyroid reflex. The thyroid reflex covers the entire area of the ball of the foot at the base of the big toe, but the most important part of this reflex is found in the half circle shape right at the base of the ball, almost 'under' the bone. To achieve sufficient stimulation,

Fig. 43.

you must get right in to the bone at the base of the ball and press 'up and under'.

With the support hand, hold the foot in the standard support grip which must be positioned close to the working hand. The fingers of the working hand grasp the foot from the inside of the instep, fingers on top of the foot from approximately half way down the big toe, and the thumb poised to work the important half moon section of the thyroid reflex at the base of the ball. With the thumb, press in and up to get right to the bone and use the 'rotating thumb' technique to work round the half circle of the ball, up to the neck and then cover the section at the base of the big toe.

Reflexes worked with Grip E
Thyroid
Parathyroid
Neck

Grip F (Figures 44 and 45)
To execute this grip effectively, the practitioner must be seated
in such a way as to be able to swivel in his/her seat so as not to
be working the foot 'straight on'. When utilizing Grip F, always
work the outside of the foot with the outer hand and support

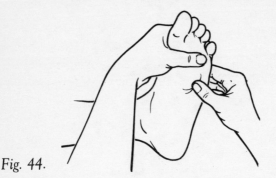

Fig. 44.

with the inner hand from the instep (Figure 44); and work the
inner side of the foot with the inner hand from the instep and
support with the outer hand (Figure 45). The pressure is, as
usual, exerted with the 'rotating thumb'.

Imagine the foot divided in half vertically. The object is to
work horizontally across both feet as if they are a single unit,
using the imaginary vertical line as the point at which to swop
working hands. This may sound slightly confusing at first, but
it definitely facilitates a smooth and flowing technique for
working the digestive area.

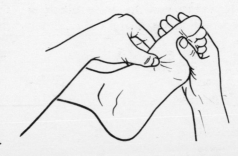

Fig. 45.

Reflexes worked by Grip F
Liver/gall bladder
Stomach, pancreas, duodenum, spleen
Small intestine, ileo-caecal valve, appendix
Large intestine
Kidneys, adrenals, ureters

Grip G (Figure 46)
For this grip, the foot is cupped in the palm of the working hand, the sole of the foot resting in the palm, leaving the thumb free to execute the 'rotating thumb' technique. The

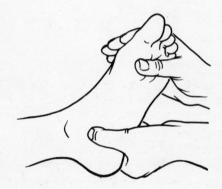

Fig. 46.

support hand is in the standard support grip. This grip is used mainly for working on the sides of the feet – the spine and bladder on the inner foot and the knee, hip, elbow and shoulder on the outer foot.

Reflexes worked by Grip G
Bladder
Uterus/prostate/ovaries/testes
Spine
Knee, hip, elbow, shoulder

STEP-BY-STEP TREATMENT SEQUENCE

The treatment sequence is divided into the same main areas as mentioned in Mapping the Feet (Chapter 4).

The Head and Neck Area – the Toes;

The Thoracic Area – the Ball;

The Abdominal Area – the Arch;

The Pelvic Area – the Heel;

The Reproductive Area – the Ankles;

The Spine – the Inner Foot;

The Outer Body – the Outer Foot;

Circulation – the Tops of the Feet.

Do not forget – the feet are worked alternately from toe to heel, organ by organ.

Easy Reference Treatment Procedure

This step-by-step sequence describes the various techniques and grips in the specific order which constitutes a full reflexology treatment. This is the standard sequence I teach, and I have found it gives optimum results.

Relaxation Techniques
Achilles Tendon Stretch
Ankle Rotation
Loosen Ankles
Side to Side
Wringing the Foot
Rotate all Toes

Head and Neck Area – The Toes
Sinus from big toe to small toe – Grip A
Pituitary gland – Grip B or C

110

Brain matter – Grip B
Eyes and ears – Grip B
Sides and tops of toes – Finger Technique 2
Chronic eye and ear problems and eustachian tubes – Grip A
Upper lymphatics – Grip D

Thoracic Area – The Ball
Bronchia, lungs and heart – Grip A
Thyroid – Grip E moving to Grip A
Neck – Grip A

Abdominal Area – The Arch
Liver, gall bladder – Grip F
Stomach, pancreas, duodenum, spleen – Grip F
Small intestine, ileo-caecal valve, appendix – Grip F
Large intestine – Grip F
Kidney, ureter – Grip F.
Bladder – Grip G

Pelvic Area – The Heel
Pelvis and sciatica – Knead Technique

Reproductive Area – The Ankle
Prostate/ uterus/ovaries/testes – Grip G
Fallopian tubes/vas deferens – Finger Technique 1

The Spine – The Inner Foot
Spinal Twist – Relaxation Technique
Spine from heel to toe – Grip G

Outer Body – The Outer Foot
Knee, hip, elbow, shoulder – Grip G

Circulation/Lymphatics – The Top of the Foot
Lymphatics, breast area, circulation – Finger Technique 3

Relaxation Techniques
Kidney and bladder meridians – Pinch Technique
Solar Plexus Deep Breathing – Relaxation Technique.

7

Self-Help and Products

SELF-TREATMENT

SELF-TREATMENT WITH reflexology can be awkward and arduous, but if you are willing to devote the time and energy to yourself, it is certainly worth the effort. There are, however, disadvantages to self-treatment. First and foremost, all-important relaxation is impossible to achieve this way. And second, the vital energy exchange between subject and practitioner – which plays a major role in the success of treatment – is lacking, as you are both practitioner and patient at the same time. Self-treatment is therefore only useful as a means of preventative treatment, general health care and first aid treatment to achieve quick relief for a condition until you can arrange for professional treatment. It goes without saying that this form of treatment could never be as effective as a professional treatment from a trained practitioner.

However, for those who are willing and able to devote the time and energy to themselves, self-treatment can have beneficial results. It can be undertaken by anyone reasonably agile, who can comfortably sit cross-legged or raise a foot onto the opposite knee.

Comfortable seating is the first prerequisite. Sit on a chair, or cross-legged on the floor or bed with cushions behind your back. If you are aware which reflexes are out of balance, work specifically on those. If not, work calmly and gently through the whole treatment in accordance with the techniques and sequence described in Chapter 6. You should be as relaxed as possible with no tension in the legs. Remember it is difficult to assess your own reflexes accurately.

A full treatment will take approximately an hour, which may be a bit much for many to contemplate. However, treatment of appropriate reflex points can be used to relieve headaches, migraines, muscle aches and other transient conditions. At the end of a treatment, always take the time to sit or lie back for approximately fifteen minutes and relax with breathing techniques.

PRODUCTS

Creams and Oils
A therapist may apply herbal ointment or oil to stimulate circulation and relax the client at the end of a treatment. It is a good idea to pamper your feet like this at regular intervals – either after a self-treatment or merely to relax and revitalize your feet. There are numerous foot creams available on the market but it is preferable to use something herbal and natural, such as an aromatherapy oil or herbal cream, for their beneficial healing properties.

Foot Baths
Famous herbalist and healer, Maurice Messegue, recommended herbal foot baths as an essential part of his treatment. He believed treatment by osmosis to be most effective, as the main ingredients which contain the healing qualities of plants rapidly penetrate the skin and sometimes reach the affected areas more quickly than if the same ingredients are taken internally. He chose foot and hand baths over hip and total baths as they are easy to prepare and because the hands and feet are the most receptive parts of the body. These can be prepared with dried herbs or aromatherapy oils infused in boiling water. Foot baths should be taken as hot as possible (but not boiling) first thing in the morning on an empty stomach and should not last for more than eight minutes.

Chemical Foot Sprays

These should be avoided. They clog the pores and prevent the feet from being able to rid themselves and the body of excretions from the sweat glands. It is not wise to suppress the ability of the body to sweat through the feet. Excessive sweating is an indication of imbalance and should not be ignored.

Shoes, Socks and Stockings

Shoes, socks and stockings of synthetic materials should also be avoided as they increase the likelihood of sweating. Plastic and rubber shoes stifle the feet, while leather allows them to breathe. The same applies to nylon socks and stockings as opposed to cotton.

Reflexology Shoes

These shoes have 'quills' which massage the feet and stimulate the reflexes while walking. Using these is not a replacement for reflexology, but is beneficial in that they promote lymphatic drainage and circulation in the feet. These should only be used in moderation as exaggerated use can overstimulate reflexes and cause discomfort.

Other Foot Aids

There are numerous varieties of 'foot aid' available on the market today – reflexology mats similar to the shoes; wood or plastic rollers; brushes and electrically operated gadgets and all types of balls like golf and tennis balls are often recommended. As with the shoes, these help tone and relax the foot and increase lymphatic drainage and circulation but should only be used in moderation to avoid overstimulation. These are only effective for maintenance of good health, and not effective in treating specific problems. None of these aids can be more effective than, or can replace, professional treatment.

When using any of the 'roller' type aids, roll them in a uniform way with an even, light pressure over the entire foot – the bottom and sides of the feet. No special emphasis need be placed on any particular reflexes. Apply this rolling therapy every day for approximately ten minutes per foot.

It is important to remember that these implements give no clue to the differing state of tissue tone or allow for accurate reflex reading and reaction. Many practitioners would advise you to steer clear of them on the grounds that no mechanical implement could replace the practised hand of a practitioner for sensitivity. They can, however, be useful as preventative and maintenance therapy.

A natural foot massage is by far the best and is probably more effective than any gadget. A walk barefoot on the beach or the grass brings the feet into contact with the earth and the energies that flow through it, and provides a revitalizing, energizing and natural massage.

VacuFlex System

Modern technology's contribution to reflexology is the Vacu-Flex System. Laser technology is replacing the surgeon's scalpel; vacuum therapy and electrical stimulation makes acupuncture more comfortable. The VacuFlex System is a vacuum system which is modernizing reflexology. By applying pressure to the whole foot at the same time, the VacuFlex 'boots' stimulate all reflex areas in just five minutes. After removing the boots, discoloration of the corresponding reflex areas remains for a few moments, providing an accurate visual diagnostic aid. People generally find the boots less painful than hand massage and children can be treated quickly and comfortably with this system. This system also includes the treatment of acupuncture meridians, stimulating these with suction cups. So it is a two-in-one idea, reflexology and acupuncture. The entire treatment takes about half an hour.

FOOT CARE

Having now seen that every part of the foot represents a part of the body, the importance of treating the feet with care and kindness is obvious.

Regular washing and careful drying will prevent cracks developing. A pumice stone and creams help soften hardened areas. Problems such as corns, verrucas and athlete's foot should be dealt with and a chiropodist consulted for persistent problems.

Feet should be kept warm and comfortable at all times. There is a good reason for this. I am, at present, living in a warm, sub-tropical climate, and have numerous clients whose children suffer from runny noses, sinus and chest problems and bladder weaknesses. In this climate the temperature is usually high outdoors, so air conditioners are common. This results in constant movement between hot and cold conditions. Most children go barefoot, and a sudden drop in foot temperature affects the reflexes as well as the related organs.

A Case History

A young male client suffered constant sinus and chest problems and asthma attacks. He responded well to reflexology treatments, but there was a constant recurrence of asthma attacks and often a slight cold. I checked his daily routine. On rising in the morning he would go straight from the warm bed into the garden (onto the cool, dew-covered grass) to let out the dogs and collect his newspaper. He would then go back indoors for a shower and walk around barefoot on tiled floors. The rapid variations in temperature his feet were subjected to was having an effect on his entire body, causing this propensity to colds and asthma. I recommended that he wear shoes to keep his foot temperature constant and his condition improved tremendously.

REFLEXOLOGY AND OTHER THERAPIES

Reflexology is an extremely effective holistic therapy, the positive effects of which can only be further enhanced by any other holistic therapy, attitude and activity. Many different factors influence each individual and therefore his ability to assimilate and respond to the healing process. Numerous conditions have an effect on our being – some in our control, some beyond our control. In order to help offset the negative effects of conditions we cannot control such as the earth's gravity, the movement of the sun, moon and stars, global and social pressures, and climate, we should make more effort to alter those conditions we can change to make them work to our advantage. The things we can do for ourselves may require some discipline and effort, but will be a great contribution to acquiring perfect health. Those we can change are diet, relaxation and exercise.

One factor under our control which has a profound effect on health is diet. Many conditions cannot be treated 100 per cent effectively unless modifications are made in diet. A good practitioner will usually enquire about diet and make some useful suggestions.

Relaxation techniques will also be beneficial as an adjunct to reflexology treatment. These include Tai Ch'i, yoga, meditation, breathing and visualization techniques. Some form of more vigorous exercise such as aerobics, swimming, jogging and the like is also recommended.

As reflexology is a holistic therapy it can be effectively and successfully combined with various other holistic/natural therapies. These include Bach Flower Remedies, herbal treatment, naturopathy, ayurvedic medicine, homoeopathy, hydrotherapy, shiatsu or any other forms of massage, acupuncture and the Alexander technique to mention a few. However, all the different methods cannot be applied together, as too much stimulation will have adverse effects.

CONCLUSION

Reflexology is expanding rapidly throughout the world. This is evidence enough of its efficacy and popularity. The main objective of reflexology is to help people attain and maintain a better state of health and well-being. It does not promise to be a magic cure-all for all people and all ills. But there can be no question that reflexology has carved a respected niche in the realm of holistic healing techniques.

Man is far more than the sum of his parts. Reflexology helps us to attune to our bodies and understand ourselves as part of a greater whole . . . to tune in to the natural laws of the cosmos and work towards a more holistic approach to life, an approach that results in a balanced and fulfilled life.

Perfect health requires discipline and energy, but the effort pays good dividends. The choice is yours – a productive, peaceful and fulfilled existence, or a life riddled with pain, anger and disease. But remember the old yogi saying: 'Health is a responsibility.'

Bibliography

Byers, Dwight C. *Better Health with Foot Reflexology*, Ingham Publishing, 1983.

Connelly, Dianne M. PhD, M.Ac, *Traditional Acupuncture: The Law of the Five Elements*, 4th Edition, The Centre for Traditional Acupuncture Inc, Columbia, Maryland, 1989.

Gillanders, Ann. *Reflexology – The Ancient Answer to Modern Ailments* Gillanders, 1987.

Goosman-Legger, Astrid. *Zone Therapy Using Foot Massage*, C.W. Daniel Company Limited, 1983.

Gore, Anya. *Reflexology*, Optima, 1990.

Grinberg, Avi. *Holistic Reflexology*, Thorsons, 1989.

Hall, Nicola M. *Reflexology – A Patient's Guide*, Thorsons, 1986.

Hall, Nicola M. *Reflexology – A Way To Better Health*, Pan Books, 1988.

Ingham, Eunice D. *Stories The Feet Can Tell Thru Reflexology*, Ingham Publishing, 1938.

Ingham, Eunice D. *Stories The Feet Have Told Thru Reflexology*, Ingham Publishing, 1951.

Issel, Christine. *Reflexology: Art, Science and History*, New Frontier Publishing, 1990.

Kaptchuk, Ted J. *The Web That Has No Weaver*, Congdon & Weed, New York, 1983.

Kunz, Kevin and Barbara. *The Complete Guide to Foot Reflexology*, Thorsons, 1982.

MacDonald, Alexander. *Acupuncture – From Ancient Art to Modern Medicine*, Unwin, 1982.

Manaka, Yoshio M.D. and Urquhart, Ian A. PhD. *A Layman's Guide to Acupuncture*, Weatherhill, 1972.

Mann, Felix Dr. *Acupuncture*, Pan Books, 1971.

Marquardt, Hanne. *Reflex Zone Therapy of the Feet*, Thorsons, 1983.

Marsaa-Teegurden, Iona; *Handbook of Acupressure II*, Ginseng du Foundation, 1981.

Nightingale, Michael Dr *Acupuncture*, Optima, 1987.

Norman, Laura. *Feet First*, Simon & Schuster Inc., 1988.

Russel, Lewis and Hardy, Bob. *Healthy Feet*, Optima, 1988.

Thie, John F. *Touch For Health*, T.H. Enterprises, 1973.

Wagner, Franz PhD. *Reflex Zone Massage*, Thorsons, 1987.

Further Information

Head Office

Inge Dougans
PO Box 68283
Bryanston
Johannesburg 2021
South Africa
Tel/Fax: 27 11 706 4206

Karen Nel
1951 Glenarie Avenue
North Vancouver
V7P 1X9
Canada
Tel: 1 604 986 7121

Cecile Myslicki
70 Parkville Drive
Winnipeg
Manitobe R2M 2H5
Canada
Tel/Fax: 1 204 253 9375

Carol Bosiger
PO Box 93
Tadworth
Surrey TK20 7YB
England
Tel/Fax: 01737 842961

Andrea Schippers
Domkeweg 23
37213 Witzenhausen
Germany
Tel: 49 5542 71463

Alberto Carnevale-Maffe
Via Procaccini 47
Milan
Italy
Tel/Fax: 39 2 311116

Karine van Niekerk
Frankenstraat 31A
2582 SE Den Haag
Netherlands
Tel: 31 70 354 304

Lena Walters
Vale Da Telha
Apartado 173
Aljezur 8670
Algarve
Portugal
Tel: 351 82 98566

Ann-Chatrine Jonsson
Varmlandsvagen 438
12348 Farsta
Sweden
Tel/Fax: 46 8 942 485

Jill Tonkovich
2222 Kilkare Parkway
Pt Pleasant
New Jersey 08742
USA
Tel: 1 908 892 7566

Ivete Maria Fagundes
Rua Jose Emmendoerter
1674
89253000
Jaragua do Sul
SC Brazil
Tel/Fax: 47 372 0192

For those who wish to pursue the study of reflexology further, Element Books publish
The Complete Illustrated Guide to Reflexology *by Inge Dougans.*

Index

Index

ileo-caecal valve, reflex to 73-4
impotence 50
infertility 35
Ingham, Eunice 9, 16
inner arm, pain in 40
inner foot, reflexes in 79-80
insanity 39
insomnia 39

kidney meridian 26, 42, 44, 58
kidneys 35, 60, 73
knead technique 97-8
knees 35, 38, 50, 60, 61, 80

large intestine, reflexes to 74
large intestine meridian 26, 32, 34, 54
laryngitis 35, 55
legs, pains in 60
little finger, pain in 40
liver 35, 51, 71
liver meridian 26, 49, 51
flower back, pain in 43, 60
lumps, 35, 44
lung meridian 26, 31-2, 33, 53-4
lungs, 35, 44, 67
lymph swellings 38, 41
lymph system, reflexes to 66

Marsaa-Teegurden, Iona 27, 32
menstrual problems 38, 55, 56, 57, 59-60, 61
meridians 5, 10, 11, 25-31, 52-3, 85 86-7, 89, 91
migraines 50, 56, 58

nails, disorders of 46
nausea 56, 60, 61
neck tension 43, 50, 54, 57
Nei Ching 32, 37, 42, 47, 49
nerves 2-3, 17-18
neuralgia 41, 57
nipples 30, 35
nose 32, 34
numbness 40

oils 113
outer foot, reflexes in 80-82
ovaries 35, 76

palms, hot 46
pancreas, reflexes to 71
parathyroid gland, reflexes to 69
pelvic complaints 38
pericardium meridian 26, 45, 46, 59
phlebitis 44, 50
pinch technique 97
pineal gland, reflexes to 65
pituitary gland, reflexes to 64-5
plantar digital neuritis 89
preventative therapy 23
prostate gland, reflexes to 78
psoriasis 31

reflexes 2, 62
reflexology 4-6, 13-18, 21-2

reflexology shoes 114
reflexology treatment 19-21, 22, 110-11
rotate all toes technique 102
rotating thumb technique 94-5

sciatica 43
sciatic nerve, reflex to 75
self-treatment 112-13
seminal vesicles, reflexes to 78
sexual libido, low 50, 60-1
shiatsu 11
shinbone, problems of 38, 44, 51
shingles 50
shoulders 33, 34, 41, 48, 50, 57, 81
side to side technique 99-100
sinuses 35, 63-5
skin, problems of 31, 33, 34, 41, 43, 46, 50, 53, 56
small intestine, reflex to 73
small intestine meridian 26, 39, 41, 57
solar plexus 44, 69, 103-4
soles of feet, burning in 44
sperm count, low 50
spinal twist 101
spine 43, 79-80
spleen, reflexes to 72
spleen/pancreas meridian 26, 36, 38, 55-6
standard support grip 93
stomach 50, 54, 55, 57, 61, 70-71
stomach meridian 26, 35, 36, 55
stress 3, 13-18, 23, 58

teeth, reflexes to 65
tennis elbow, 34, 41, 57
testes, reflexes to 77
thigh, pain in 38, 44, 50
throat, sore 35
thumbs 33
thyroid gland 35, 69
tinnitus 41
toes 35, 43, 63-7
toenails 38, 50, 88-9
tonsils 35, 66
top of foot, reflexes in 82
Triple Warmer meridian 26, 45-7, 48, 49
underarm complaints 38
ureters, reflexes to 75

uterus, reflexes to 77-8

VacuFlex system 115
vas deferens, reflexes to 78

Wagner, Dr Franz 4
Wallace, Jenny 5-6
warts 33, 54
Wei, Dr Wang 4-5
wringing the foot 102
wrists 33, 40, 48

zone Therapy 6-11, 25

122